Startup Z

Chris Dougherty

This book is for my brother, John Morris.

As always, a special thank you to the early readers Bob Dattolo and John Morris and the idea man, Steve Dougherty. Thank you for your patience and the use of your brains.

06.2027
CHAPTER 1

"Albert Tinsdale, the last of the Chance Hearings scientists still incarcerated, is being released this morning from the Pennsylvania State Penitentiary amid renewed protests by a group claiming allegiance with the Clergy Party. We have Alicia Farrah live at the scene–Alicia, good morning. What's the mood out there?"

Alicia Farrah appeared on the television holding a microphone and nodding her perfectly coiffed blonde hair. The grim red line of her mouth served as both an acknowledgment of the anchor's words and as forewarning of the utmost seriousness of the story that she was covering. "Yes, thank you, Bill, good morning. The scene here in Philadelphia is–in a word–chaotic." Alicia half-turned and the shot widened out to include a small group of people milling on a curb across the street from a large stone building surrounded by double fences topped with razor wire. The group stood quietly, signs upside down and forgotten at their sides. One woman, dressed in the black robes of a nun, yawned.

A young man in a jean jacket leaned on his sign and watched the reporter with half-lidded eyes. When he noticed the camera had turned to include them, he straightened and nudged two people standing next to him, who in turn elbowed others. At this haphazard signal, the protesters raised their signs and began to wave them in earnest, their faces pulled into tight lines of manufactured-looking fury. Their signs read, "MAN PROPOSES GOD DISPOSES" and "SCIENCE IS GODLESSNESS" and "GOD HATES SCIENCE." Behind them, a large stack of unused signs hinted at an unexpectedly reduced number of protesters.

A guard in a tan coverall uniform stood just outside a heavily reinforced gate across the street from the protesters. He eyed them with impassive boredom and cradled a machine gun across his chest. The machine gun was black and dull in the gray morning light. Another guard, the first guard's dark twin, stood cradling his machine gun almost out of sight behind the first fence, his dark green coverall blending into the shadows. On the street along the building, three ambulances sat with their lights spinning.

Alicia turned back to the camera, rearranging her features to remove the frustrated disgust.

Sitting in her kitchen across the river in Marlton, New Jersey, Cassie Ramson caught the young reporter's chagrin and snorted a laugh.

"Protesters aren't what they used to be are they, Alicia?" Cassie said to the small television sitting on her kitchen counter. "Not since the Silence Rulings. What's a reporter to do?"

On the screen, Alicia squared her shoulders as though deliberately ignoring Cassie's snide question. She went on, "A source from inside the prison has informed me that some sort of food poisoning epidemic coupled with an unscheduled 'blue-flu' is going to cause a delay of hours, if not days, before Tinsdale is released, and that–"

The shot switched back to the anchor in the studio. His face had a flown-apart, confused look, as he listened to someone off-screen. He shook his head as if he didn't understand, listened some more, and then turned his gaze to the camera. He cleared his throat.

"This is just in, all flights into and out of the Philadelphia airport have been cancelled and we're now getting word that–"

The screen went to gray and a small wheel spun and spun. Cassie sighed with irritation. Internet down. Again. It was at least the third time this week. It failed regularly–but they couldn't afford anything better.

Well, she didn't need the distraction right now, anyway.

She switched the television off and pulled her hair into a low ponytail. She took the stack of towels she'd folded while watching the morning news, shoved them into the laundry basket, and checked the clock over the stove. Ten. Two more hours until she needed to pick Lucy up at the daycare center. What else could she get done in those two hours? A lot probably, if only the couch would stop calling to her. She yawned and tilted her coffee cup, stirring the dregs. Another coffee? She consulted her already slightly soured stomach and decided against it. As many times as she'd counseled people that coffee was no substitute for sleep, she found herself caught in the same bad habits, just like when doctors used to smoke. Which she had heard about, but never seen, of course. Cigarettes had been outlawed in 2020 when Cassie was just out of nursing school and the country–hell, the whole world– was stumbling faster and faster toward the financial abyss. Thank God, she'd gotten her loans paid off fast. When the Second Great Depression happened in 2024, she and Dan had been okay. Not great, no one was great anymore, but since she was a health professional, they'd at least been able to keep their small house, and they'd been able to have Lucy.

Cassie gazed at the couch with longing and then leaned against the back of the kitchen chair to peek through the half open laundry room door. Dirty clothes were stacked in three big piles on the floor. Waiting for her. She sighed. Well, she could put a load in and then close her eyes for a minute. Last night's shift at the clinic had been rough. Some kind of mini-epidemic going on, or another flu running rampant.

She heaved herself up, stretched, and put her mug in the sink. As she began to turn away, movement from outside the window caught her eye. It looked like someone had just slipped behind her neighbor's house. Had it been Mr. Shapiro? He was retired and home most of the time, and did a lot of yard work, but still, there had been something off in the movements. Something awkward and…unsettling. Cassie frowned and leaned closer to the window, going up on the toes of her canvas sneakers, her stomach pressing against the cold porcelain of the farmhouse-style sink. A long, misshapen shadow trailed out from behind the tiny tract house next door. Was it someone (some*thing*) standing just out of sight? Was it–

Her phone shrilled. She jumped with a small yelp and whirled toward the sound. Then she laughed at herself and put her hand at her throat. Her pulse beat hard and fast under her fingers– adrenaline rush.

Her phone shrilled again and vibrated, chattering aimlessly across the kitchen table. She snatched it up. The insectile buzzing seemed too loud and the phone's erratic movement reminded her of something dying. She pressed her thumb to the screen and it glowed to life.

A picture of Donna's face appeared, smiling under the fuzzy bunny ears she'd put on last Easter for a joke. Cassie's best friend. She'd probably been watching the news just like Cassie. They liked to make fun of the overly earnest Alicia Farrah.

"Hey, Donna!" Cassie said. "Did you see Alicia's report from the prison? Ha! She—"

"Cass...you have to go get Lucy," Donna said, her voice flat, like someone in shock. Reflexively, Cassie looked at the clock again. Ten fifteen.

"It's only a little after ten," Cassie said and started back to the window. "Girl, are you already drinking? Listen, I get it...it's five o'clock somewhere, right?" Cassie grinned in anticipation of her friend's good-natured groan, but the line stayed silent. She tried to get the conversation back on track. "Hey, I just saw that goofy Alicia Farrah doing a live report from Philly and she—"

"Cass...go get her. Go now before—"

Cassie pulled the phone away from her ear and looked at the screen as though the picture of Donna could give her some clue as to Donna's confused words. Her friend smiled at her, one ear up, one ear down as the counter counted the call time above her. Cassie and Donna had been coloring eggs with the kids when Cassie had snapped that picture; Lucy's little elbow was just in the frame. Although the holiday was no longer federally recognized, she and Donna had still gotten together mostly out of habit and for something fun for the kids to do.

She pushed the video call button and waited for it to switch over. She had to see Donna's live and actual face. Something was wrong. As she thought that, her mind cross-patched and she remembered the weird shadow behind Mr. Shapiro's house. She looked out the window again. The shadow was gone. "Hey," Cassie said, the word a faint protest. She looked back to her phone. The call had dropped. She pushed redial, turned, and leaned against the counter with her back to the window. It somehow made her feel better. Once again, her mind cross-patched to a picture of herself as a little girl, pulling the covers over her head. The monster unseen was the monster defeated.

The phone burred twice, clicked to an open line. Cassie said, "Donna? Hello? Donna?" A faint hiss, interrupted by a gurgle. Cassie had heard that gurgle before, but she shied away from the association. "Donna! Donna? Are you okay? Listen, I'm coming over there…Donna?" Cassie headed for her front door with her stomach knotting, but glad she was dressed, and glad her best friend lived only one street away. "Donna? I'll be there in ten seconds. Hold on, girl, hold on." She opened the front door.

A man in a colorless suit stood on the edge of the shallow front porch, his back to her, swaying gently. Cassie nearly dropped the phone. "Hey!" she said and took a startled non-step, almost a stomp. Her hand tightened on the doorknob. A strange man on your front porch was something to be cautious of. Very cautious. Since the depression, homelessness had become rampant, despite the many laws restricting it.

The man's head jerked as if he'd heard a loud but distant sound. For a brief second, Cassie had trouble reconciling the man's flat profile, and then her synapses finally interpreted what her eyes saw: his nose was gone. *Car accident*, her mind supplied with relief and the explanation appealed deeply to her. It was a concrete problem with a concrete solution. It was probably this man's shadow she had seen next door. Most likely, he'd suffered a head injury and was wandering aimlessly. Looking for help, but confused. *Of course.*

Despite her mind's authoritative assurance, her hand–ruled by an older part of her brain–began to push the door closed. The man turned and stumbled toward her, his arms coming up. His nose was gone, yes, and one of his ears. Black, coagulated blood slicked his neck, but his eyes were…aware. Not sharp, but…

Cassie pushed the door, dropping her phone in order to use both hands. The man's weight landed against it with a dull thud and she screamed. She pushed harder as her stomach contracted in panic. The door thudded again and yawned a few inches wider. "No!" Cassie screamed, unaware that she did so. "No! NO!" She pushed, throwing her shoulder and all her weight against the door, her sneakers digging into the hardwood. It finally closed, but with a click that seemed unreliable. She turned the deadbolt and jumped back.

Thud. Thud.

Thud.

Each slam against the door made her heart race. She took tentative steps back, trying to slow her whistling breath. Her mind whirred emptily, like something cut loose.

Thud.

Each thud was progressively weaker, as though the man was losing interest in forcing his way in. *What if he's dying*, her nurse's instincts whispered. *He needs your help, Cassie. He's been in some kind of accident. You're a nurse! You have to help him!*

Cassie shook her head no, even as she took a step toward the door. Then she froze, held in place by indecision. She blinked and ran her hands over her face, pulled her hair from the elastic, and then gathered it back into a ponytail and looped the elastic around it, tightened it.

The thumping stopped.

Was he gone?

She went on tiptoe to the front window and twitched a section of curtain aside. She had to press her cheek to the glass to get to the angle where she could see the area just outside the front door. The man was still there, facing the house. He had quieted, but there was something implacable about his swaying stance. He was not leaving any time soon.

Head injury from a motorcycle accident, her mind told her, but that internal voice had grown less authoritative and more desperate. Trying to convince. *It explains the odd behavior. It explains his nose, his eyes...the...the...*

"He had eyes like an animal," Cassie whispered. Like a hyena, or a lion–not cold, exactly, but just not...not...human. Whatever had happened to the man had swept his humanity from him.

She remembered the phone and bent to retrieve it from where it had slid up against a baseboard. The screen was cracked, but the phone still worked. She dialed the police. Her hands were shaking and that surprised her–she was handling this well, thinking it through, following logical steps to resolution...wasn't she? Her body didn't seem to agree.

The phone rang three times, and then the call dropped. She dialed 911 again. It rang once and dropped. Bullshit...the call shouldn't drop. She was on the town's Wi-Fi. Bullshit, bullshit. Rage, terror, and a distressingly blank helplessness washed over her, making her feel faint. She squeezed the phone in both hands, and a scream that she wouldn't allow locked her chest and gritted her teeth.

She looked out the window again. The man was still there, still swaying, but now he faced the side yard.

Think, Cassie, think. She squeezed the phone harder as if to press ideas, solutions from it. Dan. Call Dan. Call your husband. He wouldn't answer, though, because no cells were allowed in the classroom. She wished she could text him, leave him a message that way, but texting-enabled phones had been outlawed while Cassie was in college. Now it was numbers or nothing. Most people didn't even bother to have cell phones anymore because the plans had become prohibitively expensive as the economy had worsened.

Call Lucy's school.

...*go get her. Go now before*–Donna's voice. Why had she said to go get Lucy? Why didn't 911 answer? What was going on? A deeper unease–brought on by the shadow, Donna's call, the man, his eyes, no phone–stirred her guts, almost to nausea. She glanced into the kitchen and the stack of neatly folded towels looked like something from another life. Something had changed. Something big and it was more than just the noseless, soulless, bright-eyed apparition desecrating the suburban peace and normality of her front porch.

The car was parked in the garage behind the house. Just to be safe, she would drive to get Lucy, and then go to the police. The ladies at the care center might look at her as if she'd lost her mind, but so what. Better safe than sorry.

She would call Dan on the way and leave him a message. Once she had Lucy, maybe she would drive to the Vo-Tech to see if she could get in to see him. Get him to come with her and Lucy and...*why was she thinking about getting them all in the car?*

More importantly, why was she still standing here?

Move it, Cas, she told herself and with that small, authoritative command, she was moving through the house, gathering purse and keys. There were ten long strides between the laundry room door and the garage. Always before she had lamented the lack of a decent back yard and she had told Dan a hundred times that they should sell this house and buy one of the houses in the country with football field-sized yards, but not anymore. Not with that boogieman on the front porch, and that...whatever it had been...that had cast that long shadow behind the Shapiro's house. How many 'whatevers' were out there? Had one of them gotten Donna? Maybe the homeless had finally risen up, just as the Clergy Party always said would happen. She'd never paid attention to their nonsense before; they were too strident, too reactionary. But they might have been right all along. There were so many homeless. Cas had always felt bad for them, but...

Her hand was on the knob of her laundry room door and she just stood there, frozen. She'd paralyzed herself with the thoughts of a homeless uprising.

Jesus, Cas, will you please just MOVE?

She glanced as far left and right as she could by pressing her cheeks to the cool glass–the little yard was clear–and she turned the knob to ease the door open. Her nerve endings sizzled with red caution, the small hairs on the back of her neck waved and tickled. The day was a nice one, weather wise, nice for June. Not too hot, not yet. *Stop stalling!*

She stuck her head out, looked left and right again. *Cas, go...go, go, GO...*

She went, pulling the door closed behind her and stepping with deer-like tentativeness onto the concrete steps. From there, she made her way to the garage.

CHAPTER 2

--- MAN PROPOSES GOD DISPOSES ---

!!!ATTENTION CITIZENS OF THE "FORMER" UNTIED STATE OF AMERICA!!!

Why do we say "FORMER" United States of Amrica??!! BECAUSE we are NO LONGER that great   sovering NATION born of the CHRISTIAN MORALS AND IDEELS that made it a GREAT "once"   nation!!!

The "SO-CALLED PRESIDENT" CLOONEY should be impeached and HUNG as a traitor for the   traitorous act SUSPENSION OF   RELIGIOUS HOLIDAYS.

We, of the   CLREGY PARTY, invoke on you to UNITE WITH US at the Faith BAbtist church on Charles Street on May 11, at six PM,   TWO THOUSAND AND TWENTY-4 YEARS AFTER THE DEALTH OF OUR LORD AND SAVOR, JESUS CHRIST THE   "ALLMIGHTY"!!!!!!!!!!!!!!!!!!!!!!!!!

Refreshments will be served. Also, "bring the kids"! As we will show a movie called "I HAPPILY OBEY" that many (espeshally the young) will find "most enlitening"!!!!!!

--- ---

Cassie trotted up the sidewalk, past the light-pole pasted with the peeling, three year old flyers without seeing them. The parking lot of the daycare center was empty. The employees parked out back, but there were usually a couple of cars up front. Visiting parents, late drop-offs…but it was vacant.

The empty expanse (save for her own Mazda *Zap*) re-fanned the fires of disquiet, which had begun to ease on her drive over.

The roads, although somewhat low on traffic, had still seemed normal and it had helped ease her sense of vertigo. She'd even passed a town cop sitting in the coffee-shop parking lot, trolling for late-morning speeders. In this quiet, suburban area of mostly homes with only a handful of convenience-style businesses, speeding was about the highest level of crime that occurred.

Cas had thought briefly about stopping to tell the officer about the man on her porch, but despite the calm that had settled over her, it still seemed more important to get Lucy first. She had even convinced herself that Donna had been cut off by whatever was causing all the poor phone reception, the strange gurgle she'd heard (*not a death rattle, of course not*) just one of those unexplainable phone noises. A sunspot or something could do that, right? Flares or radiation or whatever. Cas had begun to hum, but not along to the radio–that was out, too. Nothing but blank air on her six presets. She had snapped it off with something between irritation and fear. Sunflare, sunspot…whatever it was called. They showed it on the news all the time.

She knocked on the Care Center's glass door. The door was locked at all times, because that was policy, so it didn't alarm her. As she waited for either Miss Caroline or Miss Daisy to come and open the door, she turned to survey the parking lot again. Her Mazda sat like a patient little blue dog, the sun heliographing off the chrome. Across the street, a church sat blank-eyed and quiet. Next to it, a dog-groomer's lot held three cars, and next to that was a dress boutique that changed names more frequently than it changed inventory.

A woman burst out of the dog-groomer's door carrying a small, white dog in her arms. She was obviously in a hurry and nearly stumbled as her foot found the edge of the sidewalk and her ankle turned. The dog had…it had gotten into paint. It was covered in red paint. The paint had gotten onto the woman's arms, neck, and blouse.

"Geez, lady," Cassie said under her breath even though the woman was much too far away to hear her. "You need to get that dog back inside…she needs a–"

Another woman followed the first through the still swinging groomer's door. She was a big woman in jeans and a long white apron with the store's logo. The groomer. She fell onto the first woman with a garbled yell, her big arms going around her. They tumbled and landed on the sidewalk with an 'oof'. The dog popped free and danced nervously nearby, yipping hysterically.

Had the first woman been stealing that dog? Or did she…had she not paid for something? Why would the groomer attack her? It was crazy. People didn't physically assault each other…not in this town! Cassie's mind burbled with inanities as it tried to make sense of what her eyes were seeing.

The groomer wrestled with the woman, her hands gripping the back of her blouse, trying to turn her over. The woman screamed and struggled, pushing with her legs.

"Vanilla! Help mommy! Help!" the woman called, her hand stretched beseechingly to the little dog. The groomer's elbow came down across the back of the woman's head, smashing her face into the concrete and the woman grew still. Her reaching hand dropped back to the sidewalk with a thick slap.

"Hey!" Cassie yelled. The groomer looked up. Even across the parking lot, road, and sidewalk, the woman's eyes were the same as the no-nose man's had been. Cold, animalistic.

The groomer lifted her chin, her head jerking up in increments, as if scenting the air. Scenting Cassie.

Cassie turned back to the Care Center door and banged it three times with a flat palm. The glass jumped and shivered. In the reflective surface, the groomer seemed to lose interest in Cassie as she bent over the woman beneath her. The dog yipped on and on. Cassie cupped her hands around her eyes and looked into the dim stillness of the Care Center front reception area. The glass was cool and solid under her hands. A relief. She banged the door again and then stepped back, indecisive. Go around? Call? She began to fish in her bag for her phone, then remembered the spotty (non-existent) reception and dropped it again. Behind her, the dog's yipping was cut off so suddenly that Cassie was compelled to turn and look. It was gone. The dog was gone.

The groomer dragged the woman down the side of the shop's building. Getting her help? Yes, of course, that was it. She was getting help for the poor woman, carrying her inside, getting help and–

"Mrs. Ramson?"

Cassie jumped and screamed–a small, breathy yelp–and her hand went to her throat again. Strong pulse, yes, but that did nothing to help the disorienting unreality trying to wash her mind away.

A young woman in a maxi dress and long, long, pigtails stood on the other side of the glass door, her hand at the lock but hesitating. Miss Daisy. One of the teachers/school security people.

She jumped back at Cassie's scream, her hand going to her almost-flat bosom. "Mrs. Ramson!" she said and nearly tripped over her platform wedges. Her long pigtails swayed. "What's *wrong*?"

"Daisy, let me in," Cassie said, "I'm here to pick up Lucy."

Miss Daisy surveyed her for a long moment, eyes squinted. Cassie glanced back at the dog groomer's, but the groomer and the woman were gone. That calmed her a little. She hadn't seen what she thought she'd seen that was all. She'd stop and tell the cop about both things, the man with no nose and the...the fight between the woman and the groomer.

First, Lucy. She had to get Lucy.

"Mr. Ramson already came for her Mrs. Ramson...didn't he tell you?"

Cassie stepped back and dropped her arms to her sides. The girl's eyes were on the verge of panic–the whole reason the care centers were locked up so tight was to stop the abductions, but parents were the biggest offenders.

Contrarily, Cassie didn't want Daisy to call the police.

"Of course," Cassie said, as she forced her features into an embarrassed smile, "I just...I forgot. I forgot he said he was going to do that."

"Is everything all right, Mrs. Ramson?" Daisy asked with real concern (but her hand hadn't gone anywhere near the lock again– whatever trouble was outside with Cassie could damn well stay out there).

"Yes, everything is fine," Cassie said. She began to turn away. "See you tomorrow, Daisy!" She said it with a small wave and even smaller smile.

She had to drive past the coffee shop again on the way to Dan's school. She'd just pull in and tell the cop what she'd seen. Probably it was nothing, but she felt she had to say something.

As she backtracked over her route, part of her mind noted that there was even less traffic now than before, almost none, in fact.

She braked hard, as the small white dog from the grooming shop ran across the road. Its side was covered in paint (*gore...that's gore*, her nurse's trained mind said) and it was nearly hit by a Chevy *Volt* coming the opposite way. The *Volt* braked, too, and Cassie had a few seconds to acknowledge the white disk of a face that hovered over the wheel. A young man, his expression filled with dazed incomprehension. *Just because he'd almost hit a dog?*

Then Cassie was pulling into the lot at the coffee shop, relieved that the cop car was still there at the far corner, facing the road. She drove straight across, unmindful of the neatly laid rows. Let him give her hell for it, who cared? She had to let him know about—the cop car was empty.

Cassie let the Mazda glide and then braked still fifteen feet away. The cop car's window was down and lights flashed on the dashboard inside. Would he have left the window down if he had, say, run into the coffee shop?

She cut her own nearly silent engine, rolled down her window, and listened for the low electric hum of the other vehicle.

The cop car was on. Would he get out and just leave it on like that?

Cassie glanced toward the coffee shop, impatient and unwilling to wait for the officer to come back out. She dug her phone from her purse again and used her thumbprint to bring it to life. She dialed 911. The call dropped without ever ringing. She dialed again. Nothing.

A low groan wafted across to her. She dropped her phone into her purse, opened her car door, and exited in one smooth movement. Standing, she could see that the officer *was* in his car, but he was bent over sideways, tilted over onto his passenger seat. His face was hidden under one, outflung arm, his other arm folded under his body.

"Officer?" Cassie said, loath to reach into a police vehicle. "I'm a nurse; can I help you?"

The moan came again, the officer's shoulder rising and falling as though the sound was less made by him intentionally, than propelled from his collapsing diaphragm.

"Officer? I'm a nurse. I can help you," she said. She eased the door handle up, and braced for an alarm. The police had become so secretive, barely speaking to civilians anymore–who knew what they might have going on in their cars. "Officer? I'm going to touch you...I'm going to touch your shoulder." Her hand reached out, fingers shaking like delicate, inquisitive antennae. "I'm just going to put my hand on your shoulder so I can move you–" His uniform was very warm, his shoulder soft and meaty. He was a portly man, his stomach stretching his button-holes into thin ovals. Her fingers dug in. "Just take it easy and–"

The arm hanging over his face flexed like a snake and he grabbed her wrist. Cassie almost screamed but held it in check. There was blood on the seat beneath him, and it slowly dripped onto the floor mat. He was hurt, confused. She shouldn't give him reason to become even more agitated.

"Officer," she said and swallowed, "I'm a nurse and I'm going to help you." She tried to pat his shoulder but he was twisting her wrist. She grimaced in pain but tried to keep her voice calm. "Please. I'm trying to help you...you're...you're hurting me–"

The officer's body shuddered and he humped his shoulders, as though trying to force himself up. He did not let go of her hand.

"Stay still," Cassie said, "I'm a nurse. I want to–"

With a heave, the officer flopped the top of his body over, twisted at the waist, facing Cassie. His nose was not gone, but it had been smashed flat against his cheek. A big clot of bloody mucus hung, quivering, on his upper lip, and then began to slide, leaving a red, one-sided mustache on his lip. One of his eyes had been gouged. Cassie couldn't tell if the eyeball was gone or if it was still there and...mangled. The blackish maroon cavity had been stuffed with something that looked like coffee grounds. Her mind cross-patched to the coffee shop...had there been some kind of accident? Did a machine explode?

The officer's remaining eye found hers. He moaned again and then his lips tightened against his teeth in something that looked like a cross between a growl and a sneer. His eye was soulless. Just like the homeless guy with no nose on her porch. Just like the dog groomer.

What was happening? Had everyone gone crazy?

The officer bent her wrist, twisting it until her bones ground together. Finally, fully panicked, Cassie screamed. She yanked back, unmindful now of his injuries, only feeling her own pain, and dazed alarm setting in. He held her fast. He groaned again and began to rise, trying to push himself out of the seat, struggling up on one arm. The seatbelt held him pinned at the waist. He looked down and growled at his midsection. He bucked in frustration, still growling. Then he turned his head and bit at his shoulder, tearing at his uniform with the insistence of a carrion feeder.

Cassie screamed and his eye found hers again. There seemed to be a shadow of surprise there, as though he'd forgotten his captive. Instead of pushing himself up, he began instead to pull her closer. His mouth yawned open and it was filled with the same blackish coffee ground substance. Bits of it tumbled in clumps over his stretching, straining lips.

Oh God, he was trying to bite her!

Cassie screamed again and fell backward, trying to break his grip, but only managed to yank him slightly more upright. She kicked out, but the angle made it awkward, and her body was already too close to the officer's for her to get any leverage. The smell of him hit her: blood, salt, and rich rot. His mouth looked enormous, like a cave, like a pit she was about to tumble into. She knew she would die if she did. She knew she would die if he bit her.

She screamed again and pulled back, using every ounce of her strength. His other hand came up and gripped her elbow. He yanked her closer, bonking her forehead hard on the doorframe.

Everything went gray.

She floated in the gray, gathering her thoughts. Resting. It felt good. Peaceful and (*–fuck, fuck that's a cop I don't–*) relaxing like she didn't have any responsibilities or (*–did he bite her? Did she get–move her over here and–*) cares. Only the laundry and then she would (–*can't leave her here, she'll be dead in less than–leave her, leave her, we have to go, my mom–*) pick Lucy up at–

LUCY!

She snapped awake in a panic, still pulling away from the officer, scuttling like a crab on her hands, her wrist on fire and butt dragging across the warm asphalt. The officer was twenty feet away, tumbled out of his car as much as the belt at his ample waist would allow. There was a small axe buried in the back of his skull. His officer's hat sat on the pavement beneath his head collecting the thick, dripping blood.

Cassie turned in time to see three boys running across the parking lot. They were in the uniforms of the Catholic High School. They had just killed this police officer (*saved you, you mean*).

Saved me? But–

Yes, *saved you,* saved you from the *animal* that officer had become. Don't be a dumbass, Cassie. The officer, the no-nose man, and the groomer...*all* animals...something is *FUCKING* people up! Now, get your shit together and *GO GET LUCY*!

She scrambled up and then had to bend over her knees as a wave of black nausea tried to float her back into the gray. She straightened slowly, glanced once more at the fat, dead officer, then got in her car and drove away.

CHAPTER 3

Tinsdale, Last of the Chance Hearings Scientists to be Released
Donald Allen, The Philadelphia Record
June 8, 2027

Albert Tinsdale, the last of the Chance Hearings scientists still incarcerated, will be released from the Pennsylvania State Penitentiary today.

It has been two years since Tinsdale, a revered and successful research scientist working primarily in the area of genetics, was incarcerated because of discoveries made regarding the "Immortality Gene." Supporters of Tinsdale and the seven scientists working with him, said at the time that the convictions were passed down based largely on pressure from the then-powerful Clergy Party, who decried that the work was infringing upon their Christian ideals and causing persecution and ridicule of the   Christian   religion.

Johnathan Frakes, lead lawyer for Tinsdale's defense, said in later interviews that he believed the short nature of the sentences (22 months for Tinsdale and 16 months for each of his colleagues), was evidence that the conviction was handed down merely as an appeasement tactic for the decision in 2024–a decision declaring all religious holidays be removed from government and public calendars. This decision, signed into law by President Clooney and the most polarizing decision of his term, was the alleged catalyst for the so-called Christian Uprising, where hundreds of congregations, most in the Southern United States, burned down their own churches.

In an interview Tinsdale gave last month, he stated that he would not go back to his research, nor would he enter any part of the scientific arena again. "The damage has been done and the repercussions will be far-reaching, possibly even into the grave. For myself, I plan to spend as much time as possible with my wife and daughter before the beginning of the end, and I can only hope that it's not too late to do so," he said.

Some in the now-failing Clergy Party say that this statement (reaching into the grave) is a nod to Christian ideals in regards to the story of the resurrection of Christ, and that Tinsdale has 'seen the light of his errors' while incarcerated. Scientists on the other side of the fence say that it has to do with the fact that Alouitious Sparks, a then-leader in the Clergy Party's Concerned Scientists division, was given Tinsdale's former job. A decision, these scientists say, that caused errors, cover-ups, and lost data that rendered Tinsdale's research null and void.

A protest was scheduled for Tinsdale's release, but there is little anticipation of any on-going trouble as Tinsdale, himself, has already stated his intention to retire from his chosen field. "It is a great loss, indeed, for the people of this nation, even if they don't realize it yet," said Alex Gordon, one of Tinsdale's former colleagues.

– – –

Cassie drove in a haze of panic so strong that it masqueraded as calm. Her mind in neutral, she noted and discarded each car that drove past her and she barely reacted when a young man ran screaming into the road. He raised bloodied hands to her, but she swerved neatly around him and continued. She glanced at the rearview mirror and when three other teenagers overtook the young man, she looked away. She swallowed and wondered if she was getting a cold; her throat felt so sore. She would have to make sure Lucy didn't sneak into their bed–Lucy was susceptible to every germ that came along.

Cassie swallowed again and the number five popped into her head. She'd been counting the number of times she swallowed. Why was she doing that?

Somewhere to the east of her came a large bang, an explosion, as she pulled into the parking lot of the Vo-Tech. She would find Dan and Lucy, yell at Dan for taking Lucy, and then Dan would have a plan.

A plan for what?

For...for whatever was going on. Terrorists or whatever this was.

She scanned the lot. This one, too, was nearly empty, but she didn't let that bother her. It was lunchtime (*no...it's not even eleven*) and everyone was out to lunch, but Dan would be here. He and Lucy would be in the building, eating the burgers and French fries they'd bought after Dan picked Lucy up (*why didn't he call you, then? because the phones are down, duh...now shut up and leave me alone*).

She got out of the car and looked east. Whatever had exploded was now burning and a thick black cloud was expanding into the blue sky. From the direction of the cloud, she surmised that it was the auto body shop that sat on the highway at the border of Marlton and the next town over. They still had a gas pump at that shop.

She stood expectantly, head cocked, and listening for sirens, but there were none.

She sighed with disgust. What did she pay taxes for? It was ridiculous that something should just burn away unabated, unseen-to. No one cared at all. This world was falling apart.

Cassie trotted up the wide concrete steps but her hand hesitated at the outside bell that would alert security to her presence. The front doors of the Vo-Tech, like the Care Center doors, remained locked, always. Even though this was a high school, there were still abduction concerns. Three years ago, sixty-seven girls had been abducted at gunpoint from a high school in Virginia, and those girls had never been seen again.

The Vo-Tech was a hands on environment and students had to be in attendance. Not like the other schools where children mostly learned from home over the internet.

She thought for a second, tried to, as her fingers skated over the bell without pressing it. Somewhere in the deep recesses of her mind, unacknowledged, but still influencing her behavior, alarms were sounding.

She cupped her hands around her eyes and leaned into the glass at the top of the door. The lights were on. The long hallway was empty, the security desk unmanned.

The Vo-Tech was deserted.

Cassie turned to scan the lot again, looking for Dan's old Prius. There were three of them, two the same color as Dan's. He was here, then, had to be. He had Lucy and he was...*if he picked Lucy up, why didn't he come get you next?*

Cassie shook her head and pushed the bell, holding it down, pressing it. Mashing it. Willing someone to come before her thoughts, so full of treachery, could overtake her.

"Come on, come on...where are you people?" she asked and tapped her foot. She walked three quick steps left and three right, pacing, keeping her eyes on the door, arms crossed tightly at her chest, hands in tight, aggravated fists. "Come *on!*" She stomped her foot.

She looked at herself in the glass and was startled by the ugly grimace on her face. She had to calm down, what was wrong with her? She took a deep breath, like she'd learned in yoga, and blew it out slowly. Another. She pulled her hair from the band and re-gathered it, smoothing it as she tried to smooth her thoughts. She closed her eyes and took another breath. Opened her eyes. She smiled, but it wasn't a good fit and she dropped it, and simply stared at her reflection in the glass.

Something moved behind her. She spun with a gasp. A girl was coming across the parking lot. Young and slight, she could have been a freshman or maybe a sophomore. She was humming to herself and she carried her books at her chest, her head bent shyly.

The scene was so normal, so every day that Cassie relaxed.

She raised an arm. "Hi!" she called to the girl. "Do you go here? I'm Dan's...I mean, I'm Mr. Ramson's wife."

The girl did not look up, but she hesitated, and then stumbled to a stop. Head down, she swayed. Just like the man on the porch.

"Honey?" Cassie said. "Are you okay?" Her voice had grown faint, too faint for the girl to hear, and Cassie stepped back until her butt hit the glass of the door. "Honey?"

The girl's head came up by ticking, half inches. Her face was slick with dark blood from her top lip to her chin. There was a long, ragged black hole, like a shotgun wound, under her collarbone.

Cassie blinked.

The books in the girl's arms disappeared, became what they had been all along–lungs. The girl was holding her own lungs, cradling them to her gaping chest. Cassie shivered and hot bile rose like a tide into her throat. Her stomach clenched.

The girl dipped her head and tore a bite from herself. Raised her head again, chewing, the rubbery lung meat quivering on her lips.

What Cassie had taken for humming was actually a low, toneless moan that went on and on, modulated by the movement of the girl's lips as she chewed.

"Jesus Christ," Cassie whispered. "Jesus, what…what…" Rage slammed into her, so unexpected that she screamed. "What *ARE* you?" Her face turned red, then purple. She couldn't pull in a breath. Her hands clenched, nails biting red crescents into her palms. "*WHAT ARE YOU?*" she screamed again, spittle flying from her lips.

The girl's head snapped up and turned in Cassie's direction. She dropped her lungs and they dangled, half in and half out of her chest. She began to shuffle toward Cassie. Then to run.

Cassie screamed, her hands going to her cheeks. She was bent nearly double, the screams ripping out of her with strong convulsions, as if she were throwing up sound rather than vomit.

The girl's lungs bounced and banged against her chest as she ran, held only by a thin string of red tissue. Her hip banged a Prius, jarring her to the left and one lung snapped off. It fell and the girl stumbled across it, slipping, with one ankle turning with a crunch.

Cassie screamed and screamed again. Her voice began to break. She wanted to cover her eyes, bury her head in her arms. This couldn't be real. It couldn't be. It couldn't.

The girl was still coming despite her snapped ankle. She moaned and huffed, her arms reaching for Cassie as though they were three feet from each other, rather than fifteen.

Cassie slid down the glass door, her shirt rucking up, and crouched, knees pulled tight to her chest. She couldn't scream anymore, but she could cry. Hot tears blurred her vision and she was grateful for it, grateful she could no longer see with any clarity the monstrosity lurching toward her.

The girl was at the base of the steps. Her foot, turned completely on its side, was scraped raw across the ankle. She lifted it onto the first step, but tumbled to the side when she tried to put her full weight on it. The moan became a frustrated growl. Her eyes went to her foot as if she couldn't understand why it wouldn't hold her. Bone showed through the skin, the complicated interlocking bones of the ankle. She sat and pulled her leg toward herself as though going into the lotus position. She gazed at the foot hanging limply, swinging at the connection of bone and ragged skin.

Cassie shoved her hands against her mouth, stifling a rising scream. She didn't want to see anymore, and she didn't want to *be here* anymore. She should have stayed home, she just should have, there was the laundry and so much to do she could have gotten so much done today if she hadn't–

Below Cassie, at the base of the steps, the girl twisted her dangling foot and it came loose with a crunch of bone. Skin and white strands of spaghetti-like tendon stretched between the foot and ankle. The girl dipped her head, bit into the connecting flesh. Began to rip.

Cassie fell back with a sigh, collapsing into the gray of unconscious relief.

CHAPTER 4

Burlco Vo-Tech Faculty Roster, P-R

Calvin Post: B.S. Chemistry Fordham State School, M.S. Education Princeton State College
Courses: *Remedial Science, Life Science I, Algebra I*

Dr. Amanda Pritikin, PhD: B.A. Mathematics, M.A. Engineering Rutgers State College; Ph.D., Engineering Princeton State College
Courses: *Life Skills, Hospitality Fast Track, Janitorial Fast Track*

Robert M. Ralston, Esq.: LL.M., S.J.D., Harvard Law State School
Courses: Social Sciences I & II

Dr. Daniel Ramson, Ph.D.; B.A. English, M.A English Rutgers University, Ph.D. Education Oxford University (Pennsylvania State Chapter)
Courses: *Remedial English, English as a Second Language, English I, II, III, & IV*

Susan Reed, AWS GS Vo-Tech, WLD Presidio Tech State School
Courses: *Welding I, II, III, & IV*

— — —

Cassie woke slowly, brushing an annoying fly from her cheek. She'd have to tell Dan about that–the house needed to be fumigated or something. Even one bug was one too many as far as she was concerned.

"Cassie?"

And she didn't want Lucy getting bit by anything, either.

"Cas? Are you awake?"

"Course I'm awake," Cassie said. Her eyes fluttered and she rolled her head side to side, irritated. "I have to get the laundry done, and I have to pick up Lucy."

Fingers trailed down her cheek and she swiped at them again, but they got to her chin and gripped. Too hard.

"Hey," Cassie said.

"Hey, yourself," the voice said. A man, but not Dan. Not her Dan with the plan. The pressure on her chin disappeared. "You coming around? You with us?"

"Who's 'us'?" Cassie asked. It was dark, too dark to see who hung over her. "Turn on the lights, Jesus." She passed a hand over her eyes. They were starting to adjust.

"We're just being cautious," the man said, and as he did, his face resolved. He looked familiar.

The girl from the parking lot flashed into her mind and she scrambled to sit up.

"Take it easy," the familiar man said. His face was still half in shadow, but he smiled. "You're safe, Cassie. We pulled you in while she was still...while she was...you know, eating."

Three other people stood beside tall windows, looking out but keeping hidden. One woman glanced at Cassie, and Cassie recognized her...Susan Reed, the young welding instructor.

"Hey, Cassie," Susan said and then turned her gaze back to the window. Her face was grave, her movements jerky and shocky. Her short dark hair was rummaged-looking and spiky. She wore jeans and a tank top with a long sleeve button up tied around her waist and pink, thick-soled work boots.

"Hi, Susan," Cassie said, and as she did, she placed the man kneeling next to her. "Calvin," she said, "Science? Or was it math?"

"Both," he said and stood, reaching for her hand. He was about her age, mid-thirties, nondescript in the way of plain men, but his grip was strong and his forearm corded as he pulled her up. "Dan and I shared an office; Susan and Robert shared it with us, too."

At his name, another man at the window turned to nod. "Hello, Cassie, we met two years ago at Rhonda Carol's party." He was handsome, his dark hair lightly streaked with gray. Compared to the others, he was very dressed up in a button down shirt, vest, and matching slacks.

"Hi, Robert," Cassie said and smiled, then brushed absently at the seat of her pants. These jeans had been fresh this morning when she put them on, but now, they'd have to be washed and…a sense of unreality slowed over her and she put a hand to her head.

Everything had changed.

Everything.

Calvin steadied her with his hand on her shoulder.

"Where's Dan?" Cassie asked. Her voice was flat and she kept her hand over her eyes, trying to stay calm, as wave after wave of denial tried to float her away.

"He left," Calvin said. His cautious, hesitant tone made her angry and she snatched her hand away from her eyes.

"When? When did he leave?"

He squeezed her shoulder, but she shrugged out from under his hand. Rage boiled and seethed within her. She was furious that she couldn't understand what was happening; couldn't make it simple. A sharp pain twinged her temple like a warning. "When did he leave?" she asked, her voice a tight wire through clenched teeth. "When is he coming back?"

Calvin put his hands up, palms toward her. "Calm down, Cassie," he said. "Calm down and–"

"Cal, for fucks sake," Susan said, "you're just making it worse…*tell* her that Dan…" She shook her head and crossed her arms over her chest as though resolved to do what Calvin obviously could not. The shirt tied at her waist shivered and billowed as she stepped toward Cassie. "He left around nine-thirty. Right when things started getting really weird. He said–" Susan licked her lips, her eyes going briefly to Cal. "He said he was going to get Lucy and then you. He was trying to call you, but…" She shrugged. Her eyes were sympathetic but also hard. "Did you go to Lucy's school? Was she there?"

Cassie shook her head. "No, they said...they said he already picked her up." Tears stung the backs of her eyes and her throat squeezed shut, but she wouldn't cry, not right now. She couldn't afford the luxury. She had to keep herself on track if she was going to find Lucy and Dan.

She cast about the room and patted her front pockets. "Where's my purse? I need my keys."

"You can't go back out there," Susan said, "and you owe us some information, anyway. You're a nurse, right?"

Cassie shook her head, not in denial but in confusion. Susan's words were just so many nonsense syllables and sounds. Had these people gone crazy?

Her purse was against the wall under the chalkboard. She started toward it and Cal put his hand on her shoulder again. She shrugged it off with a gasp almost like a hiss.

"Leave me alone!" she said. "Jesus. You can't–"

"Cassie, listen to me," Robert said. His voice was calm and modulated. A courtroom voice. "This isn't just happening to you and Dan and Lucy. It's happening to all of us. Don't you think Susan would like to leave and get her son? Don't you think I'd like to go and find my wife? Everything has changed, Cassie," he said and another sense of unreality washed over her as he used the very phrase that had been pin balling around her head. "We have to get this figured out, and your medical perspective might help. Tell us what happened to you this morning."

At his words, it wasn't the morning that came to her mind, but her shift at the clinic last night.

Cassie worked at one of the urgent care centers that had been put in place to handle the cases not quite bad enough for emergency rooms, but not quite mild enough for the wait it would take to get an appointment with a GP.

There had been many sick people in last night, and it wasn't the usual array of cases...it was almost consistently one issue: flu. Although, some said they thought it was food poisoning because it had come on so fast. Cassie had even begun to wonder if there had been any of those small, local carnivals going on. A batch of bad hot dogs could have packed their waiting room.

Some patients even had to be sent to the emergency room two miles down the road, although most had merely been sent home with admonishments to rest and stay hydrated.

How many people came through last night? How many clinics and hospitals were there in the area, and had they all experienced the same thing?

Cassie sat in one of the desk/chair combos that had been pushed haphazardly away from the windows. She dropped her forehead into her hands and massaged.

"Cassie?" Susan said. "What's wrong?"

Cassie quelled a laugh. What's wrong? Jesus, what's *right*?

"The clinic...I was working the overnight shift last night and there were a lot of sick people," Cassie said.

Robert turned a desk around to face her and it screeched loudly. Susan and Calvin flinched, their eyes going to the windows. Robert said, "Cal, take my place, would you? Susan, keep watching outside, all right? Tell me if you see police or fire, anything official." His eyes went to the fifth person in the room—a young man—a student?—who hadn't left his post. He stood with his arms crossed over his chest, a scowl on his skinny face. "Doing okay, Ty?"

The kid gave a slight nod and Robert turned his attention back to Cassie. "Tell me what you mean," he said. "Was it more people than normal?"

"Yeah," Cassie said, "the flu, lots of it. Maybe it was...I was thinking about bad hotdogs and wondering...you know. If it was..." Her eyes drifted to the windows. From her angle, she could only see the tops of trees at the far side of the parking lot. What was going on out there?

Robert snapped his fingers in front of her nose and she gaped at him.

"If it was what?" he asked. "What were you thinking?"

"If it was food poisoning, if there was a carnival somewhere, bad hotdogs, bad burgers, something that would explain the influx of patients."

"Do you think it was? Food poisoning, I mean?"

"I don't know. Probably not, but the flu seems pretty unlikely, too."

"Why?"

"Because, there's never that many people sick at one time," Cassie said. "If you add us to the other clinics and hospitals–how many are in and near this township, eight? More than that?"

"Shouldn't you know?" Susan asked from her post at the window. Her tone held no derision, only curiosity.

"Jesus, I...let me think," Cassie said. She rubbed her eyes and then massaged her temple. Her cold fingers felt good on the hot pain growing there. "There's Marlton Memorial, Advantage Health, and GSH...that's the hospitals. The clinics are tougher, let's see, there's mine and then there's the one that feeds Advantage..." Cassie ticked them off on her fingers. "The one that feeds GSH and the orthopedic clinic...and then there's the walk-in clinics at the drugstores, and I don't even know how many of those there are."

"Holy shit," Susan said, but her tone was dull and inflectionless. She turned back to the window and rested her palms on her backside. "I never knew we had such a sick township."

Calvin snorted. "Not sick, just well insured."

Susan shrugged.

"Do you have any way of knowing if all the hospitals and clinics were overrun last night?" Robert asked, ignoring Susan and Calvin.

Cassie shook her head but then looked up, blinking, and her mouth falling open.

"What?" Robert asked. "What did you remember?"

"Tammy called Marlton Memorial...that's the hospital we feed..." At the question in his eyes, she clarified, "That's the hospital we're affiliated with." Robert nodded and she went on. "She, Tammy, called to see if they could send an ambulance for one of the patients–he was very old, very ill–but they said all their wagons were currently out. It was strange, but we were so busy that I just kind of, dismissed it. We had a lot of other things to do."

Robert sat back, his eyes intent on hers. "I think it might have happened everywhere–at least–everywhere around here. What did you do this morning? What brought you to the school? Tell me everything."

Cassie did, starting with the laundry. There was something in Robert's manner that made it easy to proceed from point A to B to C. He asked questions when he needed clarification, redirected her if she drifted, and somehow managed to keep her story from being tangled. Then she remembered. Robert was a lawyer and unlike many of the other teachers, he'd held onto his primary career. He only taught at the Vo-Tech one day a week.

When she got to the part about the girl in the parking lot, she lowered her eyes to her hands, but she could still see Susan turn from the window.

Cassie touched shaking fingertips to her lips in an effort to ward off nausea, but between the recollection and the migraine drilling into her head, her stomach flipped over on itself. The coffee she'd had this morning began to rise in her stomach on a tide of acid. She turned away from Robert, burped, and made a thick, yurking sound.

"It's okay if you're going to be sick, Cassie," Robert said, "but please do it in the ladies room, or at least out in the hall."

Cassie scrambled out of the chair with her hand pressed to her mouth, as though his words had drawn the vomit up her throat. The hallway was even darker than the classroom. Cassie's steps echoed up and down as she trotted to the door marked "GIRLS", and she made it as far as the first sink before the bile shot out of her like a hot geyser. It was brownish-tan and still smelled of her morning coffee, and she yurked again, her stomach and diaphragm clenching. She threw up three more times, finally producing only yellowy bile.

The heavy door swung open.

"Ooh, gross…at least I made it to the toilet," Susan said.

Cassie turned to her, scrubbing her mouth with a paper towel, but didn't answer.

Susan hugged herself with her bare arms and then rubbed them briskly as if cold. She scanned the room and then let her eyes rest on Cassie.

"So…you okay?"

Cassie took a deep breath and threw the paper towel in the trashcan.

"I don't know," Cassie said. "At least I think I'm done throwing up." She gave Susan a small, tired smile. "I hope."

"Yeah, I only yacked the once. You'll probably be okay."

Susan ran her hands over her arms again. She had a large tattoo of a morning glory blossom on her bicep and the vine it grew on trailed away under her tank top. Her arms were slight, but the muscles well defined, and she looked lithe and strong like a ballerina.

"You have a son?" Cassie asked remembering Robert's words, and Susan nodded once. Cassie had a tough time picturing Susan holding a baby, raising a toddler. With her tattoos and short, short hair, she just didn't look the type.

Dan rarely talked to Cassie about the other teachers and she had never thought to ask. They had a small set of friends that didn't include other teachers, only people in the medical field. Dan had never seemed to mind.

"How old is he?" Cassie asked. "What's his name? Is he in one of the care centers?"

"He's with my mom," Susan said and she must have read something in Cassie's expression. She frowned and said, "Not, like, permanently. I meant she watches him during the day while I'm teaching. He's five months; his name is Sorrow."

Cassie didn't let her expression change, forcing it to stay open and neutral. Single moms could be touchy, especially when the dads had bailed on them. Especially when they were obviously not good decision makers like this Susan with her tacky clothes and out-of-wedlock baby with the inappropriate name.

"Five months," Cassie said. "Geez, it seems like forever ago that Lucy was five months." She shook her head and smiled. "It was hard, but sometimes I miss it. That probably sounds crazy to you right now, doesn't it? You're still in the thick of it."

"No, it doesn't sound crazy," Susan said. She opened her mouth as if to say something else and then closed it, changing her mind. She ran her hands through her hair, rummaging it further. "Let's get back to the classroom. It makes me jumpy being away from everyone."

"Okay," Cassie said and pushed herself off the sink. A shiver of vertigo caused the room to shimmer, but then it settled.

Her headache had gone away, too, and now she felt more able to think clearly.

Susan held the door for her and they started down the hall.

"What happened here this morning?" Cassie asked. "Isn't there anyone else in the building?"

"Everyone else–not that there were many of us to begin with–bolted. Or died." Susan rummaged again, pulling her hair into a new arrangement of spikes. "There were, like, ten bodies in the parking lot. Well, originally. Lots of them disappeared. You didn't see any bodies out there?"

Cassie shook her head. The entire morning had been marked by a steadily creeping tunnel vision.

"I think you're probably lucky you got here at all," Susan said and then went on. "Well, so, hardly any kids showed up and Principal Frisk called everyone into the auditorium. Robert stopped Dan and me from going. He wanted to go over one of his kids with us."

"What do you mean?"

"We all counsel, you know, kids who just want info or whatever about the classes we teach or kids who are having behavioral issues or anything like that. So Robert had some questions about procedure and he wanted Dan's opinion on it, and mine, too, 'cause the student was a girl, and just because we all shared the same office. Dumb stuff, really, about excessive bathroom breaks." Susan laughed. "The student was this girl named Mary Grass, and she thinks she can get away with anything by clutching her uterus and making helpless doe-eyes. You know the type."

Cassie smiled her understanding although she was afraid someone as tough as Susan might put a lot of women in the helpless doe-eyed category.

"So anyway, we were talking about it, Robert asking did I think Mary had a problem and I said no, she doesn't have a problem because she has a clueless dude for a teacher...she's getting exactly what she wants–downtime. Robert is smart, like, book smart, but he doesn't know shit about kids."

They were at the classroom door so Susan leaned against the doorjamb and shoved her hands into her back pockets. She kept her gaze fixed down the hall. "I'll watch this way and you watch the other. Anyway, we were yammering away and then–then–"

Susan swallowed and glanced at Cassie. Her eyes were troubled and swimming with tears. Maybe Susan wasn't as cold as Cassie thought.

"All hell broke loose," Susan went on. "I think Margaret started it–Margaret Miller, the graphic arts teacher. She'd been pretty sick this morning, everyone telling her she oughta go home, but you know how some people are. I'll tell you what I think. I think she fucking lost her mind and started ripping into everyone. Whatever she had is fucking communicable as hell. Maybe not so much through the air, regular, you know, but, like, through a good, bloody bite."

"Jesus," Cassie said. She was busy trying to work out which pieces of information were facts and which were Susan's prejudices and suppositions. She couldn't believe someone suffering from that bad of a flu, would be up for an all-out assault on her co-workers.

"I think she died first," Robert said and both women jumped. He had pulled the door open behind them.

"What the *fuck*, Robert?" Susan said and brushed past him, pulling her hair straight out at the sides, making her look like a surprised and angry porcupine. "Don't sneak up."

"I didn't mean to," he said and Cassie almost smiled, and would have if not for her stress level. He looked so chagrined.

No doubt, that Susan was a force of nature.

"What do you mean, 'died'?" Cassie asked. Robert motioned for her to go into the classroom and he closed the door behind her after a final glance up and down the hallway.

"That makes no sense, Robert," Calvin said. "We've talked about it."

"What about Alfonse, then?" Robert asked. There was no anger in his voice, only a leading conviction.

Calvin shook his head and sighed, turning back to the window. His shoulders were slumped and defeated.

"What could it have been, Cal?" Robert asked. "What else, besides–?"

"I don't know…he could have just gotten up again."

"Cal, really," Robert said and placed his hands on his hips. Scolding, but cajoling, too.

He must be great in a courtroom, Cassie thought, impressed despite the overwhelming feeling of distress that waited just over the edge of her mental horizon.

"Who's Alfonse?" she asked.

Robert looked from Susan to Calvin to see if they were going to speak up, but they both kept their backs turned to him.

So Robert told her about Alfonse.

CHAPTER 5

"Dave, we have to get you to the east coast. You fly out first thing."

Dave Weathers looked up from the papers he was going over and sighed at Angela, his boss. She stood tall in his doorway, in a slightly rumpled suit, proffering a plane ticket and slim blue folder.

"Angie, I'm swamped," he said. "I've got thirteen cases of MRSA in Texas that look mutated, and another weird eye-infection thing right here in LA that might–"

"It's Atlanta that requested you," Angie said. She came into his office and collapsed into the chair in front of the desk. She yawned and swung her hair back from her shoulders.

"Atlanta?" Dave said. "Well, shit...I hope they're going to fire me."

Her lips turned up even as her eyes closed. "You wish."

"I do, sometimes. You know?"

"Dave," Angie said, "you'd shrivel up and die if you couldn't run down mysterious infections and mutated molds for the CDC."

"True, but I could work somewhere else, somewhere with less pressure. I could go work in a deli, maybe. I'm good at making sandwiches."

"Deli work is stressful, too," Angie said. "I worked my way through college in a deli." She sat straighter and laid the ticket and folder on the far edge of his desk. "Just go, okay? They're having a real problem out there and they could use your good looks to help calm everyone down." She teased him a lot about his resemblance to Superman, with his black hair and blue eyes. He could never tell if it was flirting or not. Angie had to be in her early fifties. That put her at least fifteen years ahead of him.

"What's the problem?" he asked and drew the ticket closer without looking at it.

"Some kind of epidemic based out of the tri-state area…New York, New Jersey, Pennsylvania. Fast-moving, too."

"Airborne communicability?"

"No one knows anything, yet. They have a local team en route, but they're pulling in a lot of satellite people, too. Must be big."

"Must be," Dave said and glanced at the ticket. He looked at her, startled. "Angie! This flight is for two AM! It's already–" he shot back a sleeve and checked his watch. "It's goddamn twelve-thirty. I don't know if I even have time to go home!"

"You don't, actually," Angie said. "The car is downstairs. Your bag is in it and another folder with some info about what you're getting into." She stood and stretched. Then she gave him a sympathetic smile. "Call Colleen from the car; she'll understand."

"The boys won't understand that I have to miss another soccer game," he said, but his tone was resigned. He dropped his forehead into his hands. The twins were eight and not prone to appreciating his job, not that they should. It was hard for them and Colleen, too. She was practically a single mother, at times.

"You'll be back in two days, three at the most," Angie said. She stood to leave. "They have so many warm bodies coming in for this one that they won't know what to do with everybody. Just make sure Miller knows you want to be cut loose first." She looked back at him from the doorway. "Hey…don't get any rips in your germ-suit."

He laughed and shook his head as she disappeared.

He dialed Colleen from the car. She answered on the third ring.

"Where are you going?" she asked. Her voice was sleep-muffled but not addled, as it was when she was woken from a very sound sleep. She must not have been in bed very long. There was no scold in her voice, no anger. She was a good wife.

"Philadelphia," he said and smiled, "Atlanta's involved."

In the dim room, he could sense her sudden alertness.

"Really? What's the problem?"

"I don't know yet, haven't even cracked the file," he said. "Angie told me ten minutes ago and then put me in a car headed for the airport."

"Well," she said, and her rustling sigh caused him to picture her, burrowing back into her pillows, shoulders bare. He shifted in the seat and smiled at the image his mind had made for him. "The boys are going to miss you," she said, her voice deeper. Husky. "I'll tell them you're off saving the world again...Clark." She giggled. She often teased him about the things his boss said, but she wasn't jealous; she didn't need to be.

"I'll miss you, Lois," he said.

"I'll miss you, too, sweetheart," she said and all the teasing had fallen from her voice. "I love you. Be safe out there."

"Love you, too. Hey, I'll bring you back a cheesesteak."

"Just bring me back a you," she said.

"Will do," he said and they hung up.

He checked the time again and then opened the file on his lap. The first thing he saw was a small envelope taped to the inside cover of the folder. He lifted the flap with his forefinger and tilted it; two little blue pills tumbled into the palm of his hand. He smiled. "Thanks, Ang," he said and pulled a bottled water from a side compartment. She knew he hated to fly.

He downed the Valium and then turned his attention to the few sheets of paper in the folder. There wasn't much information, just like Angie had said. A hospital in New Jersey had requested CDC assistance with a flu outbreak. Coincidentally, so had about sixty-five others in and around the area.

It was unprecedented.

It was also—like everything else—explainable and containable.

Dave closed his eyes and tilted his head back against the seat. He would rest now and try to sleep on the jet, but he had trouble sleeping during flights. The Lear the CDC used was comfortable, but small, and small equaled bumpy. Especially since they'd be traversing two mountain ranges.

Ah, well. Part of the job, part of the job, he told himself and then, he let his mind drift.

The ride to the airport was uneventful, the check-in swift and personal, the pilot and co-pilot each shaking his hand. He was to be the only passenger.

"How much will this little jaunt cost the office?" Dave asked as the co-pilot took his bag from him to stow on the plane.

"Just a tad over seventy-five, Mr. Weathers," the pilot said with a smile. He was one of a handful of pilots that the CDC chartered, and he understood the potential gravity of these flights. "You must be the man of the hour."

"I don't think so," Dave said. "This one looks to be a little more all hands on deck."

The pilot nodded but didn't question Dave further, and instead, directed him onto the plane. The cabin was tight and to Dave, slightly claustrophobic. He wasn't deathly afraid of flying, but he sure didn't love it, either. Many of his co-workers praised the easy check-in and intimacy of Learjet travel, but Dave would have preferred first class on a commercial flight.

He settled in and closed his eyes. The pilot and co-pilot murmured back and forth to each other, checking and crosschecking, and Dave let it wash over him like white noise. Maybe he would be able to rest on this flight. He was tired enough and adding the Valium on top of it should be a good recipe for sound sleep.

The plane taxied and picked up speed when it hit the runway. As it screamed into its cabin-shaking takeoff, Dave clutched the armrests but refused to open his eyes. His stomach lifted and dropped, lifted and dropped, as the pressure changed and then changed again. He found himself glad he hadn't eaten since an early dinner, and then found himself surprised that he was actually drifting off. He mentally thanked his boss again for the Valium and then he let himself drift.

He was only vaguely aware when the co-pilot came back to check on him. He took the folder from Dave's lax hands, closed it without looking, and walked it back up front. Dave wanted to protest, but he slipped into sleep, instead.

He dreamed strangely of a familiar location that had been changed beyond recognition. He was looking for Colleen and the boys and he kept asking passers-by if they had seen his family, but they all spoke a different language. No, not just different, *new*...something he'd never heard before. In the way of dreams, he realized he was holding a picture, showing it to the people who walked past. Some shrunk away from it with looks of horror. One woman averted her eyes, another stopped dead in her tracks and looked from the photo in his hand to his face, her eyes filled with shock. She said something he couldn't understand, but he caught the tone easily enough–disgust. He shrugged at her and she shook her head and walked away, muttering to herself. He watched after her. What had she seen that made her so angry?

He turned the picture so that it faced him and his stomach lurched. It was Colleen and she was lying on a tile floor, naked and bloodied. She was dead. She had a twin on either side of her and they, too, were naked, their faces were covered with blood. Dead.

He'd been showing everyone a picture of his dead family.

He struggled to wake but couldn't quite make it. He was socked in, drawn back down, tumbling along with the little pills, and dropped back into the same dream.

He walked on and on through a landscape that by turns burned and froze; sand whipped mercilessly across his face and the backs of his hands, scraping them raw. He didn't care. His family was dead. The picture started to burn in his hand. He tried to shake it, to shake the flames out, but still it burned. He dropped the picture and backed away from it, watching as the flames chewed their way inward, consuming first his children, then Colleen. Horror and grief made his stomach lift and drop, lift and drop again.

Lift and drop.

He opened his eyes.

The pilot was shouting into his headset and the co-pilot dialed frantically through the instruments. The roar of the engines was deafening and Dave could only make out snatches of what the pilot yelled.

Pilot: "–need to get this bird down, Tower, or–"

Jesus Christ, were they crashing?

Pilot: "–won't make it back to Pittsburgh; we were already re-routed once! We don't have–"

Pilot: "God*DAMMIT*, figure it out, Tower, or you'll have three lives on your hands to–"

Pilot: "–I don't give a shit, now you give me clearance and you give it to me NOW, or so help me–"

The co-pilot turned, his mouth hanging open, forehead gleaming with sweat. He gave Dave a quick, frightened glance, and then pulled the cockpit door closed.

Fuck. What the fuck? What the fuck was happening?

The pilot yelled again but Dave couldn't make out the words. He fumbled for his phone. Outside his little window, the sun was up and reflecting across the clouds. It looked beautiful. He dialed Colleen. He just had to tell her, just in case the worst happened, he had to tell her that he–the phone rang once and then the call dropped.

He dialed again. Fear tightened his chest. The boys. They wouldn't understand and they'd hate him forever. This time, the phone didn't even ring. It went to a hissing open line and then cut off.

The jet tilted down at an angle so steep, Dave's first thought was that they were crashing. He felt stuck into his seat, heavy as lead. He almost couldn't pull in a breath.

Christ! Jesus *Christ*!

He tried to dial the phone again, fumbled it; it jittered out of his hands and onto the floor. Then it slid out of sight.

The engines screamed and then screamed even louder as the jet leveled and slowed…slowed…touched down. Then it raced down a runway, bumping and jumping. Dave looked out the window and pine trees rushed by (*PINE TREES?*) a dark green blur. Everything inside the jet groaned and clacked. The piece of shit was falling apart. It was falling apart. He'd end up sitting on the runway in just his seat as everything disintegrated around him!

The jet finally stopped rolling. The engines cycled down. It shook once more, like a dog fresh from a bath, then it was still.

Dave took a deep, shuddery breath.

Then he bent forward and threw up between his feet.

The cabin door opened and the pilot came back. He was white faced, his hat askew.

"You okay?" he asked and Dave nodded, but he couldn't speak; his throat burned. He wiped his mouth and reached for his phone, but the belt still had him pinned. The pilot reached over and deftly flipped the catch, releasing him, then rummaged behind the seat and produced a bottle of water. "Here," he said. Then he collapsed into the seat next to Dave and put his head back. He ran a hand over his forehead.

Dave drank, cleared his throat, and drank again. The pilot had closed his eyes. In the cockpit, the co-pilot was still talking into his headset, his words too low to make out.

"What the hell happened?" Dave asked. "Did we almost crash?"

The pilot rolled his head from side to side and his face cramped in a grimace of disgust. Then his features smoothed out. "We were re-routed. They closed the airports."

"Which airports?" Dave asked.

The pilot opened his eyes and gazed at Dave, his expression unreadable.

"All of them," he said.

"What? How can they…what made…Christ, where the hell are we?"

"I have a lot of questions, too, believe me," the pilot said. "We were literally the last thing flying in the area this morning. Philly closed right before we got there and we were sent out here to AC instead."

"Atlantic City?" Dave said. He'd heard of it, sure, but he'd never been. It was in New Jersey, though, right? "Is this…is it common? Does it happen a lot?"

"No," the co-pilot said from his seat up front, "it has *never* happened before."

Dave looked to the pilot for confirmation and the pilot shrugged and nodded. "The closest thing was way back in 2001, when there was a terrorist attack in New York. All flights were scrambled to the ground, but this wasn't that. The AC controller said no one, *almost* no one, showed up for work this morning." His tone was one of tired disgust.

Dave looked out the window, but the pines were an unrelenting backdrop.

"Are we under some kind of attack?" he asked.

The pilot heaved himself out of the seat. "I don't know," he said. "Listen, we're as close to the terminal as I could get us. We have to hoof it over there…can you walk?"

"Of course," Dave said and stood. The pilot had to grab his arms as his knees tried to buckle under him. "Shit," he said, and his laugh was a shaky breath. "Maybe not."

"You'll be okay in a second," the pilot said and grinned. "I don't know how you'll be fifteen minutes from now, though."

Dave cocked his head at the pilot.

"Your car, your driver…they're in Philly," the pilot said.

"Oh. Yeah. I didn't think about that. I'll just call in," Dave said, and it reminded him he'd lost his phone. He scanned the floor, spotted it, and picked it up. "They'll send someone."

"You can try," the co-pilot said. He had Dave's bag in his hand and stood near the door. He pushed it open and dropped the stairs. "I can't get a call to go through on my cell."

The co-pilot steadied Dave down the short run of steps and the Pilot descended behind him. Across the tarmac, planes big to small sat in untidy disarray.

What the fuck was going on? Dave shook his head and turned to grab his bag from the co-pilot and they all began to walk. It was early, their shadows still long, but already warm.

"There's a Hertz in there, just past check-in," the pilot said. He fished in his breast pocket and handed Dave a business card. "In case you can't get your people, here's my number. I don't know what your travel situation will be for getting home, but you might need to contact me directly."

"Wait…" Dave said, and slipped the card into his front pocket. He'd had the vague idea that the pilot and co-pilot would stay with him until the situation was figured out. Now he realized that was…kind of silly. "I don't even know where I am."

"They can help you at Hertz," the pilot said, and absurdly, Dave felt hurt. They'd all been through something terrible together and he felt very tightly bonded to these two men…did they not feel the same?

Of course not. They had a job to do and they were doing it.

Well, so did he. He squared his shoulders, gripped his bag more firmly and followed them into the terminal.

Inside it was chaos, but only mild. The three of them stood and stared at the milling crowd, but Dave had the feeling that it was emptier than it should have been considering what had just occurred. Maybe a lot of people hadn't shown up for the outbound flights. Same as no one had shown up for work.

"Hertz is over there," the pilot pointed. Then he turned and put out his hand. "Good luck to you, Mr. Weathers. I hope you get where you're going," he said. "Call me when you want to go home."

"I'd like to go home right now," Dave said and he wasn't really joking, but the pilot smiled. They shook hands and then Dave shook the co-pilot's hand, too; then the two of them headed off through the concourse, gathering curious looks as they went.

Dave felt utterly alone.

He powered on his cell and dialed the office in Cali, but without much hope. Several people stared at him with something dangerously close to jealousy. He closed the phone and slipped it into his pocket. He could make the call once he got on the road.

The woman at the Hertz desk looked frazzled, but Dave couldn't see why–no one was trying to rent a car. He got closer to the counter. She was frowning down at the telephone receiver in her hand.

"Everything okay?" he asked and she jumped.

"Oh! Excuse me!" she said and tucked the phone into a space under the counter. She smiled. "I didn't see you there. I do apologize." She was middle-aged and heavy but her makeup was carefully applied and her hair styled.

"No problem," Dave said and gestured to where she'd tucked the phone. "Can't get a call out?"

"Can't get to *any*one!" she said and tried to chuckle, but there was real upset in her eyes. She was worried. "Technology...can't live without it, can we?"

"No, I guess not," Dave said. He shifted his bag from hand to hand. "What's going on here today?"

She turned her blue eyes to the concourse and blinked. "I don't know," she said. "There's been a lot of commotion. Lots of people didn't show for their flights, concessions closed, even..." She leaned across the counter and motioned him to do the same. "I think some of the controllers didn't show." Her eyes were round with scandalized shock. "That's a federal offense!"

"It is?"

"Well, I don't know, actually," she said, as she patted the top of her bosom, "but it *should* be!"

"Listen, can you help me with some directions? I need to get to…it's called Garden State Hospital, it's in–" He drew a blank on the name of the town. She blinked at him again. He remembered the co-pilot taking the folder from him as he fell asleep. Shit. He needed that damn folder! He turned to scan the crowd, but the pilot and co-pilot were long gone. His bag! Maybe he had put it in there. He dropped the bag and unzipped it and the folder was right on top. He blew out a breath and opened it. "It's in Marlton," he said, straightening. "Marlton, New Jersey."

"The whole fleet has GPS," she said and her smile widened. She seemed to revive a little at the normalcy of the exchange. "Built right in!"

"Yes, but I was wondering, you know, because of the phones. What if the GPS is out, too? I'm from California. I'll be stuck."

"Oh! Hollywood!" she said and tittered. Dave couldn't help but smile. "Marlton, was it? That one's easy. It's just two roads! You take Route 30 West to Route 73 North! It puts you right in Marlton! We're only about an hour from there."

He checked the address of the hospital. It sat right on Route 73. He shrugged.

"Okay, good deal," he said. Everything would be sorted shortly anyway. He'd most likely have a driver again and then the CDC would get him home.

Once everything was sorted.

They went over the exchange, which took longer than normal because the computer was, as she termed it–buggy. She finally handed him keys and gave him directions to the lot. "Normally, Peter would walk you out, but he didn't show up either," she said, "and I can't abandon the counter. Will you be all right finding it, Mr. Weathers?" Her concern was so genuine it warmed and bolstered him.

"Yes, I can find it," he said and thanked her for her help. He was ten feet from the counter when he turned back. "Take care, okay?" he said. "I hope you reach whoever you were trying to call."

"Thank you, Mr. Weathers, I hope so, too," she said. Her smile had become uncertain. "You take care now. It's…it's strange out there, today."

He nodded once then went to find his car. By ten-thirty, he was on the road.

CHAPTER 6

"Alfonse is…was…the custodian," Robert said. "When we heard the commotion, Dan, Susan, and I left the office to see what was happening. Alfonse was outside the auditorium and as we were coming down the hall, the first set of doors burst open and a flood of people came tumbling out. They were screaming. Some of them were bloody. Alfonse was hit in the face with the door and it knocked him back. He fell and his head caught the water fountain– it broke his neck. I'm sure of that much."

"I was coming from the office," Calvin said. He kept his eyes on the windows but his expression had become inner-turned as he recalled the story for Cassie. "It's right across the hall from the Aud. I saw Alfonse fall, too. Then he, oh man." Cal swallowed and shifted, re-crossing his arms. "He got trampled. I could see…everything. His hand got stepped on and his wrist broke, I *heard* it break!" He swallowed again. "His head was rocking, you know, as he was…as people stumbled across him, but still, he wasn't necessarily dead."

"Cal, you know Alfonse was dead," Susan said. "He was surrounded by, like, a lake of fucking blood after everyone ran him over!"

Cal's lips tightened but he didn't answer.

Cassie turned back to Robert.

"Did you see him get trampled, too?"

"Yes, we saw the whole thing. We weren't as close as Calvin, I didn't hear the man's bones break, but we still saw it all." Robert said. He had retaken his seat and Cassie clambered onto the teacher's desk, letting her legs hang over the side. She checked her watch again, almost eleven thirty. It seemed so much later. She waited for Robert to go on. Her purse was now directly behind her, no one between her and it. She would listen to what Robert had to say and then hightail it out of here before they could stop her. Dan was probably at home with Lucy. She needed to get there.

"The people kept steaming out," Robert went on. "Some, like I said, were bloody. Bite marks, I think now. Most ran straight out the front doors. A few ran deeper into the school. Alfonse was just lying there." He quieted, his hand cupping his chin, other hand cupping his elbow. "Margaret was still in the auditorium. Margaret Miller, the graphic arts teacher…did you know her, Cassie?"

Cassie tore her eyes from her purse, startled. She didn't want to be caught plotting. "No. Miller? No, Dan never mentioned her to me."

Robert looked at her a while before going on. This time though, he kept his eyes on her as he talked.

"She was kneeling in the back of the auditorium, behind the rows of seats. She was kind of slumped, her shoulders folded over. I called to her, but she didn't look up. She just stayed in place, swaying a little."

"They do that," Susan said. "They sway in place like toys that have run down their batteries."

Robert frowned at Susan who hadn't taken her eyes from the window. "It is just like that," he said. "Well put, Susan."

She shrugged without turning around. "Whatever."

"Anyway," Robert said and turned his attention back to Cassie. "Cal started down to Margaret, to see if he could help her and Susan had gone outside to see if anyone knew what was happening. Two students were standing in the hall in shock and I ushered them toward the office so I could tell someone to call 911, if they hadn't already. I didn't know yet that Principal Frisk was dead. We really didn't know much of anything."

"Not that we know very much *now*," Susan said.

"True," Robert said. "The office was empty, so I told the two students to sit and relax. I went back out into the hall just as Calvin was backing out of the Aud. I could see from his expression that something was horribly wrong. I started to ask him what happened when Alfonse started to shake."

"He was having convulsions," Cal said. His jaw tightened and he crossed his arms over his chest. "It's *live* people that have convulsions, Robert, not dead ones."

"You didn't see him, Cal," Robert said. His tone was patient, but fraying around the edges. "It wasn't like that at all. I've seen epilepsy, and I know how it presents itself. This was...a revving up."

"What do you mean? Revving up?" Cassie asked.

"I mean, it looked like...he was just kind of...vibrating, okay? But not like *he* was vibrating, but like he was *on* something that was vibrating. It looked...not like he was shaking, but that he was *being* shaken...does that make any sense?"

Cassie nodded, thinking of Lucy putting little blocks in Dan's massage chair and laughing as they shivered and jumped. She knew what Robert meant.

"Okay, so...then his arms and legs jerked. Blood went flying, spattering all over the place. Cal had closed the doors to the auditorium and was just standing there...in shock, I think...and I began to get really scared. I knew that whatever was happening to Alfonse was not...it wasn't right." He took a breath and re-gathered himself. "I yelled to Cal, told him to watch out. He was too close to Alfonse. I took a few steps toward him, because he didn't seem to hear me, and then I could see Margaret coming up the wide, center aisle..." He dropped his chin into his hand again and became still, while his gaze turned to Calvin.

After a minute, and with obvious reluctance, Cal said, "Margaret was covered in blood from her chin to her ankles. She looked like Carrie in that old, old movie about the high school girl with telepathy. She had...in her mouth...she had..." He looked at Robert with desperation.

"She had someone's scalp in her mouth," Robert said. He kept his tone even and clinical as if discussing the details of a trial that he hadn't participated in. "Forehead, eyebrows, one ear, and long blonde hair."

"Deena Sommers," Tyler Bieler said from his dark spot at the last window. Cassie jumped. She'd forgotten he was there. He was slim; the black skinny jeans making his legs look like two twigs. Black hair in a rough shock over his forehead. "It was Deena."

"Are you sure, Tyler?" Calvin asked.

"Yep," Tyler said. "I was in the Aud. I saw the bitch do it."

"Holy shit," Susan said. "That's really fucked up. Margaret wasn't, like, the nicest person, but there's no way she'd...you know...try to eat someone."

"Why didn't you say so before?" Calvin asked Tyler, ignoring Susan's contribution.

"I dunno," Ty said and turned the other way giving them his back. The vertebrae of his neck were picked out in distinct little hills. "Just didn't, I guess."

"Jesus," Cassie said. Another wave of unreality washed over her and this one brought a gray haze with it. She swayed and then leaned sharply back, catching herself with her arms.

"Cas? You okay?" Susan asked.

"No, not really," Cassie said. She scrubbed her hands over her face and readjusted her ponytail, frustrated and angry. "Are you? Are any of us? Jesus Christ. I think we're all crazy. This is some kind of bad dream or hallucination."

"No," Robert said, "it's real. Don't let yourself get too far down the road of denial, Cas."

"Alfonse grabbed my ankle," Calvin said. His words were loud and distinct like someone trying to get a conversation back on track. "He wanted me to help him, but I fell back."

"Alfonse tried to *bite* you," Robert said. "He wasn't asking for your help. He was trying to bite you."

"But he had been dead," Calvin said. His eyes were as round as marbles, his voice the plea of a child who just wants more than anything for the nearest adult to fix it. "I saw him die."

"He came back," Robert said, flat, relentless.

"He couldn't have."

"He did."

"But..."

"No buts, Cal," Robert said, "Alfonse was dead. He died and then he came back. I don't know why, I don't know how, but I know it happened."

"And his blood turned black," Tyler said. "Someone's here."

They all looked at him, their faces mirrors of confused astonishment.

— — —

Dave got out of the Ford *Current* and surveyed the building. It didn't look like a hospital. GSVT? The letters were five feet high on the façade. The GS sounded right, but the rest of it seemed wrong. He fished his paperwork out of the folder. Shit. He was looking for GS*H*...Garden State Hospital. He was at the wrong damn spot, but nothing had an address and this was the first really big building he'd come across.

He cursed and threw the papers back in the car. He was starving and he had to take a leak. Well...the hospital couldn't be much further.

"Hey!"

He'd been getting back into the car and he jumped at the voice, hitting his head on the doorjamb. He turned, rubbing his forehead. A guy was standing at the front door, leaning out, waving him away. Security, no doubt.

Schools were touchy places. Too many abductions.

"Sorry," Dave yelled. He raised his hands, palms out, in a gesture to show he wasn't a threat. "I was looking for the hospital! My mistake...I'm leaving!"

The man's wave became frantic.

"Yeah, I gotcha...I'm going," Dave said. He shook his head with irritation. "I already told you–"

"Look out!" the man whisper-yelled, his hands cupped around his mouth. "Look OUT! Behind you!"

"What?" Dave said, thoroughly confused. He turned.

A girl was standing at the rear bumper of the Ford. She listed badly to one side, swaying. She had a hole in her chest; a possible gunshot wound. Multiple abrasions. Foot missing.

Dave's surface mind ticked over each thing, clinical and precise, but underneath it screamed...*how is she still standing?! GET AWAY FROM HER!*

She lurched toward him.

He stepped back smack into the door of his car.

"Get in here!" the man in the building yelled. "Run! *RUN!*"

Without further thought, Dave turned and sprinted for the building. He had to jump over two bodies, and he nearly went to his knees when his foot caught the first step. He scrambled up, urged on by the man standing there.

"Come on, come on," the man urged. He was older, neatly dressed in a button down and vest. He pulled the door closed behind Dave. Then he bent over, hands on his knees.

"At least we didn't have to pull you in like we did, Cassie," the man said, mystifying Dave.

Dave stared at him in bewilderment, and then he turned to look out the door, certain the girl would be there, or at the least, on the steps.

She was still near his rented car. Swaying.

"What the hell is going on?" Dave said. "Is it a school shooting?"

The man stood straight and stared at him with astonishment. Then he laughed. He laughed harder and harder until tears rolled down his cheeks. He kept trying to say something. To Dave it sounded like it might be 'sorry.'

Dave turned to look out the door again. There were three bodies in the parking lot that he could see just from here. But if it was a school shooting, even one in progress...where were the police? The SWAT? Hell, the television cameras?

"Where are the police?" Dave asked. "Why isn't this being televised? Did you call–"

The man laughed even harder, completely unable to catch his breath. Was he in shock or something?

"There's a cop down the road in the coffee shop parking lot." A woman's voice. Dave turned to regard her, as she walked toward them from down the hall. She reached them and ran her hands through her short hair, her expression distracted as she watched the other man laugh. "But he's dead. Cassie said the Catholic kids killed him."

Then she said, "What the fuck, Robert, are you okay?"

To Dave's dazed mind, her words sounded like some kind of strange beat poetry, melodic but unintelligible.

The man in the vest, Robert, straightened, wiping his eyes. He had finally stopped laughing. "Yes, I'm okay, Susan. I just–" He looked at her, lost for an explanation.

"You got a little off the bead," she said and gave him a lopsided grin, but her tone sounded preoccupied. This was a woman with something else on her mind. She turned to Dave. "Are you here to rescue us?"

Dave looked from her to Robert and back to her.

"Rescue you from *what*? What the hell's going on here?"

Robert put out his hand. "My name is Robert Ralston. I'm a civics teacher here at the Vo-Tech." He raised his hand and Dave took it with a sense of surreal dreaminess. "This is Susan Reed. She teachers welding." She nodded to him over her crossed arms.

"I'm Dave Weathers. I was sent from the CDC in California," Dave said, automatically giving his credentials. "Can you tell me–?"

Robert's eyebrows shot up, corrugating his forehead. "You already know, then."

"Know what?"

"About what's happening…"

"*What* is happening?" Dave said with increasing agitation. "Christ, I'm starting to feel like…"

"Like you're losing it?" Susan asked and Dave had to nod. Yes, that was exactly how he felt.

"Why were you sent here?" Robert asked him. "Out in the parking lot, you said you were looking for a hospital?"

"Yes, well," Dave said, editing as he went along. The work wasn't classified, exactly, but it never helped to spread alarming information to the public. "There was just a concern over a rise in flu cases. Probably nothing, but we have to check it out. Just to be safe, you know, but…like I said, it's probably nothing."

Susan's lids had fallen to derisive slits. "Yeah, probably. Probably nothing at all. If you think dead people coming back to life and chomping on the living is nothing at all then, yeah…it's *definitely* nothing."

Dave stood immobile, his brain whirring dumbly like a seized computer, unable to comprehend anything she said. He'd been dropped smack into Crazy Town and he didn't speak the language…was everyone in south Jersey a complete nutjob?

The sooner he got out of here, the better.

Robert seemed to guess at least the flavor of Dave's thoughts. He turned to Susan with a mild 'back-off' gesture tempered by a smile.

"Something has gone terribly wrong here," Robert said to Dave, keeping any form or shade of hysteria from his tone, as if being careful to show he was not overreacting. "I don't know if it was what you were sent here for or not, but I think we might all need to compare notes before we decide how to proceed. There is a nurse here who had an overnight shift at one of the local clinics. I think she can tell you more about the flu, so-called, that was going around."

Dave hesitated, trying to think. He could spare a few minutes to talk to the nurse–she'd be a good source of info, especially if she had been working overnight. But he should call it in, let Angie know how he'd been detoured. He had tried to call a few times from the road, but he'd assumed his reception was out because of the damned pines.

"There's a landline here, right? I need to call my office," Dave said. "Then I'll talk to–"

A grumbling roar caused the three of them to turn toward the wide glass doors. A big man on a black and red Harley was crossing the parking lot at a speed normally inadvisable on school grounds. He wore a leather vest over a long-sleeve denim shirt, a grinning-skull bandanna tied over his head, and goggles but no helmet. The bike growled like something alive, shivering the glass. The sunlight winked and shimmered off the tall chrome handlebars.

"Oh, shoot," Robert said, "that's Floyd, the HVAC teacher. I have to let him know about that girl–"

As if his words had conjured her, the girl popped up from behind Dave's Ford. She stood, still listing, gore-streaked and swaying. Completely unsurprised, and without reducing his speed, the man on the Harley drew a short shotgun from his back and one-hand fired it, blasting the top of the girl's head off.

"Oh, *shit!*" Susan said.

Dave swore and stepped back, fumbling his phone from his pocket. In his grasping mind, this hulking monster explained not just the bodies in the parking lot, but everything that was going wrong–it *was* a school shooting! That guy had just murdered that girl!

"Is the door on an automatic lock?" he demanded of Robert as he thumbed his phone alive. "I'll call the police. You–" he said, and nodded quickly to Susan, "–go call from a landline in case I still don't have reception. Tell them we have an active shooter. Tell them–"

Susan remained planted, goggling at him with something like disgust, while Robert, who seemed to realize the gravity of their situation, was making his way to the door to check the locks. The shooter had parked his bike at the base of the stairs and he was coming up them three at a time. He was a really big dude, had to be at least six seven, six eight–how was he moving so fast?

Dave fumbled his phone again, nearly dropped it, yelled, "Move it," to Susan, and then dialed 911.

Robert fiddled at the bar on the door.

911 rang two times. Three.

The big guy was at the top of the steps, coming right toward them, the shotgun hanging from his hand as naturally as an appendage.

Dave backed down the hall, his stomach dropping.

Four rings, five.

Robert opened the door.

"Hey!" Dave yelled, his voice strident with panic. "Don't open that door! Don't–" Six rings, seven.

Robert shook hands with the murderer and Susan ran to hug him, pink work boots lifting a good eighteen inches off the ground as he gripped her up with his free arm.

Eight rings, nine, but Dave let the phone sag away from his ear as he watched the three of them; they seemed well acquainted with each other. Crazy Town had just gotten crazier. He should run, but he'd never get past them, and going deeper into the school would be the end of him–these halls belonged to the natives, they knew the lay of the land.

"Who's this guy?" the biker asked, jutting his chin toward Dave.

"Oh! I didn't introduce everyone," Robert said, and his words could have been ones from any small get-together, but his ragged tone gave away his fatigue. "Dave...Weathers, was it?" he asked, eyebrows raised at Dave and almost despite himself, Dave nodded. Robert smiled. "Dave Weathers," he continued, "This is Floyd Abby; Floyd...this is Robert. He was sent by the CDC."

"That was fast!" Floyd said, and a grin split the bush of facial hair below his nose. He reached for Dave's hand, engulfed it in his hot, meaty paw. "Nice to meetcha, Dave," he said and his voice was as deep and rumbling as the voice of his Harley. "I sure hope you can get this shit figured the fuck out."

CHAPTER 7

"Wait, go back," Dave said. "The custodian, Alfonse, you're saying he wasn't attacked?"

"No, he was down before anyone came out of the auditorium," Robert said. "He was trampled, but not, you know, bit. No one actually attacked him."

They were all in the classroom, Robert, Dave, Cassie, and Calvin, sitting in the student desks. Susan, Floyd, and Tyler were watching out the windows. It was just after noon and Cassie tried to quell her impatience. Why hadn't Dan come back here after he'd picked up Lucy and then found the house empty?

Because he's waiting for you at home, You need to go home.

She shifted in her seat as Robert talked on, telling Dave about the clash in the auditorium. Cassie had already told him about the clinic, the overrun of flu patients. It was a big deal that a CDC person had been sent here, she knew it was, but she couldn't keep her mind pinned to what was going on in this room. It didn't even seem related to her now that she'd imagined Dan and Lucy at home, waiting, worried. Now that CDC was here, even more people would come soon and get it all sorted out. It would all be taken care of. She needed to see to her own.

"–the graphic arts teacher?" Dave was looking at her expectantly and she tried to snap her mind back to the conversation.

"I'm sorry, what about the teacher?" she said. She tried to look him in the eyes, concentrate, but felt herself drifting almost immediately. What did any of it matter? Someone else would take care of it soon enough.

"I asked if you'd had a chance to examine her," Dave said, and then looked away, seeming to dismiss her. To Robert, he said, "Is she still in the auditorium?"

"Yes. I closed the doors on her. She kept, kind of, bumping against them. Then she stopped."

"And the custodian? Alfonse? Where is he?"

Calvin slid awkwardly from the desk and turned toward the windows, but his gaze was inner-turned and full of shocked grief. "I stabbed him with the flag pole. It went through him and jammed into the wall. Pinned him. Like a bug. But I had to, he–"

When Cal stopped speaking, Dave looked questioningly at Robert.

"Cal," Robert asked, "do you want me to tell the rest?"

Cal nodded without turning.

"Alfonse had Cal by the ankle and Cal had fallen back. Alfonse was snapping at him, trying to–I know it makes no sense, but Alfonse was trying to bite his leg–"

"He *did*…he did bite me," Calvin said, his voice strangled with horror. "He bit me on my calf." He turned and his face was white, his eyes shimmered with desperate tears. He addressed Dave. "Am I going to get it? Whatever they had?" He stepped closer, his hands curling into fists. "Tell me!"

"I don't know; how could I know that?" Dave asked, standing at Cal's approach. The desk screeched backward.

"You're from the fucking CDC!" Calvin said, his voice rising. "You should–"

"Okay, hold on, just hold on," Susan said. She got between Cal and Dave, her palms on Cal's chest. "Just calm the fuck down for fuck's sweet sake."

From his post at the window, Floyd tossed her an admiring glance. Obviously, she was singing his tune.

"Cal, listen to me," she said. "You've got jeans on…he didn't bite through them."

"No, that's right," Cal said. He relaxed a little, his hands unfolding, but his voice remained wary. "It pinched me though, his teeth, I mean. I felt them pinching. If he broke the skin, then saliva or something might have–"

"Well, let's see it, dummy," Susan said. She smiled at him, a one-sided grin. "Long as the skin's not broke, you should be fine...right, CDC?"

"You're asking *me*?" Dave asked and pointed to himself, fingers splayed with somewhat stagey surprise. "Hey, listen, there are tons of variables, tons of things I don't know. I can't just–"

"What*ever*." Susan snorted derision. "Cal, roll up your pants. Let me see."

Cal sat so fast it looked like he'd collapsed, but he rolled up his pant leg with ready ease, even though his fingers trembled as he did so. He raised his eyes to Susan and she bent to inspect the area just under and halfway behind his knee–the meaty part.

"Just bruised and even that doesn't look so bad," she said. All the brusque swagger was gone from her voice and she patted his calf. She smiled up at him. "You're okay, ya big baby." She helped him start to roll his pant leg down.

"Wait," Dave said, "we should, I mean, someone else should confirm–"

Susan turned with a swiftness that a snake would have admired. "Confirm *what*?" she said as she rose. "Confirm that I'm not *lying*? Or confirm that I'm not too stupid to see if the skin is broken? Huh?" She'd come dangerously close to Dave, her arms waving as she got louder. "Which is it?"

He put his hands out, palm up to her. His face was open with astonishment, and Cassie thought, not a small amount of fear. It was almost funny, watching little five foot five Susan intimidate the man who had a passing resemblance to Superman's alter ego, Clark Kent.

"No! I'm not...I didn't mean..." He took a deep breath and closed his eyes. "Okay, let's all calm down," he said. Then he looked from one person to the next, maintaining a few seconds of eye contact with each and Cassie wondered fleetingly if that was in the CDC training, some kind of confrontation-diffusing behavior.

Probably the guy was just used to people falling in with him because he was so handsome.

"Yes, I would agree with Dave," Robert said. He tucked his fingers into the small pockets on his vest. The gesture looked odd, but habitual. "We need to calm down and think rationally, not go off half-cocked at imagined slights."

Susan bestowed Robert with a look scathing enough to peel paint. But she held her peace and returned to her post at the window.

"I'm going to call the Atlanta office from your land line," Dave said, "and find out what's going on. Then we can–"

"It's cell or nothing, buddy," Floyd said. "Big truck smashed the telephone pole straight over right down the street. Phone'll be out for a good long while."

"But my cell isn't working," Dave said, and to Cassie's ear, his tone had an almost petulant quality.

"Well," Cassie said and stood up. She gathered her purse to her chest, holding it high as though it were a shield. "I'm leaving. I have to go home and find my husband and daughter. I'm sure they're waiting for me there."

Calvin stood. "Yeah, me too. No offense, but I'm sick of this room. I'm going to head over to Laurelton and see about my mom."

"There hasn't been anyone outside since Floyd got here," Susan said. A thin ribbon of hope slipped through her voice, raising it. She looked expectantly at the group. "Whatever was going on, maybe it's stopped."

"No," Floyd said without turning from the window he watched over. His tone was flat and firm. "There probably are other regular people out there, but if they're smart, they're hiding, just like us. You can't go out there, Cassie."

It seemed strange, him using her name when they'd just met. She had met the other teachers at functions, but never Floyd. Dan had told her a few laughing, raucous stories about him, but Cassie had never found anything endearing in the things Dan told her.

"Well," she said, nearly sighing the word. She ran a hand across her forehead. Exhaustion that teetered on the edge of depression was making her logy. "I'm going anyway. I have a car. Nothing will happen to me."

"Cassie, listen," Floyd said and startled her by taking her upper arms in his hands. The small adrenaline rush of anxiety it caused in her brought him into sharp focus. He was gentle, his fingers barely denting her skin. "There's nothing but monsters out there right now. I'll make you a promise," he said, and tightened his grip just slightly. "Stay until two, maybe three, and let's see what happens. Then, if nothing has changed, and you still want to go home, I'll go with you. I'll take you on my bike."

"But I have a car," Cassie said, dodging his bargain. "It's almost fully charged. I'll be fine."

"I don't think so," Floyd said. "You haven't seen it out there."

"I *was* out there!" Cassie said, irritated, her fear making the irritation so much worse. "It was practically deserted...the roads, the stores, everything! I had no problems getting around. There were so many people sick last night that I think a lot of them just stayed home."

"Could be," Floyd said. He gave her arms a quick squeeze and then dropped his hands. He turned restively and considered the windows. "That could very well be, but I'll tell you this...there's a lot of them out there now."

They all turned to look out the windows as if expecting that his words would have conjured a ravaging horde. It was just as quiet outside, the sun strong now, and hot. The main road, Route 70, stayed deserted.

"Floyd," Calvin said, "it's not that I don't believe you, trust me I'm not saying that...but look out there." He raised his hand to the window; compelling them not just to see, but to believe. "There's *no* one. The road is deserted! Where are all the people you're talking about? Where are the–"

"No, Floyd's right," Cassie said, suddenly reversing. While Cal spoke, the certainty had risen in her like a hot tide. "He's right. Just the fact that Route 70 is deserted...there are always cars out there, Cal. *Always*. Not just people from Marlton, but from Laurelton, Hillton, Mayville, Cress...it's a main thoroughfare to the city! Jesus, where is everyone?" Agitated by the beginnings of fresh panic, she stared at the circle of eyes fixed on her. "Where did they all go?"

CHAPTER 8

Dave watched as the others argued, glad the attention had been taken from him. He slid his phone out and put his thumb on the screen to unlock it. The phone searched for Wi-Fi, found the school's, and locked onto it. Dave skated his forefinger over the numbers, knowing he should call the office first, but he dialed home instead. It rang three times and cut out. He dialed the office. It clicked and seemed as though someone answered, but all he got was the hiss of an open line. There was something disturbing about the echoing nothing in his ear, so he hit 'end.'

"Why don't the phones work?" he said, mainly to himself, but Calvin heard.

"It's the lines and switches," he said. "No one's out maintaining the equipment. That stuff can fail pretty quickly."

"Let's see," Cassie said and pulled her phone from her bag. She dialed Dan's cell. It rang ten times and went to voicemail. "Voicemail," she said to the others and then tried to smile. "That's progress, at least." She turned away, but Dave could still hear her clearly. "Dan, please call me. Are you at home? Sweetie? Tell Lucy I love her. Okay, well, I love you. Call me back."

"I have to run out to my car for my bag," Dave said. "I have a folder out there with all the office numbers and the other agent's cells. Maybe we can get some news on what–"

"You can't go out there–"

Susan said just as Calvin said, "Dave, weren't you listening to–"

Floyd raised his hand in a clenched fist, silencing the room. His head down in a listening posture, he slowly lowered his arm. Susan began to speak and he shushed her with a glance. He touched his ear...*listen.*

They all listened. One by one, they drifted closer to the windows.

At first, all Dave heard was a sigh, like wind through the trees and he cocked his head at Floyd as if to ask "So?" but a glance at Tyler convinced him to listen again. The boy's eyes were slitted half closed with suspicious fear...what could the kid hear that Dave could not?

"Oh my God," Cassie said, her voice quiet, barely audible above the sighing wind. Dave realized that the wind had gotten louder; much louder. He looked out the window, checked the tree line, the sky. Was it a tornado or what? Was New Jersey even prone to tornadoes?

"You're looking in the wrong direction," Cassie whispered. She touched his cheek with cold, shaking fingers, drawing his face down, until he was looking out at the highway. Still nothing. He took a breath to ask and then she pushed his face, gently, until he was looking east.

Then he saw.

A crowd of people, maybe fifty, was coming down the highway. For a brief second, his spirits rose, despite the fear on Tyler's face, the coldness of Cassie's fingers...lots of people had survived whatever had happened! Now it was over, and they could all go out! They could all–

His heart seemed to stop beating.

The crowd was bedraggled, bloody, as if returning from battle, but it was more than that, so much more. The closer they got, the more he could see how far beyond disheveled they were...they were torn apart.

People were missing arms to the elbow, to the shoulder. Some limped, some slogged along, barely able to keep up. Clothing was torn, bloodied, and in some cases, missing. Hair ripped out, noses caved in, eyes dangling like ripe fruit from ocular nerves. At the end of the unlovely parade, people with one leg, no legs, people who seemed to be semi-paralyzed, dragged after the rest.

They all hummed and sighed; a toneless, insectile rasp of vibrating vocal cords...it was what Dave had mistaken for wind in the trees. They moved slowly. Their eyes, when they were close enough for Dave to see, were alight with awareness, but no humanity.

When the morbid crowd passed directly in front of the school, shuffling, sighing, and moaning, everyone in the classroom stepped back from the windows. No one had to tell them to do so; instinct compelled them.

Once the crowd was just out of sight, Dave looked across the room. Each person stood blinking and disoriented, as though coming out of a dead sleep, and Dave saw his own horrified confusion reflected in each of their faces. The silence accumulated around them like deep water, and each person seemed reluctant, or unable to speak. He ran his thumb over his cell and considered why he hadn't been able to get through to California. Whatever was happening here hadn't been happening in Cali. Not when he left. In his mind's eye, he saw a wave that started on the East Coast and traveled in, flowing west, covering the country bit by bit.

Taking out everything. Everyone.

— — —

Cassie sat again, still finding it hard to keep her mind pinned to this room. That crowd...she'd recognized some of those people.

"Let's take a look at Alfonse," Dave said, "and that other teacher, the one locked in the auditorium. Maybe...I don't know. Maybe it will answer some questions."

"You guys go do that," Susan said. "I'm going to the caf to get us some water and food. Granola bars or something. Tyler, do you want to come with me?"

He shrugged but moved nearer to her. He was so slim and dark in his black shirt and black jeans that he looked like her shadow.

"I'll come to the caf with you, too," Calvin said.

"I think it would be important for you to come with us," Dave said. He said it in the tones of his official capacity. "You were one of the initial witnesses."

Calvin hesitated and Susan glanced up at him. She settled her hand in the crook of his elbow, squeezed, and shot Dave a slit-eyed look of disgust. "Come on, Cal," she said, her eyes not leaving Dave even as she spoke to Calvin. "You come with me and Ty."

"Hey, listen you guys–" Dave said, but Robert put a hand on Dave's arm, "let him go; he doesn't want to see Alfonse. What he did was entirely justified, but still…"

"Fine," Dave said, "but I want Cassie along with us. Cassie?"

"Me? Why?" she asked. She'd just been sitting back down, trying to calm the shake in her knees. She wasn't sure what that crowd meant to her plans to find Dan, and was still struggling to sort it out. Yes, she'd recognized some of the faces…not to put a name with necessarily, but she knew that she'd seen them around town. Dan hadn't been among them, and she had to hold onto that. Dan hadn't been sick, so he was fine, and since he was fine, then Lucy was fine, too.

She just had to get to them. Somehow.

But the pompous jerk from the CDC was still talking, distracting her from her good thoughts. It was so annoying.

"You're a nurse, Cassie," he said, as if reminding her. As if she *needed* reminding. Pompous. Asshole. "You'll see things other people might not. Also, you saw a lot of this sickness, right? At the hospital?"

"Hospital?" She felt completely lost. She couldn't figure out his words or what they might mean to her. *Because they mean nothing*, her inner voice cried. *Nothing he says matters…you don't know him! He's not even FROM here! Cassie, find Dan! FIND LUCY! You have to–*

"Cassie," Floyd said, his mouth suddenly disconcertingly close to her ear. His voice was not loud; it was calm, almost confidential. "Cassie, I'll help you find Dan, but you have to help us first. Deal?" She turned to look at him and as she did, she felt a new reality settle a little more firmly around her. She had to humor these people if she was ever to get out of here.

"Yes," she said and stood. She was glad that her knees had stopped shaking. In fact, she felt calmer than she had since seeing that monster on her front porch this morning. More…in control of herself. She patted her hair and smoothed the front of her t-shirt. She glanced into her bag. Keys, good. No problem.

"Cassie," Floyd said. His hand hovered near her shoulder but did not connect. "I think you might be in shock. Do you feel like you're following everything that's going on?"

She looked at him and then from Robert to Dave. Dave eyed her with uncertainty as though ready for any nonsense she might pull next. He thought her an hysteric. Typical hysterical woman. Leave it to a pompous asshole man to judge her. As a nurse, she got tons of this kind of attitude from the doctors, and this Dave was just like them.

The rage that bubbled up burned away some of the fog just enough for her to see that she was, actually, behaving oddly. This was not her normal self. Not at all. She had to pull herself out of it, she had to…had to…

This time, she was acutely aware of the fog when it began to roll over her thoughts again. For a second, a bright spark of panic made her want to slap herself, pinch herself awake. Then that spark, too, winked out in the fog. Her shoulders relaxed, everything seemed fine. Some part of her started to insist that everything *really was okay*. Once she got away from these nut-jobs, once she had Dan and Lucy, once she was home making dinner…everything would go back to normal. No monsters, no fighting, no dying. Laundry, dinner, television, bed, work tomorrow, kissing Dan goodbye, taking Lucy to school. Everything would be back the way it had always…*always*…been.

She wanted that–normal–more than she wanted anything else.

She turned to Floyd.

"You'll help me get everything back the way it was?" she asked.

His eyes squinted in concern. He reached for her again, kind of patted the air near her without making contact.

"Cassie, it can't go back to the way it was," he said. The leather vest creaked as he raised his arm to gesture to the windows. "You saw that out there. You saw what people have become."

She shrugged lightly, but didn't look toward the windows. "They were sick. Probably heading to the hospital."

"They weren't *sick*. You saw that," Floyd said, "Cassie, they all looked as though they'd been hit by a train." His tone was firm but still compassionate. Behind Cassie, Dave blew out a frustrated breath. Floyd raised a hand to him.

"They *were* sick, Floyd," Cassie said. She shook her head and tried to smile. She crossed her arms over her chest, glad of the solid weight of her purse against her stomach. "Everyone has some kind of flu. That's all. You're making too much of it."

Floyd stared at her for a lengthy, uncomfortable moment. She met his gaze for as long as she could, then she looked down. He was just trying to intimidate her. Big, bad, biker, right? Picking on a woman. She shook her head.

"Cassie, listen to me—"

"What is it then, Floyd, if they aren't sick?" she asked, her voice hot and sarcastic with defensive anger. "Did everyone suddenly have car accidents? Did a train derail? There are no trains in this town. None."

"They're all dead, Cassie," Floyd said. "Everyone in that group, shit, maybe everyone in the entire tri-state area. You don't want to admit it…but you *know* it, don't you?"

She laughed but it was an ugly, barking sound.

"What the hell are you talking about?" she said. Even to herself, her voice sounded overdone in the disbelief department. That made the panic leap in her like a frenzied, clawing animal. "You're crazy! You're all crazy, and I don't have to sit around with you and…and…go crazy with you!" She strode past Floyd, expecting him to grab her, ready to fight, but he never made a move to stop her. At the doorway, she turned and with a hitch in her voice, said, "I'm going. I'll…once Dan and Lucy are with me…I'll, I mean we'll…we'll come back. You'll see by then that everything is fine. No problem."

Floyd nodded. "Okay, Cas," he said, "but I'm coming with you." He raised his hands, palm out, placating. "Just to help; just to see. All right?"

She nodded, but just once, and her expression stayed grim. She was unable to admit the amount of relief his words invoked in her. The thought of those empty streets, the odd and disturbing things she'd seen this morning, worried her more than she wanted to let on. She was glad to have his company.

Floyd pulled the shotgun from its sheath on his back and handed it to Robert. "Keep this handy, just in case. You might need it and I still have my forty-five." He patted his side with one large paw.

Robert took the gun but held it at a distance from his body as though it might burn him. He looked at Floyd with growing dismay.

"Hey, wait," Dave said. "Listen, we have to take a look at this Alfonse guy. I think it's important."

"Catch up with the others in the cafeteria and stay there," Floyd said. "Wait for us to come back."

"But...this Alfonse...we need to–" Dave said.

Floyd grinned, and even from where she stood in the doorway, Cassie could see a weird, twirling glee in his eyes.

"Don't worry about Alfonse. We can check him out when we get back. After all–" Floyd said, his grin widening, "he's not going anywhere."

– – –

Cassie drove.

Floyd struggled to get comfortable in the tight space. She marveled at how much smaller he made the car seem. Maybe that was why he rode an old-fashioned gas powered motorcycle, so that he wouldn't be crammed in. Probably he would have preferred to take his motorcycle to her house, but once they had Dan and Lucy, there'd be no way to transport them back. Without conscious thought, Cassie had already changed her mind on staying in the house and now pictured Dan and Lucy coming to the school...she wasn't able to picture anything after that. Not yet.

Even this quick ride through town showed her that nothing would be going back to normal any time soon. Not, at least, until someone in authority came along.

"Someone will come soon," she said to Floyd, as if to reassure him.

He raised his eyebrows. "You think so, huh?"

Annoyance pierced her like a needle, and a sharp pain started up behind her eyes. "*Yes* I think so. They'll send the National Guard."

All the survivors might have to go to a shelter for a while. Just like anyone in a natural disaster, but she and Dan would get through it. They'd been through a lot together. And they were lucky, too, to both have jobs, even though Dan's teaching salary was a joke, barely above the minimum wage. Still, they were lucky considering the times. "They'll get this all sorted out."

"I'm starting to wonder about that," Floyd said. He gazed out his side window and she snapped a glance in that direction, too. There was a black cloud that might be from the fire she'd seen earlier. If it was, then there must be more things burning, as the cloud was too big to be an hours-old fire. Especially since, by now, the fire department should be on it.

Cassie stopped at a red light at the larger highway. She waited, watching the light, tapping her fingers with impatience. She could feel Floyd's eyes on her.

"What?" she said without taking her eyes from the signal.

"Cas," Floyd said, "just go."

"What? I can't just *go*…it's a red light," she said as if spelling it out for someone slow or maybe foreign. "I'm crossing over, not making a right." She shook her head.

"There's no one on the roads," Floyd said. "It's completely deserted out here. In case you hadn't noticed."

She pulled her eyes from the light and with some reluctance, she looked left and then right. There were a handful of cars sitting dejectedly, like left behind toys; none of them was moving. She frowned. The road they were on was deserted, had been since they left the school, but it was a smaller road, only two lanes. The six lanes she was looking across, though, should have had something moving on them. Someone.

"Hey," she said and hope dawned in her, almost as hot as the earlier panic. "Hey, Floyd, it must be an accident…a big one. Everything is blocked and no one can get through. All those people we saw, they were…survivors of it. Like, when there are those sudden ice storms and people pile up on each other. I saw one on the news last year where there were over a hundred cars and trucks involved! No one had been ready for the conditions and the cars just couldn't stop. They just kept plowing into each other and it kept getting worse and worse..." Cassie saw it in her mind; saw exactly how it could happen. An accident so bad that not even rescue workers could get through. People injured and dazed, leaving their cars, walking...

"But it's June," Floyd said, and for a brief, confused second, she thought he was talking about a person. June, who? She stared at him in bewilderment, unaware the light had changed to green.

"There's no ice, Cassie. Not even rain. Sky's blue as anything."

She glanced at the sky as if to check his words, but she already knew the sky was clear except for the smoke from the fire. He was right. Even if there had been an accident...it wouldn't be a pile up situation like the one she'd seen on TV. The conditions weren't there.

"Green," he said and she glanced at the sky again, confused. Then she saw the light. He meant the light was green. She could go.

She couldn't get her foot to move. She nodded to herself then shook her head. "Floyd, where is the National Guard? Why hasn't anyone come?"

"I don't know," Floyd said, but there was a hesitation in his words. He tapped her knee and that seemed to release it. She put her foot on (what she still thought of as) the gas pedal. They rolled into the intersection and through it.

"Why hasn't anyone come?" she asked again. She kept her eyes firmly on the road although there was nothing to watch for. But she couldn't look at him. She was afraid to.

"I don't think anyone *can*," he said. His words were mournful and he sighed, but Cassie remembered the twirling, delighted gleam she'd seen in his eye back at the school. He went on, "I don't think there's anyone left."

CHAPTER 9

Robert and Dave made their way down a corridor lined with posters, each of which extolled the virtues of trade work. They passed a glass enclosure with the word "OPPORTUNITIES!!" hand-lettered above an assortment of recruitment posters. Mechanics, drivers, line-cooks, medical, apprenticeships for electrical and plumbing–all the things that make the world go around, Dave thought. He suddenly wished he'd gone to a Vo-Tech instead of going into research. Non-trade degrees were barely good for anything and he'd been lucky to get in with a government agency right after graduation. It would be nice to make the kind of money a tradesperson made, especially electricians–they cleaned up.

"You like teaching here?" Dave asked. Robert hadn't spoken at all since Floyd left and he seemed to be sinking into a black mood, barely even making eye contact.

"It's a good supplement to my law practice," Robert said.

"You're a lawyer? I've heard that doesn't pay very well."

"Well, no, not since the market glut back in the early two-thousands," Robert said. He cocked an eye at Dave and then smiled a little. "Neither does teaching, but between the two, I get by."

"I looked into teaching, too, but if you're not teaching a trade…" He shook his head.

"Yes, you're quite right. Without some certifications, all the bachelors, masters, and doctorates in the world don't mean much of anything. Susan and Floyd both have lucrative careers outside of this Vo-Tech…they just like to teach. For me, it's a necessary second income, and for them, it's something interesting to do. That and they do make quite a bit at it."

A sign for the cafeteria pulled them left. It was a large space and set up like a restaurant. Booths lined two of the walls and tables with wooden chairs–not the cheap aluminum ones he associated with his own college caf–were dotted throughout. There was seating here for a least two hundred.

Across the back wall was a long kitchen sitting open and exposed to the dining area–it was the only way in which the cafeteria differed, visually, from a restaurant. There were at least eight stainless steel refrigerators, ten commercial-grade stoves, sinks with tall, goose-necked faucets. Big slanted mirrors hanging above everything would give people in the cafeteria a perfect view of the prep stations. The entire kitchen was set up for teaching.

They followed the sound of voices to a long pantry behind the prep area where they found Susan, Calvin, and Tyler standing at the back, faced away from the door.

"We should ration everything," Susan said. "We have no idea how long–"

"Ration? Susan, you're way, *way* over-reacting…there are a million granola bars at least. Look at these giant bars of chocolate, and the canned goods! We could live here for years and not run out of…" Calvin turned a can to face him, "pinto beans! Not that I'm dying for pinto beans, but we're not going to be here long enough to use even an eighth of what's here."

Tyler hefted a box of individually wrapped chocolate chip cookies as if testing their weight.

"Tyler, do you want a cookie? Take one," Cal said. He opened a granola bar and downed half of it in one bite. "Grab extra of everything and we'll take it back–"

Robert cleared his throat and the three turned. Tyler dropped the box of cookies and they burst open along one seam. Cellophane crackled as the cookies poured out.

"Jesus, Robert," Susan said, her hand on her chest, "what the fuck?"

"Sorry," Robert said, "I was just–"

"Where's Floyd?" Susan said. She took a step toward him, her face drawing down in lines of concern. "Did you see Alfonse?" She looked past him to Dave. "What did you make of it?"

"We didn't see Alfonse yet," Robert said. "Floyd and Cassie left and Floyd said we should–"

"*What?*" she said. "They went *out* there? Did Floyd lose his mind?"

"Yes or...no...I mean...yes, they went out there, no, I don't think Floyd lost his mind," Robert said. "Not that I know him well enough to say. I think Cassie was losing hers, though. Or, at least that's the impression I got. Not that I could say for sure, of course."

"You sure equivocate a lot," Susan said. Her hands had gone to her hips and she regarded him with a contemptuous twist of her lips.

"Susan, give him a break," Calvin said. He put the beans back on a shelf. "He's right...he wouldn't be able to answer anything you're asking."

She turned to Calvin. "Then he could have just said that, right? Instead of all this..." she tucked her chin down and made her voice deep and self-important, "well, I really couldn't say, old bean; yes and no, but it's not in my bailiwick, you know...harrumph, harrumph."

"For Christ's sake, Susan, lighten up," Robert said. "What's wrong with you?" His tone was more mystified than disgusted, but there was a *little* disgust in there and it was enough to deflate her.

Her shoulders dropped.

"I don't know," she said. Her eyes, when she met Robert's gaze, were full of honest apology. "I'm sorry, Robert. I'm just, like, really stressed, and it's coming out all wrong. It's just that I want to go home, too, you know? I want my kid." Her voice broke a little and she shrugged her shoulders once as if trying to shake off the brief weakness.

"Me too," Dave said, breaking into the conversation. The picture of the wave traveling east to west had popped into his mind again. "I have two boys, twins. They have a game today and I wish...I really wish I'd just stayed the hell home."

They stared at each other in mutual understanding and finally, Susan smiled, even though her eyes stayed sad.

"Well," Cal said, "I've got a ninety-inch television I'd very much like to see again before the looting starts. So maybe we should all leave."

"Maybe we should," Dave said. "We might be making all this out to be worse than it is." His mind flashed an image of the morbid parade of people they'd just seen, but he dismissed it. There was likely a good explanation, some kind of industrial accident, chemical plant explosion, maybe a train wreck–none of those possibilities had been explored. They'd all just been making each other crazy. "Can you tell me how to get to Garden State Hospital? It must be close by."

Susan looked from Calvin to Robert and raised her shoulders. "What do you think? Should we leave?"

"I think so," said Cal. "Listen, even if something happens, we know we can meet back here, right? This is a good home base."

"Absolutely not," Robert said, but he seemed tired and his words lacked authority. Even his natty dress was beginning to look worn down. He pulled out a chair and sat.

"Yeah, okay, good," Susan said, as if Robert hadn't spoken. "Listen, Dave, GSH is further down 73. You'll recognize it from–"

"You'd be crazy to go out there." Tyler's voice. He was still in the back of the pantry, half-hidden in the shadow. They all turned to look at him.

"Ty, listen," Susan said, "I'll go with you and we'll go to your house first if that–"

"The dead are rising," Tyler said. "You all saw it. You saw those people on the street." The proclamation was flat, and Tyler's voice quietly declarative. Delivered from the shadows, his words had the strength of prophecy. A harsh chill ran down Dave's back.

"Ty, listen," Cal said, "this is some kind of group hysteria, and we have no idea what we saw, not really. We've jumped to too many conclusions already. I think getting out of here, finding out what's going on...that will put everything back into some kind of perspective."

"You already said it." Ty directed this to Robert, but Robert didn't raise his head. He seemed lost in his thoughts. "That janitor, you said he died and came back to life. What about Mrs. Miller?

She died and then she got up. Then she ripped Deena's fucking head off."

"We can't be sure of any of that, Ty," Cal said and his voice was climbing, defensive. "We didn't–"

"You put a flag pole through him, Mr. Post," Ty said, "and he kept moving. He was wiggling like a bug. You *did* see that." Despite his words, Tyler's tone was calm, bordering on indifference. "And I saw Mrs. Miller keel over. She was right in the front row. The principal was talking but I was watching her...I knew something was going to happen. She looked dead even before she died, if you know what I mean. She fell forward right out of her seat. Mr. Keely kneeled right down next to her and he yelled, 'someone call the nurse; call 911' and he was holding her hand, taking her pulse. He looked up at Mr. Anders and shook his head like, 'no pulse', and by then, everyone was kind of milling around. We could all feel it...that feeling like something was really, really off. Everyone was right on the verge of panicking, just like last year when me and some friends were at the Acadia seeing a movie, and all a sudden, we smelled smoke. Then you could see as it traveled down the rows, people kind of looked around and started whispering to each other. A few stood up. Then everyone did, like they'd been told to do it." He unwrapped a cookie and took a bite. The others looked at each other questioningly.

Susan said, "Ty, what happened next?"

"Well, the lights came on and an announcement said for everyone to leave and there was just a small electrical fire and no one was in danger so–"

"No, I mean, what happened in the aud, with Mrs. Miller."

"Oh," Ty said. He took another bite of the cookie, chewed and swallowed. "So, okay, like, you could tell how everyone was getting jumpier, like they smelled smoke, and people were just standing around, talking. I was watching Mrs. Miller and Mr. Keely, cause I didn't think it was a good idea for him to be so close to her, you know? And he was looking up, looking at Mr. Anders and he was saying something I couldn't hear. Then Mrs. Miller kind of started to jiggle, like, all over. Then she sat straight up and bit Mr. Keely's shoulder. He turned to her, like, surprised or something and she ripped out his throat. It was fucking fast, dude. Like a snake or something. Mr. Anders jumped up and he was yelling, but you couldn't make it out. It was mostly nonsense, like he couldn't get his shit together. He was covered in Mr. Keely's blood. Then everyone started screaming and headed for the back doors. I kept watching Mrs. Miller, cause I was thinking, you know, like, someone has to tell the cops, right?"

Robert was watching Ty with renewed interest, his eyes sharpening. He opened his mouth as if to ask a question, but Ty went on, oblivious.

"She grabbed Deena next and Deena's a pretty small chick, so Mrs. Miller didn't have any, like, problem gripping onto her. She pulled her hair, making her head kind of snap back, and she…man, first she ripped open Deena's neck, and then she chewed Deena's face…ripped her hair and all right off."

"Jesus, Ty," Susan said, as she raised her hand to his thin shoulder, "you saw all that? Are you–"

"Did either Mr. Keely or Deena make it out of the auditorium?" Robert asked. Dave wondered why it mattered. Christ, what the kid was talking about…it was madness. It didn't have anything to do with why he was sent here; it couldn't. He had to get to that hospital–things would be saner at the hospital.

"No, neither of them," Ty said. "When you all closed the doors, you shut them up in there together."

"Why didn't you say something? Tell someone?" Dave asked. "They might need help; they might be–"

"The only thing they are is dead," Tyler said, "and anyway, what are you gonna do? Call an ambulance?" He took a last big bite of the cookie, finishing it off.

"Jesus Christ," Dave said. Now it was his turn to pull out one of the cafeteria chairs and fall into it. It was like a trap. A maze where each corridor bumped you up against a reality that couldn't be changed, no matter how hard you tried to deny it.

"We have to go and check the auditorium," Robert said, "and see if they're still alive, see if they need…any help we can give them."

"No," Cal said. He squeezed a granola bar in his hand, crushing it in an unconscious gesture of distress. "I'm not going back there."

"Cal, we have to," Robert said. He drew himself up and centered Cal in his gaze. "Number one, because we have to see if either Deena or Bob Keely need any assistance we can render, and number two, I think Dave needs to see Alfonse. Maybe this is a disease and Dave might recognize some signs or–"

"I highly doubt that," Dave said.

Robert turned to him. "Which do you doubt? That it is a disease or that you might recognize it as such?"

"It's definitely not a disease," Dave said. "Disease doesn't work that way because it's not that fast. There are three other stages of disease before you even begin showing symptoms, much less dying. Something as fast acting as you describe would be more along the lines of a toxin, or maybe some kind of nerve gas. It might also begin to explain the people on the road. Maybe the country is under attack." He thought of the CDC coverall suits and masks that were required anywhere a contagion was suspected, and wished he had one to put on right now. Although, it probably wouldn't do much good against a nerve gas.

"That could be it," Calvin said. There was a light of hope in his eyes. "That makes a lot of sense. Think about the nerve gasses in the past and what they were capable of making people do…wasn't there one that made people dance?"

"That was a plague in the eighteen hundreds," Dave said, "nothing man-made. But to your point, yes, nerve gasses can have some very odd and–this might be the most important part–fast acting effects."

"Then why were so few people affected?" Susan said. "I mean…we only know about Margaret and maybe…*maybe* Alfonse."

"That girl in the parking lot," Dave said.

"Maybe," Susan said. "Maybe her. Maybe the people we saw on the road, but we don't really have any idea. Do we? I mean, we're okay. If it had been something in the air, then–"

"It could have been in the water," Dave said. He'd ruled out food-borne bacteria–the numbers of the ill just didn't support it.

"That could be what caused so many people to be sick yesterday and into last night. There are five water or food borne bacteria: Salmonella, Shigella, E.coli, C.parvum, and Cholera."

"Cholera! I've heard of that one," Susan said. "Isn't that deadly?"

Dave laughed and it felt good to do so. It loosened something in his chest that had been tightening like an impending heart attack. "No, actually, none of them are deadly to healthy people, but it could put a lot of them in bed."

"What kind of attack would that be?" Robert said. "Giving people diarrhea does not seem like much of a statement…not from terrorists capable of abducting and killing schools full of children."

"I didn't say it was a terrorist attack," Dave said. He sobered, realizing the implications of the statement he was about to make. He considered not saying it, but then went ahead, anyway. They needed to know. "The janitor…if he'd had a fever, then it might explain the seizures you said he was having."

Cal swallowed and looked from Dave to Robert to Susan. "If that's all it was–Cholera or something making people sick–then I killed Alfonse for no good reason. I killed him just for being sick, and Floyd killed the girl in the parking lot. If that's the case, then he and I are murderers."

"The only thing we can do," Robert said, "is go and find out." He put a hand on Cal's shoulder. "We still don't know anything."

Cal nodded and Susan grasped his hand to squeeze it, but her face had gone white and sick. If the whole thing had been an overreaction on their parts, then they were all partially responsible for what had happened to Alfonse, Deena, and Bob, if they'd been left to die in the auditorium.

The five of them decided to go together…to *stay* together. It was one thing to speculate on a relatively harmless contagion, but it was another to face the relentless reality of the dark and echoing hallways. Regardless of how the mind tried to equivocate, the nerves spoke a red-alert warning across every inch of the skin. Something had gone terribly, horribly wrong.

Dave's thoughts turned and twisted like a worm on a hook and he vacillated between grim dismay and a disturbing urge toward black laughter. Diarrhea seemed a thin (and watery) answer to the puzzle of the empty school, the seemingly empty town. He thumbed his cell again, dialing first home and then the office. Voicemail at the former, nothing at the latter…the phone rang on and on. He counted twelve rings before he hung up. Congestion would make the calls drop (he thought) so the problem wasn't congestion any longer. So, what was the problem? He saw the wave again, traveling east to west, relentless as a tsunami. He shuddered and shoved his phone back into his pocket.

"Jesus fucking Christ," Susan said. Her voice was a strained whisper. Dave walked into her and then Tyler bumped into him. Robert and Cal had already stopped, their eyes fixed and horrified.

Dave followed their gazes and the idea of Cholera or Salmonella or any kind of bacterial infection became a non-starter in the category of explanations.

The janitor was on his knees, facing them. A flagpole had been pushed through his torso and lodged into the drywall behind him. An American Flag was half sunk into his chest, the rest cascading down to puddle on the floor around him. It was soaked with blood.

He looked like some kind of crazy war protester gone too far; so compelled by his ideals that he had impaled himself on the flag in order to make his point.

He was looking right at them.

Black granules plugged his nostrils. He moaned and the sound was as senseless as wind rattling through a gutter. He raised one arm as if asking them to come to his aid. His other arm hung limp; there was a large bump where his shoulder had been separated. His eyes were bright and he looked from one of them to the next, moaning. He lunged against the pole, but on his knees as he was, he could not get the leverage to push himself up. But white drywall dust sifted down onto the floor–the pole would not hold him forever.

He lunged again, awkward and moaning. The black that jammed his nostrils broke free and ran over his distended lips, catching there like a sudden mustache.

More drywall dust kicked out of the hole and the flagpole wiggled loosely.

"That's not a disease," Dave said. He had already taken a few steps back. "He's not…it's not a nerve toxin, either." Panic seized him and squeezed his heart. "That pole isn't going to hold him. We better get–"

Next to them, the auditorium doors thumped, and then thumped again. A small chorus of distinctly inhuman moans–like an answer to the janitor's–oozed out under the doors. Another thump and the doors pushed open by half an inch before falling back into place.

Whatever was in there didn't seem to know about the push bars that would open the doors, but soon, they were going to bump into them by default.

"We have to get out of this hallway," Dave said, "right now."

CHAPTER 10

Dan's car was in the driveway. He was home. He was safe. A rush of relieved happiness brought tears to Cassie's eyes. "He's here. That's his Prius," she said to Floyd without turning to look at him; she couldn't take her eyes off Dan's car. It brought home to her all at once how much she had doubted that he'd be here.

She reached for her door handle.

"Cassie, let me go first," Floyd said, a restraining hand on her arm, "just in case."

"In case of what?" Cassie said. She sat back, exasperated but also, face it, a little relieved. The empty streets and quietly deserted neighborhood were working on her nerves. She scanned the black windows of her house and a dazed feeling of unreality came over her. As if it were no longer her safe haven, her sanctuary…but Dan was in there, and Lucy. *Then why does it look abandoned?*

She shook the thought off, anger replacing the creeping dread.

"I'm going," she said. She opened her door. The passenger door clunked open, too, sounding hasty and annoyed, but when she glanced across to Floyd, he was looking at the house with calm regard. His hand hovered under his vest.

"Is that a gun?" she asked. Jesus, what did he think this was? The Wild West? A movie? "Floyd, you don't–"

"Something is *wrong*, Cassie," he said. He stared at the front door as if he couldn't tear his eyes away. His voice dropped. "Don't you *feel* it?"

She did.

But she didn't want Floyd to shoot Dan by accident.

"Fine, but I'm going in first. Jesus, Floyd."

He shook his head, but motioned for her to go.

She felt weirdly awkward proceeding in front of him. She was too aware of the gun–even, of his very presence–as foreign. It was disorienting in such otherwise familiar surroundings. She climbed her porch.

"Be careful opening the door," Floyd said, his voice so close and low it could have been a thought in her head. Her fingers faltered on the cool metal of the door handle. Floyd breathed at her back and irritation flared in her. He was making her crazy. She opened the door.

"Dan?" she said. "Dan? I'm here; I'm home. Are you–"

Lucy ran to her from the kitchen. Her small sandals tapped on the hardwood floor. "Lucy!" Joy and relief poured into her at the sight of her daughter. Cassie knelt, her arms spread wide. She laughed even as tears prickled her eyes and everything blurred. "Lucy! Lucy!"

Orange fire appeared in her peripheral vision. Something hot passed by her face and she shied to the side, her shoulder coming up, but she kept her eyes on her daughter.

A hole appeared in Lucy's forehead. Her small body slammed backward as though pushed by a giant's hand.

What?

Cassie swayed on her knees, blinking at her daughter. Lucy had the same pink t-shirt and darker pink shorts that Cassie had put her in that very morning. One little foot bare, the other still in the white sandal they'd bought last Saturday. Lucy's toes peeking out over the edge of the sandals like tiny, round faces. A smudge of blood on the bottom of her bare foot, like a checkmark.

What? What–?

The entire world had become silent. Something shoved her from behind, sending her forward. She got her hands up just in time, landed on her forearms. Two sets of feet danced before her, occluding her vision. Boots and loafers. Dan's loafers. She'd know them anywhere.

She shifted, the floor grating across the thin bones in her arms. Found Lucy again. "Lucy?" she said, but only heard it as a dim echo, a vibration along her skull. "Baby?"

She levered herself up, crawled forward on her hands and knees. The floor vibrated under her hands. A weight on her back, sudden and shocking, nearly toppled her over. Then it disappeared. The floor shook as something crashed to the hardwood next to her.

She kept going. "Lucy? Baby?" Still silent...echoing and lost somewhere in her skull.

Her hand on Lucy's cold ankle, the buckle on the sandal cutting into her palm. "Lucy?" She shook her daughter's leg and the movement traveled up, shook Lucy's torso. Her head rocked side to side. Cassie pulled.

Strong hands appeared in her armpits. Yanking her away from her baby. She kicked and one hand disappeared. She toppled sideways as more orange fire, more heat, erupted next to her.

Lucy's ankle was still in her hand. Cold. Still. Cassie pulled, dragging her baby to her. Black granules, like a dark halo, ringed Lucy's head. Granules oozed from the hole in her forehead.

Her eyes were open but glazed.

Dead.

Cassie dropped her daughter's ankle, her fingers frozen with shock.

She screamed without sound. Something dragged in her throat. Like a cat clawing. She tasted blood. She screamed again.

Lucy! LUCY! PLEASE!

Hands in her armpits again, digging and rough. Cassie screamed and kicked. Was pulled back. Toward the front door. Dan on her left. Slumped over. Dead. Shot.

Shot by Floyd.

Dan no no NO! Dan! Lucy! Please PLEASE!

Silent. Silent world. Blood in her throat. Floyd dragging her. Dragging.

Sunlight on her side, hot across her face. Blinding after the dim room.

The porch under her feet as she scrabbled to get upright.

The hands dragged and dragged, keeping her off balance.

She fell back and looked up.

Porch ceiling. Blue. Blue, blue sky. A bird.

None of this was happening.

She closed her eyes and hot, yellow shapes bled under her lashes.

None of it was real.

It couldn't be.

CHAPTER 11

"Move," Dave said. He gave the kid a small shove. "Go, go, go."

Tyler turned as if more than happy to obey, but then turned back, his hands spread in dismay. "Where? Where do we go, man?"

Dave didn't know where they should go...how could he know? He looked at Cal, but Cal was watching Alfonse with dumbstruck horror. Robert had pushed himself against the far wall, cringing at the muted thudding of the auditorium doors. Susan pulled and yanked at her own hair, grimacing. They'd all lost their minds.

"See thirteen!" she said. "Guys? See thirteen."

Her words made no sense to Dave at all, and he became even more convinced of her madness, but Tyler nodded at Susan, a grin drawing across his features.

"See thirteen," he said. "Yeah, fuck yeah! Totally!"

Susan grabbed Cal's arm, yanked him around. "Cal...see thirteen...Robert? Come on!"

Without further discussion Cal, Susan, and Tyler began to trot back the way they'd come. Robert followed but spared Dave a glance, taking in his confusion.

"It's her classroom. Her shop," Robert said, and then Dave understood. C-13. He trotted after Robert, catching up, one ear trained back to the thumping and thudding behind them.

"Why does she–" he said and then his cell phone rang in his pocket.

Susan and the others stopped and turned, staring at him in surprise as if they'd never heard a cell phone before. *Look how quickly it becomes a novelty*, he thought. Then he fumbled for the phone, lifted it to his face.

Home.

He scanned his thumbprint. "Colleen! Colleen, can you–"

She was crying, sobbing, her breath coming in hitches and gasps. Dave's stomach dropped out, his heart constricting. He felt cold settle around him and sink into him. Part of him welcomed it.

"Sweetheart," he said. "Can you hear me? Colleen?" He scanned the row of eyes on him–Susan's eyes, especially, filled with dark concern. He turned away, putting his hand over his free ear, pulling his shoulder up even though the thumping behind them in the hall had grown quiet. "Sweetheart? Can you–"

"Deh, deh, the b-boys…are d-deh…" More sobs interspersed with unintelligible half-words, but Dave knew suddenly and with the force of a wrecking ball–he knew what she was saying.

"The boys are *dead*? Colleen? Is that what you're telling me?" His voice was a thin and reedy whistle, although he tried to control it. He didn't want any misunderstanding between them. Her sobbing was interspersed now with choking coughs. She couldn't breathe. "Colleen? *Colleen!*" Impotent rage and helplessness swept him by turns making him feel dizzy. "*Colleen!*"

"Yes," she finally choked out and the one coherent word seemed to calm her. Or numb her. She sighed and in that empty, shuddering breath, he heard the winding down of her consciousness. Had she…had she done something to herself? Taken pills or–? "They're both dead." Her voice was as flat and emotionless as a recording. "But it doesn't even matter, does it? Nothing matters now, Dave. Nothing."

"Colleen, sweetheart," he said, "don't…don't say that. I'm coming home. I'm coming right now and I'll fix it. Whatever is wrong, sweetheart, I'll *fix* it." The wave appeared again and this time it flowed and flowed, highlighting the distance between him and her. The insurmountable distance.

She began to cry again but this time it was weak, almost a whimper.

"Colleen? Listen to me, listen, I–"

"It's all gone," she said, whispering. "I love you, Dave. I love you. But don't come home. It's all gone. It's all done."

"Sweetheart, what's gone?" he asked but he already knew. Hadn't he already seen it? The empty everything. The girl with the broken off foot. The janitor impaled on the flagpole but still alive; somehow still alive. Tears blurred his vision and he pinched the bridge of his nose to stop the headache that was beginning to pound through his sinuses. "Listen to me," he said, his voice as steady as he could make it, "I'm coming. I'll be there in…I'll *be* there…Colleen? *Colleen*?"

He looked at the phone to see if the call had dropped, but the seconds ticked calmly over. He put it back to his ear and Colleen was speaking.

"–love you, too, but don't come home. It doesn't matter. I love you. Don't–" She sighed again and this one spoke of both resolve and utter defeat. "–don't come home, Dave. I…I've been…bit. Ellie bit me and…I'm bleeding too much to…"

"Colleen, listen, hang up and call an ambulance, you have to–"

Her laugh was muffled, barely there. He suddenly saw her as clearly as if he were in the bedroom with her, curled in the mass of pillows and downy comforter on their bed.

"There are no ambulances, sweetie," she said with the faintest hint of the marital, scolding tone wives reserved for especially dumb husbands. Her papery chuckle came again.

Dave tried to smile. Couldn't.

He hitched in a breath and it caught in his throat.

"Sweetheart…Colleen…" he said. He didn't know what else to say. She was so incredibly distant from him, far on the other side of the country, but she was also as clear to him as if he were lying beside her. As though they were snuggled face to face, weaning away a quiet morning. The sunlight across her shoulder. The sleepy pink of her cheeks. Her beautiful eyes. Her smile. "I love you," he said, and he nearly choked on the words. "I love you, Colleen."

"I love you, too," she said. In his mind's imagining, she closed her eyes, her lips curled into a secret smile. He leaned across the pillows to kiss her nose and the call dropped.

"God-DAMMIT!" he said and threw the phone across the hall. It slammed into the wall and fell to the floor in front of him. He kicked it and roared in his frustration and anger. "Mother-*FUCKER*! God-*DAMMIT*!" Ha hammered the wall with his fists, ripped down a poster, ripped down another. His sons were dead.

His wife was dead or close to it. The rage distorted his vision; the cursing whipped his adrenaline. "FUCK! FUCK! FUUUUCK!" He found one of the display cases. Punched it, breaking the glass into long, deadly shards. Grabbed the edges of the case and pulled; pulled again and grunted. It started to give, the bolts holding it in place screaming through the drywall. He screamed, the sound both primitive and modern–grief as it has been expressed throughout time.

He barely felt the hand on his shoulder, barely heard Susan as she started to yell. His entire focus was on the display case, and he wanted to destroy it, murder it,. Ruin it. Another hand on his bicep, pulling. He snatched his arm away and turned on his assailant with a growl. Robert was staring past him down the hall. He pounded Dave on the shoulder, yelled. Behind him, Calvin was pulling Susan away and Tyler shifted from foot to foot as if he couldn't decide which direction to go.

"Dave, come on! He's loose!" Robert said and yanked Dave's shoulder again. "Come on, come *on!*"

Dave turned to look back down the hall in the direction of Robert's gaze and all thought was driven from his mind. Alfonse, the janitor, was coming toward them. The pole through his chest was impeding his forward momentum as it whammed and butted into the walls at each staggering step he took. He looked like a dog with a stick too big to fit through the back door.

Each time the end of the pole bounced against the floor, it jammed further into his chest and the flag disappeared by another inch like a magician's handkerchief trick. A trail of black crumbles snaked out behind him in a scattered and entirely senseless s-pattern.

His mouth was ringed with dried blood, his teeth clotted with something that looked like black and shining snot. His eyes were pinned to Dave's.

"Jesus Christ," Dave said and staggered back, stepping on Robert's feet. Robert caught him by the shoulders and shoved him upright.

"Follow Susan and Calvin," Robert said. He smacked Tyler on the back, and Tyler shook his head as if waking from a dream. He looked at Robert with shocked incomprehension and Robert pushed him. "Tyler, *go*."

Tyler turned and bolted after Susan and Calvin, his sneakers squeaking on the floor. Dave followed, staggered once, then righted himself and ran. He felt slow and clumsy in his hard-soled shoes, as Tyler sprinted away from him with ease. He couldn't stop seeing the janitor's bright and searching eyes. They were like the glass orbs of a taxidermied animal. But somehow alive.

Tyler turned a corner and disappeared after Calvin and Susan. A hot wash of panic made Dave speed up. He would be lost if he lost sight of them…would they wait? He glanced back reflexively, hoping he'd put enough distance between himself and the janitor.

Robert was on the floor, his back to one of the auditorium doors. The janitor loomed over him, arm swinging. Robert's legs had become tangled in the flag hanging from the janitor's chest, He kicked and screamed as the janitor fell toward him. The pole hitched up against the baseboard and the janitor hung over Robert, swaying like a marionette, his fingers inches from Robert's upturned face.

"Tyler! Help me!" Dave yelled down the hall and headed back toward Robert…then he hesitated. Heavy thumps came from the auditorium and the door next to Robert shivered. Dave scanned the area but there was nothing he could use as a weapon.

The janitor grabbed for Robert again with his one working arm, but the pole impeded his reach. Robert screamed, trying to backpedal out from under the janitor, kicking the red and white striped folds away. His head hit the wall, hard.

"Robert!" Dave yelled and his paralysis broke at the sight of the bloody circle on the wall behind Robert's head. He started back down the hall. Behind him, Tyler was screaming for Susan to come help.

The janitor grabbed the pole just below where it emerged from his chest, and holding it steady, shoved himself further onto it with a determined moan. He swiped at Robert again, his fingers able this time to catch in the man's hair. Robert screamed, but it was a murky, half-unconscious sound. Next to him, the auditorium door thumped, coming open a half an inch before settling back into its frame. Robert began to slump over, eyes rolling up, eyelids fluttering. The janitor yanked Robert's hair, drawing his head back. The extra weight caused him to slide further down the pole until his mouth was less than half a foot from Robert's vulnerable face.

Fueled by pure panic, Dave took three lunging strides and slammed into the janitor. They sprawled across the floor, sliding as Dave scrambled to right himself. Adrenaline helped him bounce to his feet in a maneuver that sixteen-year-old him would have found cool, then he jumped back and readied himself for an assault.

The pole through the janitor hitched up against the facing walls and pinned him in place. He lay on his side and kicked like a dog running in his sleep. He moaned and the sound was the rattle of loose bones in a lightly padded coffin.

"Robert!" Susan was halfway down the hall, Cal right behind her. She had a large wrench in her hand. Cal had a long piece of rebar.

Thank God; reinforcements, Dave thought. He leaned over his knees and hitched in a long, shuddering breath.

Susan slid the last five feet to Robert, the wrench clanking on the industrial tiles. "Robert? Robert!" She reached for him with tentative fingers. Her eyes darted between Robert, the bloodstain on the wall behind him, the thumping auditorium door, and the slowly kicking Alfonse. "Robert? Can you hear me?" Calvin stood behind her, his eyes glued to the janitor.

"Mr. Post!" Tyler said, his voice ragged. "Kill him! *Kill* him!"

"Huh?" Cal asked. His eyes went from Tyler to Robert back to Tyler. "Kill who?"

"Kill the janitor!" Dave said before Tyler could get the words out. "Cal, kill the goddamned janitor!"

Susan patted Robert's cheeks and he rolled his head side to side and opened his eyes. "Susan?" he said.

Cal looked at Dave with horror. "I already did. I killed him before!"

"Kill him again!" Tyler said, yelling and nearly dancing in his agitation.

"Tyler, help me with him," Susan said. She alone seemed calm in the midst of the chaos, her voice pitched low and steady.

"Robert, can you sit up? We have to get you out of this hallway." The door thumped open by an inch and settled back.

Tyler squatted next to her. "What should I do?" he asked and his voice, too, had calmed.

"Here, help me lift him," Susan said. Together they got Robert in a seated position. "Get under his arm and–"

"How am I supposed to kill him *again*?" Cal asked Dave. Anger and fear tripped his voice up and down the range of octaves. "How do you kill someone *twice*?"

Dave shrugged his shoulders, dazed. It was a good question, but he didn't have any answers. He sidled carefully past the janitor, his back pressed to the wall.

"Hurry," Susan said, "he's going to get loose any second. Once we're in my room, we can barricade ourselves in." Her voice stayed even, and Dave found himself responding to it, his shoulders relaxing. Options. There were options. Always.

"Let me help you," Dave said. He reached for one of Robert's hands.

The door opened and a monster fell out. It landed facedown and lay still.

Susan screamed and fell back, dragging the half-conscious Robert with her. Tyler scrambled away on his hands and feet, crab-like, his eyes pinned to the monster. He hitched up against Dave's legs, and Dave grabbed Tyler's shoulders and pulled him out of the reach of the janitor. Calvin stood with the rebar in his hand, grimacing and shaking in shock.

"Cal! Kill it!" Dave yelled. The monster, small and almost skeletal, was still face down, but moving groggily. Behind the monster, the door thumped again.

Cal turned to Dave. "I c-can't–that's D-Deena...Dee Sommers...she's a...a *student*!"

Dave looked at the monster again and this time the clothes registered: a kick-pleated skirt and pink blouse. But she was covered in gore and her head was a blood-covered skull trimmed in ragged flesh. Dave remembered what they had told him. The girl had been de-gloved by another teacher.

The door thumped again.

"Jesus Christ," Dave said. He lifted Tyler and something pulled in his back as he did it. "Help Susan," he said and pushed Tyler toward Susan and Robert. Robert was awake but still groggy.

The monster–Deena, she's *Deena*, a *girl*, not a monster!–was on her hands and knees, her head hanging like a tired mule's. Black granules pattered down onto the floor under her. She moaned and it was a lighter, smaller sound than the janitor's moans, but no more human.

Susan and Tyler had Robert on his feet between them. Dave bent to retrieve Susan's wrench and nearly dropped it in his surprise at its weight. He gripped it tighter. "Get him to your classroom," he said to Susan, "we'll be right behind you." She nodded, and she and Tyler turned with Robert and started away.

"Cal," Dave said. Cal was watching Deena, the rebar gripped in his hand. She was struggling to get her feet under her. Her head still hung, hiding her face and Dave was glad of that. He grabbed Cal's shoulder and the man pulled back with a gasp. He stared at Dave in horror as if not sure who he was. Dave raised his hand, palm up. "Cal…it's me, Dave. Listen to me…"

The door thumped again. Then the one next to it thumped, too.

"We–we have to see if she's okay," Cal said. Dave glanced back at Deena. She had crumbled onto her side. Her throat was not just torn…it was gone. Ragged bits of meat and tendon dangled and shivered under her chin, and again at her collarbones, but between was just a blackish-red cavity. The knobs of her spine appeared and disappeared as she struggled to right herself again.

Dave took a deep breath to suppress the nausea rising in his gut. That was not a survivable injury–she would have bled to death in seconds of her carotid being torn.

He turned back to Cal.

"She's *not* okay…she's *never* going to be okay," Dave said. Cal couldn't seem to tear his eyes away from the girl. The auditorium door thumped again. "We have to go, Cal. Before the others get out of there. Before the janitor gets loose." He knew all at once that he and Cal should kill the janitor and the girl, that if they didn't, it could spell more trouble for them later, but how?

Look at the injuries they'd already sustained! They were still…mobile. Not alive, exactly, but certainly ambulatory.

What more could he and Cal possibly do to them?

"We have to go," Dave said. He tried to keep his voice calm like Susan's, but his nerves were sizzling, near to their breaking point. He hefted the wrench and tightened his grip for the comfort of it. The janitor kicked and one end of the pole pinning him in place bounced free. "Cal…you have to show me where Susan's classroom is." The janitor tried to roll onto his back, but the pole stopped him. Deena scrabbled back to her hands and knees. She began to crawl toward them, turning her dangling head owl-like as if to see them better. Cal watched her with horrified fascination.

"Cal! Calvin, listen to me!" Dave grabbed the man's chin and yanked so that Calvin faced him. The door thumped open and dropped back. "We have to go," Dave said, and Cal's eyes cleared.

"I can't kill a student," Cal said.

"You won't have to," Dave said, but a chill ran tripping fingers down his spine and he thought the promise he'd just made would soon have to be broken.

The janitor's hand wrapped around Dave's ankle. Dave gasped and swung reflexively, hitting the janitor with the heavy wrench. It landed on his humerus, breaking the big bone with a crunch and the moan turned into a groan, and then cycled up to a high-pitched whine. Now, both the janitor's arms dangled uselessly, but he continued to kick, his hands grasping at nothing.

Dave grabbed Cal's wrist and pulled. "Come on, Cal," he said.

Finally, Cal turned away from Deena and once she was out of his sight, he seemed to find a little more of himself. He followed Dave down the hall.

At the first bend, Dave looked back in time to see one of the auditorium doors fly open and a man fall out, tripping over Deena. A woman tumbled out after him. They were both covered in blood, and as dead as Deena and the janitor. And just as animated.

That was it, wasn't it? They were *animated*, as if some other force controlled the shells of their bodies, but they weren't *alive*.

Dave stared at them until the woman's head turned, her eyes finding his. Then he followed Calvin. He tried to pay attention as they made their way through the halls. At this point, he wasn't even sure where the entrance was–he needed to get back to his car. He patted his pockets as he ran. Where were his keys? His phone? He couldn't remember where–

Colleen's death hit him, and the boys...all dead. This town, the entire east coast, dead. California, dead. The whole country? Dead?

He stopped running and bent double. He put a hand to his chest and tried to pull a breath of air, but it seemed his heart and lungs were refusing to work. Locked up. Seized. Colleen was dead. The boys were dead. What did anything else matter? He crumbled to his knees, still trying to breathe. He should just lie down, stop trying. What did it matter?

Behind him, a hollow rattling clank as Cal pulled the emergency gate across the entire hallway and secured it, trapping the dead. Then a hand on his back. "Are you okay, Dave? Dave?" Cal's voice and he sounded scared, concerned, but who was Cal? Someone he'd met less than an hour ago...so...

What did it matter?

What did *any* of it matter?

"Dave?" Cal said. "We have to keep going...is it...is it your heart? Are you okay?"

"Cal! Hurry!" Susan was yelling from a short distance away. "It's Robert! Something's wrong! Please hurry!"

A hand in his armpit, pulling. "Come on, Dave, come on," Cal said. "You can't stay here." The one they called Deena had reached the gate, her thins arms reached through as she moaned, her face pressed against the metal.

Who cares? Dave wanted to say but couldn't. Calvin pulled him up, moved him forward. His knees tried to collapse, but Cal yanked again, and again.

"Come on, help me," Cal's voice. Was he talking to Susan? And the kid? Tyler? "Dave, help me," Cal said, "we're almost there. We'll be safe in just a second."

So what? Colleen...the boys...dead. Everyone...dead.

Dead.

They rounded into a set of double doors. It was a shop, large machines across the back wall, cases and cases of supplies, and workstations. Tools of every size hung across pegboards. A flock of rolling stools huddled like scared sheep in a back corner.

Susan was kneeling by Robert. She had put a cushion under his head.

Dave stared with incomprehension, his thoughts far away. Cal released him and he stumbled, but managed to keep his feet. Behind them, the double doors closed with a thud. Susan looked up from where she knelt next to Robert, her face white, her hair pulled into disordered spikes. Her mouth worked as she tried to find words that seemed reluctant to come. Finally, they did.

"Robert is dead."

CHAPTER 12

Cassie kicked and screamed, twisting in Floyd's hands as he dragged her backward through the door. At the porch, she relaxed all at once and the dead weight almost made him drop her. He dipped at the knees, solidified his grip, and dragged her across the neat lawn to the passenger side of the Mazda, keeping an eye on the yawning front door, too aware of the gun tucked into his jeans instead of at the ready in his hand. He leaned her against the back wheel and lifted her sagging head. Her eyes were open, but she had checked out. She stared over his shoulder.

"Cassie?" he said. He looked the house again and still squatting, opened the passenger door. "Can you get in the car? Cas? Cassie?"

Her eyes came to his. They were dull, without light. Her pupils were contracted to pinpoints in the bright midday sun.

"I'm going to kill you," she said. Her voice was as flat as her gaze. There was no menace, no anger.

"Okay, but for now, you have to get in the car," he said. He looked at the house again. There had been another one in there somewhere, he was sure of it. "Come on, Cas. Ass in the seat."

She let him lift her, even helped as much as she seemed able, but her body thrummed with tremors. It was shock, probably. He maneuvered her into the car.

"Kill you," she said and it was more of a mumble, her eyes slipping closed as her head dropped back onto the headrest. Her lips were going blue. He had to get her back to the school and get some help. Could someone die of shock? He didn't know.

He pushed her legs in. Closed the door. He rounded the car, drawing his gun, his eyes glued to the front door. He wished it were closed.

Once in the driver's seat he glanced at her. Her skin was very white, and the area under her eyes a deep, unhealthy brown.

"Cassie, I think you're going into shock," he said and started the car. He reversed down the driveway and out into the street, bumping over the shallow curb. Now the house was on Cassie's side of the car.

"Can you tell me what I need to do to help you?" Floyd said. He didn't have much hope of an answer from her; she'd gone lax again, staring at nothing. He put the car in drive, hating the almost-silence of it, the ubiquitous whine. He hated all such electric vehicles. Give him gas any day of the week, brother. Give him the oil and stink and power...not this ozone fart machine.

"It's h-him," she said and he started, surprised. She was stuttering but coherent, as though merely cold.

"Who?" he said and glanced past her at the house. A man in a suit stood on the porch. Swaying. He had no nose. "Who the fuck is that?"

Cassie didn't answer. Floyd took one last look then shook his head, dismissing the man. He was already becoming accustomed to the gore show.

They purred away and Floyd wished with all his heart that they could have roared, instead.

The drive back to the Vo-Tech was surreal. As they wound through Cassie's neighborhood, he kept thinking he saw movement out of the corners of his eyes–curtains twitching, shadows shifting behind windows–but when he turned to look, there would be nothing. He began to feel more and more uneasy. As deserted as the place looked on the surface, how many people were crammed into those houses? How many had gotten sick overnight? How many had died...nearly everyone?

Would they all rise?

It was hard to assimilate, and his mind wanted to turn away from the information. The conspiracy and doomsday nuts must be going crazy right now. If any of them were left.

Floyd flicked on the radio. Dead air. No static, just...nothing. As though no one had gone to work today, and those that had, well, they were most likely coming to the realization that work had been cancelled. Maybe forever.

Floyd didn't have a television in his apartment, and so hadn't seen any news this morning. He didn't know whether much had been reported about what was happening, but probably not. Whatever it was, it had been goddamned fast. In the old days, the internet might have been able to keep up and information might have been passed ahead of the wave of this mysterious illness, but not now. Internet barely existed except for business use, games, and government record keeping. Sometimes, the gamers were able to get news out, but it was so often misinformation that most had ceased to rely on it.

A car passed him going the other way, a tiny, three-wheeled Tesla *Muskie*, and Floyd and the other driver–an older man–stared at each other with something like fascination. Floyd tapped the brake in case the guy wanted to what? Compare notes? But he kept going, so Floyd did, too. How many people like him, Cassie, and the others at the school? How many people existing in a daze of disbelief trying to come to terms with what the world had become overnight?

He didn't know.

On his left, movement caught his eye and he snapped his head around. Someone was just ducking behind the library. It looked as though he or she were dragging something. The last thing he saw was a pair of sandaled feet, toes up, the heels catching on the cement.

"We're almost to the school, Cassie," he said, "hang in there."

He glanced at her. She stared straight ahead, expressionless. Her hands were folded in her lap.

"Cassie?"

No answer.

The highway had a few more cars on it than they had seen earlier. Two were distant but moving, others looked as though they'd been abandoned. Floyd counted five bodies scattered around a minivan. It was on the other side of the median, but it looked as though at least two of the corpses had been shot in the head. Another was still moving, arms swinging listlessly. Something other than good-Samaritanship urged him to stop, but he kept going. Whatever their story was, it was not part of his narrative, at least, not yet. He had to get Cassie to the Vo-Tech first.

They pulled into the parking lot. Tyler appeared at one of the sets of double doors. He must have been waiting just out of sight, watching for them. Floyd drove to the steps and parked next to his Harley, ignoring the neatly lined spaces. Tyler opened the door and motioned them in, but his eyes were pinned across the highway. The Vo-Tech faced a small strip mall consisting of a WaWa, a nail salon, and a dry cleaner. Three people were making their way across the lot in the direction of the Vo-Tech. They were rumpled and bloodied, but at this distance, Floyd couldn't see their eyes.

He hustled around the Mazda and opened Cassie's door. To his surprise, she swung her legs out and stood, pulling herself up slowly, as though she were an old, old woman.

"Cassie?" Floyd said. "Let me help you."

She pushed his hand away without making eye contact. She trembled and took a shuffling step. Another. Floyd glanced at the three across the highway–they were closer; almost to the edge of the strip mall parking lot.

"Ty, hold the door," he said. He bent and lifted Cassie into his arms, and carried her up the steps. She didn't protest, but she didn't help, either, her arms hanging limp and unresponsive. He set her gently on her feet and she swayed, still not looking at him. He turned to Tyler. "Take her to Susan and the others. I'm going to watch those three across the road and if–"

"Mr. Ralston's dead," Tyler said. He had made no move toward Cassie.

"*Robert* is dead?" Floyd asked, as though for clarification.

Tyler nodded and shrugged, his fingers tucked into the tight front pockets of his jeans. "Yeah, he, like, had a heart attack. Or something."

"What? When?" Floyd asked but shook his head right after and put a hand up even though Tyler hadn't yet said anything. "Just…take her to Susan," he said. "I want to see what the deal is with those three."

"Yeah, okay," Tyler said. He looked Cassie up and down as she stood silent, facing the wall. He kept his hands in his pockets. "How do I, like…get her going?"

"I don't know," Floyd said. He had already turned back to the door. The three were on the highway now and still advancing. They didn't interact with each other and that struck him as significant. But it could just be fatigue if they'd been through…something. "Take her by the hand. She'll probably walk with you."

Floyd glanced back to see Tyler had taken Cassie's hand, but the contact made him blush a deep red. He looked like an embarrassed kid whose mom was trying to kiss him in front of his friends. He began to walk and Cassie followed.

"What happened to her?" Tyler said, but he was a teenager and his tone leaned more toward mild revulsion than empathetic sympathy.

"I shot her daughter and husband," Floyd said. At his words, Cassie's head twitched, but she remained otherwise expressionless. Tyler blinked, his mouth dropping open and eyes going wide.

"For real?" Tyler asked.

Floyd nodded and Tyler started away again, tugging Cassie along.

"Fucking harsh, dude," Tyler said.

Floyd didn't bother to answer. The people were in the Vo-Tech parking lot. It was two men and one woman, Floyd could make out that much. One of the men was young, maybe only as old as Tyler. The other man and woman looked to be in their mid-forties. A family? Floyd found it hard to believe. The young man tripped and fell forward. The woman knelt next to him, while the man's head swiveled as he scanned the area around them, keeping watch. He caught sight of Floyd and raised his arm in a wave. They were not animated dead, not like the others they'd seen.

They were survivors.

Floyd opened the door and waved them forward. Some instinct stopped him from yelling. The man nodded to Floyd, a relieved grin on his face. He waved again and then bent to the woman, said something to her. She looked up and smiled, too, and said something to the young man.

He stood, finally, with help from the man and woman and they started across the parking lot. The kid limped, but they were still moving quickly. The man grinned at Floyd again and waved. Floyd couldn't help smiling back. These three looked wasted. Whatever their story was, the Vo-Tech was probably a haven for them.

They went around a Honda *Zizzer* and between a Prius and a scooter. Halfway across the lot sat an old, gas powered conversion van–a delivery van with *LaDoll Food Service* scrolled on the side. As they drew even with the van, the back doors opened and a worker in blue coveralls tumbled out. He landed face first with a meaty thud, not even trying to get his hands up to cushion his fall. Then he laid there, his limbs working as though he was trying to swim. His movements were sluggish, and to Floyd, familiar.

The man slipped out from under the kid's arm and said something to the woman, motioned her to go on. Then he started toward the worker on the pavement.

Floyd leaned out the door. "Hey! Don't go near that guy!"

The man hesitated, then waved and nodded and the woman turned to look at Floyd, her face unreadable. Then she started forward.

The worker shuffled his arms, his face planted squarely into the blacktop. The man was almost to him.

"Don't!" Floyd yelled. "Leave him! He's already dead!"

The woman stopped. Her expression was one of distrust as she looked at Floyd. They must not know yet, must not have had as many encounters.

Now, the man knelt by the worker on the ground, his hand on his blue-covered back. A low murmuring came across the lot, but Floyd couldn't make out the words. The woman stood, undecided, the kid swaying on her shoulder. His eyes were at half-mast…was he sick?

A man in a white chef's coat fell from the back of the van. He landed on the man, knocking him sideways. The woman screamed, backing away, and the kid under her arm, nearly tripped again.

The chef-coat man grabbed the man's upper arm and bit, tearing away a chunk of skin and fat. The man screamed and the woman screamed as if in answer.

"Peter!" she said and staggered back again.

The man struggled, but he was pinned by the chef-coated man. The chef found the back of the man's neck, bit and ripped, and then bit again. The woman screamed and dropped to her knees, the kid crumbling next to her.

"Get up!" Floyd yelled. There was no hope for the man, but the woman and kid could still make it. "Come on!"

The man's screams tapered down to a strangled garble. The chef knelt above him, a ridged tube in one hand. The man's esophagus. Blood surrounded them in a puddle, gaudy sprays of it splashed across the white van doors.

The woman's voice broke and she sat, panting like a gut-shot animal. The kid next to her had either passed out or died. The chef continued to chew, bringing the esophagus to his mouth like a sausage and biting off chunks. The first man who had tumbled from the van swam on, limbs moving at the same lethargic pace.

Floyd had to help. He had to help them. He pulled the gun from his waistband and started down the stairs. "Lady!" he said, trying to whisper and still make himself heard. He didn't want to draw the attention of the chef. "Come here! Come this way!"

The woman's eyes found his and a kind of distracted hope cleared some of the terror away. She knelt, lifted the kid's arm over her shoulder. "Help!" she yelled. "Help me with him, please!"

The chef's head shot up, his cheeks distended, his chin covered in blood. He moaned and began to stand, but he was clumsy and slow.

Floyd was at the bottom of the stairs. He kept the gun pointed down, as he didn't want to shoot the woman or kid by accident. Adrenaline thrummed steadily through his system. "Lady, come on!" he said. "Hurry!"

A chorus of moans, loud and agitated, came from his left, over near the administration parking lot. A small crowd, at least a dozen people, were coming from that direction. Floyd's stomach dropped. He'd never get to her in time and he didn't have that many bullets. He backed up one stair. The woman screamed again. She hadn't seen the new group yet, because she was too distracted by the kid she was trying to drag with her. He was dead weight. "Help me with him!" she screamed. "Help me!"

"Leave him!" Floyd said, his voice still low but threaded with panic. He backed up another step. The moaning grew louder, counterpointed by the slapping of feet on pavement as they picked up speed, drawn by the woman's screams. They stumbled over each other, bounced back up, and kept going.

The woman finally turned, and saw them. She screamed, hitched the kid up to her side and screamed again.

"Stop screaming!" Floyd said, but it was too late. They were keyed onto her like good hunting dogs on a scent. He backed up the rest of the steps and crouched. They fell on her, swarming over her and the kid and at the last second, Floyd saw that the kid was still alive.

But not for long.

As quietly as he could, Floyd stood and opened the door. He backed in, keeping his eyes on the roiling knot of people. It was a confusion of limbs, teeth, and flesh. Blood splattered and an eyeball popped free and sailed toward him, trailing nerves and bits of flesh.

"Holy shit."

The words came from behind him. Floyd blinked but couldn't take his eyes from the carnage.

"Floyd?" Cal said. "What happened out there? What's going on?"

With a gesture, Floyd cautioned Cal to lower his voice. They watched with matching expressions of despairing horror.

A few of the attacking crowd had begun to wander away as though the frenzy didn't hold that much interest for them. Or as if they'd already forgotten about it. One of them, a young girl in a bright spring dress, held an arm—the young man's arm. Her fingers were intertwined with his as though they were holding hands, but the arm ended just below where the elbow should have been. The small white bones peeked out below the ragged edge of skin. Bright drops of blood littered the pavement, drawing a line from the girl back to the still-feeding mass. She lifted the arm and licked a rill of blood up the side as a child would lick a melting ice-cream cone.

Floyd sighed as the adrenaline drained away, leaving him tired and sick to his stomach. He should have done something, been quicker. He should have saved them, but how? How do you kill something that's already dead?

"Floyd, we have to go to Susan's shop; everyone is there," Cal said, his voice quiet and almost distracted. "Robert is dead. We have to…I don't know…do something."

Floyd nodded without taking his eyes from the parking lot.

Sometimes, the infected people died, like when he'd shot the girl in the parking lot this morning and then Cassie's daughter (which was hard to think about, but he'd had no choice…the girl would have killed Cassie), but sometimes they didn't, like Alfonse. According to Cal, Alfonse had died, come back, and been run through with a flagpole to no ill effect.

When Floyd had shot Dan in the chest, Dan hadn't fallen. He'd had to fight Dan and Dan had nearly gotten Cassie, had nearly bitten her legs as she struggled toward her daughter. Until he'd shot Dan a second time.

Nearly took the top of the guy's head off, in fact.

The minivan on the highway popped into his mind. The two corpses he could see clearly had both been shot in the head.

In the head.

Was that the key to killing them?

CHAPTER 13

"Lay down! Lay DOWN, Robert!"

Susan's voice met Floyd and Calvin as they got close to the welding shop. Floyd pulled the gun from his waistband and motioned Cal to stay behind him. They pushed into the classroom.

Susan stood in the middle of the shop, Tyler behind her. She held the big wrench in both hands slung at the ready over her shoulder like a baseball bat. Robert swayed fifteen feet from her, vest open and tie pulled askew. His chin was slicked with saliva. A long workbench, waist height, had him confused as he tried several times to climb over it, not seeming to realize he could have gone around.

Cassie sat unconcerned on one of the rolling shop stools, facing the wall, her shoulders slumped over. Her ponytail was half out of the band and her hair stuck up in a snarl on the side of her head.

"For fuck's sake, Robert!" Susan said. Bright panic snapped through her voice. "You're sick! Lay the *fuck* DOWN!" She seemed unaware that Floyd and Cal had come in behind her.

An idea bloomed into Floyd's mind like a dark flower. They could get something figured out if he could make it work. He turned and handed the pistol to Cal. "If it looks like he'll attack, shoot him in the head."

"But I don't–" Cal said and nearly fumbled the gun. He looked at it with alarm as though Floyd had just handed him a small but dangerous animal. One that might bite.

"Just point and pull the trigger," Floyd said and another manic, twirling grin appeared on his face. "Nothing to it. Just don't shoot anyone else." He turned away but then turned back, thinking of something. "But if you *do* shoot someone else...just make sure you shoot them in the head."

"Don't shoot him!" Susan said. She tossed the words over her shoulder, not taking her eyes from Robert. "He's just...just..."

Floyd spotted a heavy length of chain coiled neatly on one of the benches.

"Susan, talk to him," Floyd said. "Keep his attention."

"Robert! Robert, look at me!" Susan said. She waved the wrench, drawing his eyes. "Lay down, Robert! You're sick! You have to–"

"Yeah, Mr. Ralston!" Tyler chimed in. There was an odd note of glee in his voice...maybe because he was yelling at a teacher. "Lay down, dude! You're, like, totally *sick*, man! Lay down! Lay–"

They went on yelling as Floyd skirted the room, keeping his eyes on Robert. He lifted the chain from the table, slowly enough to dampen the slithery noise of the links, and tested its weight. It would tether, he decided. He glanced at Cal who stood to the side with the gun trained shakily on Robert.

"Cal," Floyd said in a whisper, drawing the man's attention. *Don't shoot me*, he mouthed. Cal nodded and pointed the pistol down.

Floyd walked up behind the swaying Robert, a length of chain dangling loose between his hands, the rest wrapped over his forearm. When Susan saw his intent, she redoubled her efforts, waving the wrench as she yelled. Tyler slid around her and took a few steps toward Robert, yelling and laughing, sounding on the verge of hysterics. Susan reached to pull him back. Robert moaned and reached for them, trying to get a knee on the workbench.

Floyd threw the chain over Robert's head and stumbled back, drawing Robert with him. Robert's moan became a strangled caw and he clawed at the chain around his neck. His body against Floyd's was cool and somehow spongy although Robert was not overweight. It was as though his organs had turned to foam.

Floyd pulled tighter and Robert began to kick. He threw himself side to side, trying to wrench free. Floyd realized he hadn't exactly thought this whole plan through. He had Robert, but now what?

"Susan!" Floyd called out, his voice strained. "Padlock? Do you have a–"

She dropped the wrench and spun to another workbench. Pulled open a drawer. Slammed it closed. Pulled open another. Rummaged. Turned with a yell of triumph.

"Here!" she said and held up a large Yale lock.

Floyd kept the chain taut. Robert's hands scrabbled at the links. Two of his nails peeled back and then broke off. Floyd's stomach churned at the sight. *You've seen worse*, he told himself, swallowing back the bile, but it was the close up of it, the small crunch-snap he heard even over Robert's moans.

Then Susan was there and she reached to put the hasp through two links of chain. Robert pulled the other direction and Susan fumbled the padlock. It dropped to the floor. Flailing, Robert kicked it away.

Floyd growled in anger, sweating, his arms growing fatigued. He had to get Robert over, get him down on the ground so Susan could hook the chain. He heaved to the side with a yell while hooking his leg in front of Robert's ankles. They both went over. They hit the ground and Robert's face crashed into the hard floor with a wet smack; it should have killed or at least dazed him, but he continued to pull at the chain around his neck, fingers scuttling. His moans became muffled. He squirmed and bucked beneath Floyd like a cold and muscular snake.

"Hurry, Susan!" Floyd said. "Tyler, sit on his legs!"

Tyler landed on Robert's legs with a thud as Susan snapped the padlock through two links of chain, forming it into a collar around Robert's neck.

"Attach the end to something," Floyd said, his voice wheezing as he grappled with Robert. "Can you find–"

"Of course I can. It's my shop," Susan said as she searched for the other end of the chain in the snarl of links. She found it and stood, casting about. "There!" she said. Several industrial hooks had been drilled into the concrete wall to hold heavy equipment.

"Will that hold him?" Floyd asked after a glance at the hooks.

"Yes," Susan said. She made her way to the wall but came up five feet short. She turned and yelled, "Can you get him closer?"

Robert bucked and moaned, snapping his head side to side as if trying to get it around far enough to bite. The black coffee grounds flew each time his head snapped and Floyd dodged to avoid being hit by them. He shot a desperate glance at Susan. "I can't let him go!"

"Just hold on! We'll pull you!" Susan said. She wrapped the chain over her bicep and cinched it tight. "Tyler, Cal...*help* me!"

Cal set the gun on the nearest worktable. He got to Susan just after Tyler. They pulled. Floyd and Robert slid three inches and stopped. His legs now free, Robert kicked and flopped like a fish, Floyd rocking on his back.

"Shit!" Cal yelled. "Again! PULL!"

This time, they were able to move the men a foot.

Robert's struggles had not diminished, but Floyd's strength was flagging.

"Cassie!" Susan yelled. "Help us! Please!"

Cassie turned on the stool, blank-faced. Floyd had a sudden and sinking realization that Cassie would never do anything to help him. She hated him.

"Cassie!" Susan yelled again. "Help us pull them!"

Cassie stood, some of the blankness draining away. Without a word, she trotted to them, added her hands to the chain.

"On three, pull as hard as you can," Cal said. "One, two...*three*!"

They all pulled as one, Tyler tumbling backward, Susan yelling. A reddish black smear appeared under Robert as they slid the last few feet. Susan pushed the chain over the hook.

"Move!" Floyd yelled. "Get out of reach of the chain!"

Cal lifted Tyler and pulled him to the side of the room. Cassie and Susan darted to the other.

Floyd rolled off Robert, and with an effort, rolled out of his reach. Robert's hands tugged at Floyd's pant leg and with reflexive panic, Floyd yanked it away. He scrambled onto his hands and knees, then his feet, still moving away from Robert, his breath wheezing out in tight, panicked exhalations.

Robert pushed himself onto his knees. His nose was flattened across his face, split open and dripping the black coffee-ground substance. His eyes were still bright with cold menace but beginning to haze over. He reached for Floyd, jerked up against the chain and moaned. Reached again. Fell over. Pushed himself up. Reached again with a long, trembling moan, as the chain rattled and jangled behind him.

Floyd collapsed against the wall near the door and let himself slide down. He watched Robert with frank fascination. Floyd was exhausted, but Robert was as lively–or well, *energetic*–as when they'd begun their struggle. How could that be?

Floyd wiped a hand across his forehead and it came away slicked with sweat and grease. Susan and Cassie watched Robert with the same intensity; they looked almost hypnotized at the horror of Robert's appearance.

On the other side of the room, Cal reached a shaking hand to Tyler. Tyler let Cal pull him up and then he started brushing off his skinny black jeans, sending small white clouds to float around his ankles. Cal blew out a long breath and then picked up Floyd's gun from the workbench.

He went to Floyd, giving Robert a wide berth. He sank down next to him and handed him the pistol.

"Here," he said, "I don't want it." Then he tipped his head into his hands and sighed. It was almost a sob.

"I gave my shotgun to Robert when I left. Where is it?" Floyd asked. Then, just realizing, he said, "And where's Dave?"

"I'm here," Dave said, entering the room from the hallway. He held the shotgun in one hand, a duffle bag in the other. He scanned the room, taking in the chained Robert with only mild surprise. "What's going on?"

"Well," Floyd said as he heaved himself up. He brushed off his vest, ran his hand over his beard to check for blood or…anything…that might have come from Robert. "We're going to try a little experiment."

— — —

"Stop it!" Susan yelled. Her voice was shredded with anguish. She held her hands curled into tight fists at her sides. "Floyd, that's *Robert*. You *know* him!"

Floyd stood just out of Robert's reach. The gun in his hand was not yet raised, as he tried to decide where to shoot the other man. He'd been trying to keep his mind on a clinical plane; how could he shoot Robert otherwise? Shooting Dan had been bad enough, shooting his and Cassie's daughter had been the worst thing he'd ever had to do, but it had been something he'd done instinctively to save Cassie's life.

The anguish in Susan's voice was making it hard to keep his cool. He glanced at her.

"He's not Robert anymore, Susan," Floyd said. In his peripheral vision, Tyler nodded, agreeing. He'd been watching Floyd intently and seemed almost eager for the 'experiment' to begin. *The kid's a little creepy, when you got right down to it,* Floyd thought.

"You don't *know* that," Susan said. Tears began to roll down her cheeks, and next to her, Cal shuffled his feet. Susan glanced at Cassie as if expecting her to do something, but Cassie had resumed communing with the wall.

"Floyd," Susan went on, "what if this is *curable*? What if we could save him? It's Robert...he's your *friend*, Floyd. Remember when he gave you that advice about Julie? Remember when he helped you get your money back from that shady broker? He wrote that awesome letter and then he–"

Floyd lowered his forehead into his hand. Robert moaned and threw himself against the chain over and over. He'd not lost one ounce of his vitality even though his windpipe seemed to be collapsing as the chain began to dent his throat.

Susan pressed her point. "Let's just try to talk it through. Can we do that at least? Maybe Dave has some ideas. Maybe...I don't know. Maybe we can get something figured out. We *have* to get this figured out. Even if we can't save Robert, we have to know what's going on for ourselves! We have to–" Her voice finally broke. She dropped her head and collapsed onto one of the stools, her hands clasped between her knees. Her voice, when it came again, was choked and stilting. "My mom and kid were both sick last night, Floyd. If there's no cure for...whatever this is, then there's no point to any of this for me."

This last seemed to reach Cassie even in her fugue state. Her gaze came around and she rolled her stool to Susan's and put an arm across her back. Susan turned to Cassie, leaned her face against Cassie's shoulder, and cried. Cassie hugged her hard, her own cheeks wet with tears as she stared into the empty space of the shop.

It was good Cassie was finally showing some emotion, Floyd thought, as he watched the women, but her empty gaze didn't sit well with her actions. She hadn't come all the way back.

As important as it seemed to Floyd to follow through with this line of action, shooting Robert in front of her wasn't likely to help the situation along.

"Okay," Floyd said, relenting, "let's talk it through." He turned away from Robert with something that felt like relief. As much as he had been anxious to try his 'experiment,' Susan was right...in some ways it *was* still Robert standing there. "Dave? I nominate you to lead the discussion."

"Me? Why me?" Dave asked and looked up in surprise from where he'd been digging through his duffel bag.

While Cal had had to wipe tears from his eyes after watching Cassie and Susan, Dave seemed to be almost deliberately ignoring the situation going on around him.

"Because you're the closest thing we have to an authority," Cal said. He had shuffled closer to Susan and now he patted her on the shoulder. She looked up at him with a brief, unhappy smile. Then she sat straight, but kept a hand in Cassie's.

"Yep," Floyd said, "plus, you're CDC and have a better understanding of what's going on here, or at least, a better *chance* of understanding it. You're our most analytical mind, since Robert is...you know...changed."

Dave sat back on his heels, shoulders dropping, a pair of sneakers in his hand. He looked around at the group, his face white with strain. He looked down, seeming to consider the old Nike's. Then he shook his head.

"Guys, listen," he said and then fell silent again. As if it was what he had intended for them to listen to, Robert moaned and clanked against his chain. He moaned again and the end of the moan pulled up into something like a whimper. He stepped forward, snapped back. His arms reached and swung, his eyes pinned to Floyd. Stepped forward. Snapped back. Moaned. Did it all again.

And again.

One by one, their gazes went from Robert back to Dave. Dave shook his head, staring at Robert. A sheen of what might have been unshed tears glowed in his eyes.

"If that's what is going to become of everyone...if we're all going to end up like that, regardless..." Dave looked at each of them in turn. Floyd raised his hands and took a step back at the cold, dead expression on Dave's face. "I don't want it," Dave finished. His eyes went back to Robert and a creeping, dawning horror filled his eyes. "Is that what my wife looks like right now? Is that what...what she *is*? And my boys?" He swallowed and dropped his hands to the shoes on his feet. He picked at the knots, his fingers shaking, and then, with a grunt of anger, he pulled the shoes off. He stood and flung them across the room. One sock had pulled partway off. He stood breathing heavily, vulnerable in his stocking feet. He swiped at the tears on his cheeks and took a long, shuddery breath. The expressionless mask dropped back over his features.

"I don't want it," he said.

Floyd looked at each member of the group. Susan's spiky hair was flat and defeated, her thin arms wrapped around herself. Cassie was nearly catatonic, staring blankly, her mouth open. Cal had walked away, hands jammed in his back pockets, as if to distance himself from the situation. Dave sat to put his sneakers on, concentrating as though the task occupied every bit of his attention, trails of tears unacknowledged on his cheeks.

Tyler stared at Robert with bored, half-lidded eyes. When Tyler felt Floyd's gaze, he looked back and shrugged like, what now? He was still remarkably unaffected.

"It's, like, your call, Mr. Abby," Tyler said.

"You can call me Floyd, Tyler. School's out, probably for good."

"Yeah," Tyler said, his gaze going back to Robert, "whatever."

Thank God for disenfranchised youth, Floyd thought and it held a modicum of dark humor. His mind handed up a quick picture of him and Tyler riding off on the Harley, Tyler blasting away at the affected, laughing like one of those loonies in old westerns. Behind them in the school, Robert, Susan, Cassie, Cal, and Dave wandered the halls, moaning and disconsolate. In another flash, they were all back in this room, lying still with bullets in their heads. Floyd's bullets. For an instant, the idea glowed like a black diamond, enticing and rich. Relieving, too, in its implication of drastically reduced responsibility.

Floyd shook it off.

"Don't be a dickhead, Abby," he said under his breath. "You can pull them together."

But how? He had an idea, and it didn't involve group hugs and sing-alongs. It didn't involve discussing their feelings and talking it all through. At least, not yet. His idea might tear them apart, but did that matter?

He had to try.

Floyd strode to where Dave sat, still hunched over his sneakers. He placed the pistol at Dave's temple. Dave's mouth dropped open and then he froze.

"Where do you think, Dave?" Floyd asked, his voice neutral. "The temple? Or..." he lifted the gun and put the barrel at the top of Dave's head. "Right down through? You have a better understanding of physiology than I do, Dave. So which will it be?"

"What...what are you..." Dave's voice blew out like a shaky candle flame. "Floyd?"

Susan jumped up from the stool and it rolled away, chattering in panic. Cal looked at her over his shoulder, alarmed by the sudden movement.

"Floyd!" Susan said. "What the *fuck* do you think you're doing?"

Dave had begun to shake. Floyd kept his finger carefully outside the trigger, but Dave couldn't see that. He also blocked it from Susan's sight.

"I'm helping Dave," Floyd said. He glanced back at her. She looked angry, but she also looked fearful and despairing. Not good. "I'll help you next, Susan."

The effect on her was immediate. "The hell you will, you fucking prick," she said and took a step toward him. Her brows had drawn together. "I'll fucking take that gun and–"

"Floyd, put the gun down, you're not helping," Cal said. His hands ground together and he licked his lips. "For Christ's sake."

"You're next after Susan," Floyd told him with callous disregard. Satisfaction flowed into him when Cal balled his hands into fists, but he didn't let the approval show on his face, not yet. Keeping his tone cold even though he hated his next words, he said, "I'll kill Cassie last. She's halfway fucking dead, anyway."

Cassie, sitting on her stool and staring at the floor, seemed at first not to hear. Then her head came up, her eyes on Floyd. They were clear, with a hard shine. She sighed and shook her head. "I know what you're doing," she said. "Asshole." She stood and tugged the trailing elastic from her snarled ponytail and then gathered her hair back together, smoothing it. She pulled the elastic over the end and then doubled it. She put her hands on her hips and gazed at Floyd. Her eyes were heavy with fatigue but clear and now, her own. She was back. She said it again, "I know what you're doing."

"What? What the fuck is he doing?" Dave asked. His hands shook at either side of his head as if he were gearing himself up to reach for the gun. "Does someone want to clue me in before he fucking kills me?"

"What does it matter to you?" Floyd said, his voice a pitiless growl. He put his mouth close to Dave's ear and shouted, "You're already *dead*!"

Dave ducked and rolled out from under the gun. His breath came in a hissing gasp as he crab-walked away, scuttling on his hands and heels. "Fuck you!" he said to Floyd. "I'm not dead! Fuck you! Fuck you!" Spit wet his chin and anger replaced the fear in his eyes.

Floyd shrugged and tucked the pistol back into his waistband. "Well, okay then," he said and his voice was mild. He glanced at each of them in turn. "Since we all seem to want to live..." he walked to Dave and put a hand out. "Let's talk."

CHAPTER 14

<u>Diagnostic Notes/Marlton, New Jersey</u>
<u>JUNE 8, 2027</u>
<u>David Weathers, Agent</u>
<u>CDC of the United States of America</u>
All notes herein are confidential and classified and are considered to be under the sole proprietorship of the CDC of the United States of America. Any dissemination of the contained information, whether verbal, written, or electronic (either via facsimile or posted online or to any website, including personal sites such as blogs, social media, etc.) shall constitute a Federal offense and can be prosecuted in a court of law. Conviction will result in detainment for a period of time discretionary to the Federal court and is not subject to appeal.

– – –

As dictated to self (DW being the party taking notes)
Symptoms. Initial onset of the disease manifests as flu-like with symptoms including chills, muscle aches, and cramping. Sometimes accompanied by diarrhea and/or vomiting. [These symptoms were not witnessed by me personally, but were relayed to me from Cassie Ramson, RN, who was on shift at Advantage Urgent Care on the evening of June 7 into the morning of June 8.] Further investigation required. Blood samples, stool samples, charts, clinician notes, etc. unavailable ~~at this time~~.

Transmission. It seems at this time, with ~~very~~ extremely limited info, to be transmissible through contact such as a bite. Initial onset is inexplicable at this time, but possible sources (taking into consideration the scope of the disease) would have to be water- or food-borne. Possibly air-borne if the survivors have some sort of built in immunity to the initial disease. Further investigation required.

Estimated Casualties. Innumerable. The disease seems to have decimated the entire country. ~~Anecdotal evidence shows that the disease took an east to west course, starting in~~*. Further investigation required.*

Estimated Deaths. Innumerable. The disease seems to have decimated the entire country. Further investigation required.

Conclusion: further investigation required.

– – –

"You have to put the part about the dead coming back to life," Cassie said. She tapped the clipboard in Dave's hands. "It's important to have that in the record."

"Cassie, I can't put that," Dave said. His voice showed his level of dismay. "No one would ever believe it!"

"Everyone alive now…" Cassie said, "…will believe it. We all already know." She smiled and the smile was a trifle grim, but it still looked good. "It's no secret, Dave."

He stared at her for a long minute, then dropped his eyes back to the notes. He began to write:

~~*Conclusion. Further investigation required.*~~
Ongoing manifestation of symptoms. Individuals who seem to die from the onset of the disease (the flu-like symptoms)–

Cassie tapped the page again, pointing to a specific portion of his notes. With a small half-smile, Dave said, "You're braver than me. Can I put your name on this?" Then he bent over the notes again.

–Individuals who ~~seem to~~ die from the original disease (the flu-like symptoms) reanimate within a twenty-four hour period of time (the timing and sequence of events need further investigation). The reanimated individuals display a new array of symptoms such as cold skin, thickened–and in some cases, granulated–blood, high

tolerance to pain, high tolerance to trauma, a sort of rabies-like aggression, and an inability to 'die' again. Disturbingly, (and this parts needs a LOT of further investigation, a fuck load of it, in fact, since it could affect all survivors) individuals unaffected by the initial flu-like disease who die of another cause can still manifest the secondary set of symptoms. To put it bluntly, you can die of a heart attack but still reanimate as one of the undead. (An interesting side note to this: the initial cause of death seems to have no bearing on the reanimated individual.)

Conclusion. Further investigation needed on all aspects of the current situation. Comprehensive conclusions unlikely as most people are now reanimated corpses and the number of survivors is unknown. One thing I can put as VERY conclusive; we're horribly fucking outnumbered.

— — —

Dave looked up at Cassie as she finished reading over his shoulder. She snorted a small laugh through her nose and looked at him, eyebrows raised. "It gets a little unprofessional at the end, Dave," she said. "Can you live with that?"

"Something tells me I'll never have to face any HR repercussions," he said. He looked across the cafeteria table and his eyes were met by expectant looks. "Want to hear it?"

"More than anything," Susan said, the sarcasm in her voice tempered by a tired smile. She yanked at her hair and leaned her head against Cal's shoulder. He yawned but gave Dave his attention. Floyd sat with his chin tilted against his chest, his blond Viking beard nearly covering his folded arms. Crumpled wrappers littered the table.

Outside, the sun was going down. It had been an incredibly long day.

Dave read them his notes.

When he finished, he put the clipboard down and fiddled with the pen. "It's not, uh, comprehensive. I realize," he said, "but as a start, I think it's a good one." His eyes skated over Floyd and away. The big man had put things into perspective for him, it was true, but Dave could still feel the barrel of the pistol on the crown of his head. He didn't relish the feeling.

Yes, things had snapped into perspective, but that didn't mean he missed Colleen any less. It didn't mean that he could so easily get over the death of his boys. The grief process was not being hastened so much as it was being buried, and nothing good came from buried feelings. His eyes found Floyd again, and in his gut, he recognized a feeling that was the warm beginning of hate.

"I think it's good enough for now," Floyd said. "Now we need to decide what to do next."

Cal gave him a blank, questioning look. Floyd went on, "First, if everyone agrees, I want to test my theory. Susan? Can you go along with me on it?"

Susan nodded without opening her eyes.

"Then we have to decide what we want to do after that," Floyd said. "Stay here? Go somewhere else? If we go somewhere else, we have to have a reason why. I don't think we should go running all over the township like panicked chickens."

"I think we should try and get to Atlanta," Dave said. He'd been giving it thought as he wrote out his notes. "The CDC building is there. If anyone were buttoned up and ready for this, it would have been the people there. And it's pretty close, isn't it?"

Cal laughed and Susan sat up abruptly, blinking sleepily.

"Sorry, Susan," Cal said, and then he turned to Dave with a good-natured smile. "Your geography's a little off, unless you think a twelve hour drive through undead-infested country is 'pretty close.'"

"Jesus," Dave said, "I guess I was thinking of it in terms of flying. I guess that's out."

"What if they all die off, or, like, rot away, or whatever," Tyler said. It was the first time he'd spoken since they'd all trooped to the cafeteria to eat and regroup. "Maybe they'll all just kind of, like, stop moving. We haven't seen any of them."

They all turned to look out the windows. They'd not turned on the lights in the cafeteria as some instinct told them to be discreet, and the world outside had gone a dusky purple. Lights were on in some of the buildings and shops. The streetlights had come on. The traffic signals continued to blink through their red, yellow, green pattern.

"Who knows," Dave said, "I guess anything is a possibility. Maybe they don't go out after dark. Even better, maybe they grouped up and migrated away." He was thinking of the crowd of them they'd seen on the highway today, traveling in a kind of pack. "But we're going to need some long-term solutions, too."

"What do you mean?" Cassie asked. She picked at a cookie as far down the table from Floyd as she could get without her avoidance of him looking too obvious.

She must have feelings about him as mixed as my own, Dave thought.

"What are we going to do tomorrow, next week, next year? Dave said. "Winter, starvation, lack of water...hell, basic sanitation? What about all those things? The phones are effectively gone and electricity won't last forever. We're going to starve or freeze to death."

Cal's face had gone dead white. "Fuuuck," he said barely above a sighing whisper, "I hadn't thought of all that. I hadn't thought past today, to tell you the truth."

"I think that's why it's important we make Atlanta at least a long term goal," Dave said. He sensed resistance from Floyd although he couldn't have pinpointed why he felt it exactly. Just something in the set of the big man's jaw.

"Okay, but now for the short term," Floyd said. He pushed back his chair and rose and Tyler did the same, but no one else.

The beginning of the mutiny? Dave thought.

"We have to be together on this," Floyd said quietly. "What's it going to be? Find something out or wallow in our ignorance?"

The room became still and seemed to slip further into darkness, as though their decision darkened the heavens themselves. Finally, Susan stood.

"I'm with you," she said and she tried to smile but her tone belied her unease.

"Me, too," Cassie said and Dave was surprised. He would have thought she'd hold out till the end. Dave stood at the same time as Cal.

They all went back to Susan's shop.

– – –

There were only two windows in the shop to accommodate the much-needed wall space of the welding equipment, and neither the parking lot nor the streets were visible—just the wide grassy expanse of the school's side yard. They decided lights were worth the risk and Floyd flicked them on as they entered.

Robert, who had quieted and wandered into a corner, turned as fast as a striking crocodile and ran toward them. The chain brought him up sharp and his feet went out from under him. He landed on his back with a hard thump that made Cassie cringe. That fall alone could have been enough to paralyze him, but Robert jumped up and redoubled his efforts, fresh as he'd been earlier. Only his eyes had changed, glazing over even more, leaving them smoky and blind looking.

"Okay," Floyd said, "I've been thinking about it. I'm going to shoot him in the thigh. Maybe I can get him in the femoral artery." He checked with the others who had stayed grouped at the door.

"It's your call, Floyd," Cal said.

Floyd looked at each of them and then walked to Robert. He raised the pistol.

"Wait!" Dave said.

Floyd turned with something like annoyance on his face, but Cassie saw relief there, as well. She was glad to see it.

"I think you should put on some kind of coverall," Dave said. "You're at pretty close range. What if something flies up and hits your eye or lands…you know…in your mouth."

They all cringed at the idea and Susan fished in a closet for a pair of Dickies that would fit Floyd. Once he was suited up, she fit a welding helmet over his head. She unzipped the coverall, tucked his beard down into it and zipped it back up. She gave him a little smile and snapped the faceplate down.

"I can hardly see!" he protested.

"You'll get used to it," Susan said with the offhand casualness of someone who'd said the same thing to countless students. "Just let your eyes adjust." She went back to stand with the others.

Floyd walked to Robert again, holding the welding helmet steady in his free hand, adjusting it up and down. Robert reached for him and a moan rattled through his chest and throat sounding like air through a can.

Floyd raised the pistol, adjusted the helmet again, and shot.

A large, ragged hole appeared in Robert's trousers at the bend in his thigh. Robert fell against the chain and then crumbled to the floor.

Susan yelped, "Robert!" just as Tyler screamed, "Holy shit! You, like, shot Mr. Ralston in the dick!"

"I didn't shoot him in the dick!" Floyd said, his voice both muffled and flustered under the faceplate. "And don't call him Mr. Ralston, in fact…" he turned to the others and ripped the helmet off, his face was full of horrified anger, "don't call him Robert, either. Don't fucking call him anything! He's NOT ROBERT!"

"You're right," Susan said, "I'm sorry. It just flew out. I'm sorry, I'm…" She shook her head. New tears stood on her eyelids. She went to Floyd and patted his cheeks where his own tears had leaked, reluctant and telling. "I'm sorry," she said. "I know this is hard."

He gave her a one-armed hug, his eyes closed, seeming to draw strength from her.

Behind them, Robert struggled to regain his feet.

The chain had cut deeply into his neck, embedding itself in the flesh. He reached for Floyd and Susan. His moan had a choked off quality. They turned to look at him. A thick, blackish red substance dripped from his pant leg on the side where Floyd had shot him. Other than tilting slightly to that side, he was as lively as he'd been since he'd risen.

"Get back," Floyd said and gave Susan a gentle shove, "I'm gonna shoot him again."

This time, he shot Robert in the chest.

Robert spun and fell onto his face, the moan cut off in mid-breath. The chain rattled as it hit the ground behind him, scattered and chaotic.

He lay still.

Floyd glanced at the others, the faceplate of the mask making him look alien and strange. He shrugged, hands up and questioning. Then he turned and took a step toward Robert.

Robert's arms twitched, then his legs. He was up in less than a second and he stood, his back to them, swaying. There was no tear in his vest, but a dark patch appeared between his shoulder blades, slowly blooming to the size of a saucer. Black crumbles fell from beneath his shirt to plop and patter to the floor. He seemed disoriented–turned off–as he swayed quietly.

"I think–" Dave said.

Robert turned and lunged at Floyd. Floyd stumbled back with a startled yell. He raised the pistol and shot Robert in the head.

Robert went down like dead weight, all animation gone. A final wheeze of air forced its way out between his gray lips.

Then the room was silent.

Cassie counted thirty seconds. Sixty. Ninety.

If he were going to get back up, wouldn't he have done so by now?

Floyd glanced back at them again, his arm up in a stop gesture, cautioning them to stay put. He walked guardedly to Robert, the gun up and ready in his hand. He shook Robert's thigh with one heavily booted foot.

Robert didn't move.

Floyd squatted down next to him and Cassie held her breath as he lifted the faceplate of the welding mask. If this were a horror movie, Robert would choose this second to lunge forward and rip Floyd's face off. She wanted to call out a warning, but something cautioned against it.

Still, Robert didn't move.

Floyd shoved his shoulder, tapped his cheek. Nothing.

Robert was finally gone.

Cassie went to Robert and knelt. She took his wrist in her hand and felt for a pulse, didn't find one. Of course, he might not have had one before, either. The man's skin was stiff and cold. It had a tough consistency, almost rubbery. Certainly not freshly dead. She blinked and it was Lucy's ankle in her hand…just as cold, just as rubbery. Just as dead.

She shook the image away.

Floyd had not moved. He stared at Robert's gray face with fascination. Cassie reached to close Robert's cloudy eyes and then Floyd looked up at her. His eyes were filled with anguish but he was trying to smile. "Guess I was right," he said. His voice was strained. "Shot to the head kills 'em. Now we know. Now we–" He dropped his forehead into his hand and one terrible sob escaped his throat. Cassie put her arm around his shoulders, disliking the heat and the bulk of him, but letting her nursing instincts push that aside for now. Beads of sweat clung in his beard and he stank of sour sweat.

A wind had begun outside, sighing through the pine trees. She wished she could go outside for some fresh air. She also hoped–for reasons she couldn't define–that it would rain.

"We need to get you some water," she said. "Floyd? Let's get you out of those coveralls and get you something to drink."

He looked up. "A whiskey would be nice," he said, his voice rough with emotion.

"I think I can accommodate you on that," Susan said. She went to a desk, felt around deep in the back of it. "Let's see...somewhere back here...here it is!" She pulled forth a bottle of Jack Daniels. "I confiscated it from Billy Hayes."

Floyd stripped and sat in the desk chair. He tilted the bottle to his mouth and took a long swallow. Cal leaned against the desk.

"Guess I'll take a pull," he said and reached for the whiskey. Floyd handed it over willingly.

Susan sifted through detritus on the desk surface. "I know I have a mug here somewhere," she said.

"Do I have cooties?" Cal asked and she gave him a quick, distracted smile.

"At least we know how to take care of the four trapped in the auditorium hallway," Floyd said. "Then the building will be secure."

Dave said, "I think sound draws them. Did you notice, when we first came in, he was just standing there? And when Floyd...shot him, you know, in the chest? When he first got back up, he didn't see us and it was like he forgot we were there. Remember?" He tucked his notes under his arm and reached for the bottle. Susan was still looking for her mug. Cassie joined them. She wouldn't mind a sip of the whiskey.

"That sounds right," Cassie said. Maybe that had been why her instincts had told her not to yell out. Maybe some part of her mind had already put two and two together.

Susan blew dust out of a mug and frowned at it. "That might have been metal filings. I don't think I can drink out of that."

"If sound does draw them, we're going to have to reconsider any 'experiments' using the gun," Cal said. "It's too damn–"

The shotgun went off with a deafening blast.

Cassie stooped and threw her arms over her head. Dave and Cal both ducked and Floyd rolled out of the chair, hitting the ground, hard. Susan turned, her hands on her hips, the only one used to loud noises in the shop.

"Tyler!" she yelled. "What the fuck?"

Tyler stood over Robert, the shotgun in his hands. Robert's arm had been blown off at the shoulder. Black grit, charred skin, and flecks of gore decorated the concrete in a wide spray pattern. Tyler looked at Susan, his eye already swelling and turning purple where the gun had kicked back. His mouth hung unhinged in shock. "I never shot a gun before!" His tone was somewhere between triumph and shaking fear. "Holy shit! That was, like, so cool! That was–"

"Sshhh!" Dave said. His face was white and spittle dotted his lips. He motioned them all to be quiet. "Listen!"

Outside, the wind had picked up. It moaned and howled making Cassie's arms pull into gooseflesh. Dread contracted her stomach into a cold knot, but what was so dreadful? It was only a summer shower.

"It's going to rain," she said and couldn't help the small note of pleading in her voice.

Dave's eyes locked onto hers. "I don't think it's that kind of storm."

CHAPTER 15

They stayed at the very back of the hallway as far from the front doors as they could get, while still being able to see out into the parking lot. They stood shoulder to shoulder in the dark and Cassie couldn't tell if the shaking was her own, or the result of her shoulder pressed to Cal's on one side and Susan's on the other. Her mind was filled with cold dismay.

The parking lot was packed with the shambling undead.

They moved in an almost tidal influx and outflow, dotted throughout with dark eddies of confused limbs. Some moved quickly while others struggled to move at all, lunging wildly from side to side as they tried to walk on broken or missing feet and legs. Some merely swayed in place like crank-driven toys winding down. The parking lot lights glinted blackly on open wounds, twinkled on exposed bone. Some were naked, some half-clothed, but pajamas seemed to be the garment of choice for more than half. There were elderly ones, middle-aged, teenagers. Hardest of all for Cassie to see…there were children. Lots of them.

A small brown and tan dog, some kind of terrier mix, walked at the heels of a girl who looked to be eight or nine. The girl wore Hello Kitty slippers and a white nightgown; the front was streaked with what could have been vomit or something worse. The dog stared up at her with head-tilted confusion. He barked and barked again, his little feet coming off the ground. Cassie couldn't hear the barking from where she stood inside the building, but the terrier's movements were unmistakable. The undead girl paid no attention and wandered deeper into the crowd. The terrier stared after her, uncertainly taking a step forward and then hesitating. He barked again then trotted in another direction. He seemed to search the faces of the snaking crowd. Then he disappeared among them.

They moaned and it was the same sound repeated in varying tones, almost like a song sung in rounds, nonsense syllables becoming unintelligible through repetition.

"There's so many of them," Susan said, her voice barely louder than a breath. "Remember the ones on the highway? Are these the same ones? It can't be...there weren't this many."

"Maybe they just hadn't risen yet," Dave said. "People have most likely been dying all day. Either from the original flu or other causes."

"You think it was the gunshots that drew them?" Floyd asked. "How'd they hear it over their own racket?"

In Cassie's peripheral vision, Dave shook his head and his troubled expression said he didn't know; how could he know? To Cassie, it seemed the most likely explanation–the shotgun, especially, had boomed like a cannon.

Half a dozen of the reanimated stood at the glass doors, looking in. One of them–a young man, possibly early twenties– stepped into the glass over and over, his head hitting it with every step, boinging hollowly. The skin on his forehead had begun to peel away. It hung in tattered flaps, exposing his skull.

Others had wandered away as if they had already forgotten what had drawn them in the first place. One unfortunate–its gender indeterminate–had tumbled down the wide concrete stairs breaking both ankles. It tried to stand but toppled over each time. How long would it go on trying? Cassie's mind offered up a picture of a half-rotted corpse, eyes fallen in, ears, nose and lips gone, tendons creaking against element-bleached bones...struggling still, over and over, to stand. When would it stop? Once all the connective tissue had finally rotted away? Or would it keep going until its brain had decayed to sludgy mucous?

"At least they can't, like, get in here," Tyler said. As if in direct contradiction to Tyler's words, the young man stepped into the glass again and this time, it starred under the blow from his forehead.

Cassie gasped and Cal voiced a startled, "Shit!"

The effect on the young man was immediate. His mouth yawned open, impossibly wide and black. He moaned deeply and then, as if he had learned something, he smashed his head into the glass with more force than before. Small pieces broke away from the chicken wire holding the panes together. They tinkled to the industrial tiles and lay gleaming like false diamonds.

Others that had begun to wander away turned back, while still more of the undead began to swarm the stairs. The half dozen at the doors turned to a dozen. Two dozen. The moaning became a roar and Cassie was reminded of an interview she'd seen on the news of a woman who'd lived through a tornado; the way she had described the sound... "Like a train," she had said, pushing back her thin, tangled hair as she dragged deeply on a home-rolled cigarette. "But not like a real one, like a dead one...a ghost train."

That woman's eyes had been blank with trauma and the horror of the things she'd seen and at the time, Cassie had felt a deep well of pity for the woman, but she'd also felt something else, hadn't she? Complacency. Maybe with a dash of superiority as the camera panned to the trailer park, half the homes tumbled like a child's toys. What fool would choose to live in a tin can in Tornado Alley? Now Cassie felt she could trump that woman's horror and she no longer felt complacent...her carefully ordered life had just crumbled around her. The luxury of judgment was gone.

"I think we should barricade ourselves in the shop for now," Susan said and her voice was soft but authoritative. "They'll get through–eventually–if we keep standing here."

"Or they'll forget again," Dave said, but he fell in behind Cassie as they made their way back down the hall.

Cassie cast one more look over her shoulder. Heat lightning flashed across the far horizon, unaccompanied by thunder. The eyes of the undead lit up, seeming to snap with fleeting sparks. Seeming alive.

– – –

"Let's all get some rest. It's been one long ass day and we need clear heads to get some shit figured out," Floyd said. He was pulling orange squares from a metal cabinet. FIRE AND FIRST AID BLANKET was printed in black on the front of each. "Susan, how many of these do you have in the shop?"

"Four," Susan said. "The machine shop has some...automotive...the labs might, too. We can get them tomorrow." She hoisted herself onto a workbench and leaned her forehead into her hands. They had turned the lights off, just in case it might somehow draw the undead. The night was clear and bright and cold moonlight filtered in through the two windows, giving just a hint of light. "We may as well try to sleep; we can't go anywhere tonight, not with all those...things...out there."

"Things?" Dave said. He didn't know why, but he felt uncomfortable with her use of the word. It seemed somehow offensive. Whatever they were now, each one of them had been people and not very long ago.

"Yeah, *things*," Susan said.

But her bristling was desultory and she didn't raise her head.

Floyd offered a blanket to Tyler, but Tyler waved him off and kept his eyes on the wide, grassy side yard that lay outside the shop windows. Floyd shrugged and handed one to Cassie, one to Susan, the third to Cal, and the last one to Dave.

"I'm going to put this over Robert," Cal said. Robert's body was a vague hump in the dark room. "I won't be able to sleep with him just lying there."

"I have some plastic we can use instead," Susan said. "Keep your blanket. Use it as a pillow at least." She'd gone to one tall cabinet and drew forth a large roll of heavy, milky plastic. "Help me with it?"

Dave watched with hypnotized fascination as they walked to Robert's body. He was still tethered to the chain, his arm ten feet away in the spray of blackish crumbles.

"What about that?" Cal said, indicating the arm. The corners of his mouth were turned down in distaste.

Susan looked at Robert's arm with a mirrored frown on her face. "I guess you could kind of kick it over here," she said.

"I don't want to touch it," Cal said, "not even with my foot."

"Me either," Susan said and her sigh was a long, exhausted exhalation. The plastic whispered and crinkled in her arms, as though in agreement.

Tyler trotted to them, picked up Robert's arm by the hand as if to shake it, and tossed it onto Robert's torso with a casual, "Head's up!" It landed across Robert's chest. The hand hit the floor and the knuckles cracked.

"There you go," Tyler said, unconcerned. At their astonished expressions he said, "My pop does crime scene clean up. I've seen, like, way way worse. NBD to me, dude."

Dave's stomach churned and sour bile worked its way up his throat. Susan must have had a similar reaction, because she covered her mouth with her hand, dropping the roll of plastic. With haste, Cal bent to unroll a section and tried to spread it over Robert, but he hadn't unrolled enough.

"Here, let me..." Susan said. She drew a penknife from her pocket, unrolled more plastic, and slit it off the roll. She and Cal shook it out and wafted it over Robert and his arm. It landed with a hush and they both stepped back as if reluctant to be hit with the outrush of air.

"We should tuck it under or something," Susan said. "In case, you know, of infection." She pulled two pair of heavy gloves from a hook on the near wall, tossed one pair to Cal and drew on the other. "I should have thought of these before," she said.

Cal lifted Robert as an orderly would lift a comatose patient, rolling him from side to side, as Susan worked to shove the plastic under. They wore identical expressions of horrified distaste. When they finished, Susan threw the gloves in a far corner and went to the desk to retrieve the bottle of Jack Daniels. Cal was close on her heels, his face deathly pale in the moonlight.

With the body covered, Dave's stomach settled, but he found his eyes straying to that milky, man-shaped pod over and over throughout the night. He couldn't sleep. Every time his eyes began to close, he saw some horror from the day–the plane's rough descent, the limping girl, the janitor sliding the flagpole through himself with grisly ease–and he jerked awake, heart hammering in his chest.

When his eyes were open, he turned and twisted with thoughts of Colleen and the twins, whamming him over and over onto the spike that was the truth of their deaths, tearing his guts out. He was so far from California, so far from home.

He was an outsider here. These people all knew each other and it gave them at least some small comfort in this wildly horrific circumstance. Not so for him.

Finally, when he judged the time to be around four in the morning and had decided to give up on sleep, Cassie crept to where he lay, dragging her blanket with her. Her eyes were as bloodshot and bleak as his felt. It had been her husband who had taught here, Dave remembered. So she might know these others very well, either.

Cassie sat down next to him and he sat up so that they were face to face. In barely audible whispers, they began to talk.

— — —

"You can't leave. We have everything we need right here," Floyd said. "Food, weapons, water, facilities, and once we get those four in the auditorium taken care of and the doors reinforced, the building will be secure. We're inside, out of the elements. That doesn't matter that much right now, but in the fall? In the winter? It will mean everything once it gets cold. Forget the rain and the snow, the cold alone will kill you."

"We'll be in Georgia long before then," Dave said. "I'm sure that Atlanta is still viable; they were prepared for a pandemic."

"Like this?" Floyd said, motioning to the windows, indicating the world beyond. "This seems like it might be a little outside the realm of planned for emergencies."

Dave stood up from the stool he had occupied. He glanced away from Floyd and gave a small shake of his shoulders, dismissing Floyd's concerns. There was some validity there, he could admit that much, but not enough to derail his plan.

"How are you going to get out?" Floyd said. "You won't get ten feet before they're on you."

"I already looked out front and there's no one there," Dave said. "They've forgotten us already, or, who knows, maybe they've all finally died, *really* died. Listen...I'll get word back to you somehow. Then you can join us at the CDC."

Floyd crossed his arms over his chest and gave him a long stare. Dave told himself not to shift or equivocate–his decision was made. Floyd was imposing, but Dave didn't fear him. In his old life, someone like that might have caused him alarm, but not now. He was focused on the next step of getting to the CDC and–at least for now–doing his best to forget that Colleen and the boys were gone. He would mourn them later, once everything had been settled.

It was easier for him than for Cassie. She'd watched Floyd kill her family.

That's why she was joining Dave; there was nothing for her here, either. Not anymore.

They had discussed it in the early morning hours, finding a commonality between them that was at core, the belief they didn't belong, not with this group.

"Dave, you can't go," Susan said. Her face had a deep crease down one side where she'd lain against the blanket. Her eyes were bloodshot. "We need your help. Jesus Christ...you're the only one with any kind of background in communicable diseases! Besides Cassie, you're the only medical professional we have!"

Cassie turned from where she'd been staring out the window. "You're really going to be upset with me, then, Susan," she said, "because I'm going with him."

Susan turned on Cassie, her eyes flying open with shock. "You...you *can't*! You...Jesus Christ, Cassie! What are you thinking? Listen...forget about us, forget that we need you...think of yourself...you'll get killed out there."

"I think we have to take that chance," Cassie said her voice held in a careful neutral. "Susan, you could come with us. Cal? Tyler? You're welcome to come along, too."

"Guess I'm odd man out?" Floyd said with a humorless grin. Cassie didn't look his way or acknowledge his words. He went on, "I get that you hate me, Cassie, but don't put yourself in jeopardy because of it. We have a good set up here. There's even a decent gym! We'll all need to start getting stronger in order to face what's out there. I was going to recommend a daily regimen for each of us to include strength training and cardio–we'll have to be able to run, right? Because we'll have to make forays out for food and more weapons. Even if–"

"You like this," Cassie said. Her voice was barely above a mumble and she kept her eyes on the floor. Dave would have assumed that she was intimidated by Floyd, but her hand on the back of a chair, white knuckled and shaking, showed the deep well of anger she carried.

"What are you talking about?" Floyd asked. He huffed out a skeptical laugh. "No one in their right mind would *like* this."

Finally, she looked up at him, hitching her purse higher on her shoulder. Her eyes were miserable and brimming with hate. "You *do*, though," she said, and took a step closer to the big man. "You love the chaos, don't you? And the violence. I know about you. Dan told me...the motorcycle, the drinking, prostitutes, and the fighting. You shouldn't even be a teacher here. They shouldn't let you around kids!"

Dave's stomach turned as Cassie berated Floyd and he tried to prepare himself for a physical altercation, but Floyd merely sank back into his chair, making it squeak, and refolded his arms across his chest.

"Well," he said, "I guess that's not too much of a concern anymore."

Cassie shook with rage and angry tears overflowed her lashes. "You're some kind of monster. I knew it as soon as I saw you."

Susan took a step toward Cassie, her hands coming up in a commiserating gesture. "Cassie, let's think this through. Maybe we *should* all go together. Let's talk about it at least, but you'd have to let Floyd come, too...he's not the monster you think he is. Really, he's not, if you knew–"

"Shut up!" Cassie snapped and Susan's mouth dropped open in surprise. "Don't defend him to me. Stick with him if you want–I'm sure it'll be just another bad decision in a long line of bad decisions for you–but don't try to defend him."

"Bad decisions?" Susan said. Indignation colored her cheeks. "What are you *talking* about?"

"Those tattoos! Your weird career!" Cassie said. Rage pulled her face into ugly lines as she yelled. "That child you had out of wedlock. And naming him *Sorrow*, for God's sake…*those* bad decisions!" Her eyes were slits. Spittle flew from her lips.

For a second, Dave reconsidered the idea of taking her with him–she looked completely insane.

Susan turned away, hugging herself. Cal looked from Susan to Cassie. He shook his head. "Cassie, what are you talking about? Susan didn't have Sorrow out of wedlock. Her husband died in a car accident five months ago."

The anger drained from Cassie's face leaving it pale and incredulous. "What?" she said, her voice barely audible. "But he's…she said Sorrow is five months old."

"Yeah, it was stress that brought on her labor," Cal said, his eyes on Susan's thin back. "Her husband was driving home from work and one of those older-model self drivers slammed right into him. He died in the hospital and Sorrow was born later that day. In the same hospital. It was…" His mouth twisted and he shook his head. He hadn't taken his eyes from Susan.

Cassie's mouth worked but nothing came out as she looked from Susan to Cal and back to Susan.

Dave hefted the bag he'd packed and took her arm.

"Let's just go," he said and led her to the shop door.

Floyd stood and Dave tensed.

"Listen…" Floyd said. His voice was surprisingly gentle as he laid a hand on Dave's shoulder. "Just reconsider. It's too dangerous out there. Cassie? Everything you said, it's…we're all confused right now, but we can get this worked out. I know we can. Please…stay."

Without looking at him, Cassie shook her head. She hunched over as if trying to make herself smaller. Her ponytail hung greasy and dispirited down her back.

Dave gripped her arm more firmly but looked at Floyd. "We'll get word back to you," he said.

"It's fucked up all the way around," Floyd said, "and it's not true, Cassie, what you said about me. I'm not enjoying any of this, especially not…you know…what I had to do to Dan and your–" Her shoulders flinched as if he had raised a hand to hit her even though she still hadn't turned to look at him. "I hate this whole thing. I swear to you I do. But we can be smart about it now that we're here, can't we? We...we can carry on."

Cassie turned her head slowly, as if she heard puzzling, far off sounds. Her eyes were wide and rimmed red with exhaustion as she took him in. "Maybe you can," she said, "but I can't. Not if I stay here. It's too...it's too much." Tears made fresh tracks on her cheeks but she seemed unaware of their passage. She turned away again.

Dave stood undecided for a fraction of a second. He could feel Floyd's eyes on him, compelling him to make a decision.

He did.

"Take care," Dave said. He dropped the bag and shook Floyd's hand. Then he picked up the bag again and led Cassie through the door. He said, "You all take care of yourselves." Cal gave a half-hearted wave but Susan didn't turn around.

"Wait," Floyd said, "Tyler, go with them and lock the door once they're out."

Dave's stomach dropped at the thought of the door locking behind them–locking them out. Of course, they had to do it for their own safety.

"Take this," Floyd said and handed Dave the pistol. Dave reached out automatically to take it. It was warm from its place on the man's hip and he found himself disgusted by the heavy feel of it. He shook his head and handed it back. "We'll be okay," he said and tried not to see the shock turn to disgust and then pity in Floyd's eyes.

"Suit yourself," Floyd said and re-holstered the pistol. "I guess that means you don't want the shotgun, either."

"Won't need it; we'll be traveling by car," Dave said with a confidence that was beginning to wane. "Those things aren't smart enough even to open a door...they're not going to get us."

"No," Floyd said, "but they might not be the only monsters out there."

A thrill of fear caused Dave's back to crawl but he controlled the shudder that wanted to shake his shoulders. The condescension Floyd was laying on him was thick enough; there was no reason to give him another thing to judge by.

"Well, like I said," Dave said, trying to keep his tone brisk. "We'll get word back to you."

Floyd nodded and crossed his arms over his chest. He stepped back and turned away as if dismissing them.

Dave hefted the bag again, getting a good grip on it. Tyler bounced on his toes in the hallway beyond the door, impatient to get going.

Dave looked from Floyd to Cal to Susan.

None of them looked back.

He and Cassie left.

CHAPTER 16

Tyler watched them drive away in Cassie's *Zap*. In Tyler's opinion, that car sucked, but not as bad as the Prius, which was everywhere. At least the Mazda *Zap* had a little bit of personality, especially in that electric blue color. Cassie must have been making some pretty good coin. Tyler was going to get a Tesla. Once he could afford it, which would probably be around the time he was a hundred, the way shit was with the economy. Then he remembered that there was no economy anymore. He could just go and find a Tesla. Take it. Then he could stop using his old man's beat the hell up gas guzzling Toyota. That sucker had over three hundred thousand miles on it. Thinking of the car reminded him that his dope was in the glove box.

Of course, it would be retarded to go out there just for a few ounces of grass. He could probably go through all the lockers and find ten times that amount. Fuck, even the teacher's lounge probably had some hanging out with the old lady teabags.

The Toy wasn't parked very far away, though, and it would be easier than searching the school. It was right on the other side of the cafeteria. If he snuck out real quick, no one would even have to know.

He jittered in place, undecided.

This whole sitch was a balls up, but what the fuck? As an upside, no one could tell him what the fuck to do anymore. No old man yelling at him that he was a skinny waste of air when the old man himself was just a glorified fucking janitor...just like that Alfonse guy stuck to his flagpole. Was the old man stuck like that somewhere?

Tyler kind of hoped so.

Fuck it. He had his keys and he'd go get his dope.

No sweat.

He scanned the parking lot, taking in the several new bodies lying among the handful of cars. Must'a got their heads knocked. Closest to the stairs, the chick with her head blown off by Floyd was looking even worse for wear. Her body was beginning to bloat, like the deer you see beside the highway. Her stomach was pushed up against her dress like she was growing some kind of gas-bubble baby in there.

Tyler grinned. A gas-bubble baby…that was fucking gross! If his friends were here, they'd all crack up at that one. Not because they wouldn't feel bad for the girl who had probably been a student here–of course, they'd feel bad–but cracking up was better than bawling our eyes out.

If he ran out there, he'd have to leave these doors unlocked. If something, you know, happened to him, then he was basically screwing the teachers inside.

Not that anything was going to happen to him. He was just going to run out and run back. NBD.

He pushed the heavy door open, being careful to hold the push bar in so that it wouldn't clack. He scanned the lot and the street. Across the street. Nothing moved. He let the push bar out slowly and then eased the door closed behind him. A light breeze ruffled the hair on his forehead. His arms rashed out in gooseflesh and his stomach rolled and fluttered with nerves. Fucking baby. Man up. Maybe he should go back for the shotgun, but if he used a shotgun out here, they'd probably swarm him like fucking piranhas. He patted his pockets, found the one with the key, and pulled it out. Okay. Okay, fucking GO!

He trotted down the steps making sure his sneakers didn't slap on the concrete. It was already hot and the sun cooked his legs in his black jeans. Sweat itched in his armpits. He couldn't blame that on the heat, though. That sweat was fear.

Once at the base of the stairs, he doubled back to the building and slipped behind the bushes that grew against the concrete wall. The sharp branches picked and scratched at his skin and clothes, and then he was through. The concrete was cold and the area between bushes and building was tight and musty.

He wouldn't be completely hidden from sight, but he'd be camouflaged pretty well. Dry sticks and mulch rustled at each step. Damn, louder than he'd thought it would be. He slowed his pace and glanced down to try to find the best path.

He walked face-first into a spider web.

It clung and tickled and his first instinct was to run, screaming, tearing the shit from his sweaty face–what if the fucking spider was in his fucking HAIR?!–but he couldn't panic.

He took a deep, shuddering breath, pulled his shirt up, and scrubbed it across his face. Took another breath. He had to stop being squeamish. That shit would get him killed.

When he continued on, he kept one arm up, his forearm acting as a kind of spider-web battering ram, because he had to keep his eyes on the ground. He'd already stepped on one skeleton that looked as though it might have been a cat and he'd seen three dead mice in various stages of decay. The bushes were fucking nasty; how did kids make out back here?

He got to the outside corner of the building and stopped. Peeked around, just to be safe. It was clear from here to the cafeteria–if you ignored the spider webs strung across at what seemed to him to be ridiculously close intervals. Like an obstacle course thought up by someone involved in the planning of hell.

He took another breath and deliberately pushed it out of his mind. The dope was totally gonna be worth it.

From here, he could see the Toy sitting in the lot in front of the cafeteria. Almost there. He clenched the key harder, letting it dig into his palm. Then he started forward. He kept his arm up again, his eyes cast down. The bushes whispered against his jeans. Twigs poked him sharply in the bicep.

Around the cafeteria, the bushes changed to trees, the ground to black mulch. Tyler hesitated at the edge of the bushes, reluctant to lose his cover. There was no movement in the parking lot. None in the street beyond. He'd be okay. As long as he stayed quiet.

He trotted across the sidewalk and through the parking lot, snaking around the handful of cars between him and the truck. He kept his pace light and he felt good, really good, as he dodged the other cars, feeling like he was doing old-fashioned parkour. Nothing could touch him. He was a panther, a ghost. He almost wished now that there had been more obstacles…something he could have climbed and something he could have jumped off of.

At the Toyota, he took a second to breathe. He bent over, hands on his knees, but kept his head up and his eyes open. All his senses seemed heightened, ultra-sharp.

He pointed the keyfob at the Toy and…BEEP! BEEP! WAH WAH WAH! BEEP! BEEP! BEEP! WAH WAH–

Oh, fuck! He'd hit the alarm by mistake.

Behind him, something scraped across the blacktop. He hit another button on the key fob, pressing frantically, and nothing happened. He'd hit the alarm again. He threw a panicked glance over his shoulder. A man stood behind a Chrysler SUV. Half his arm was gone, one of his eyes, too. The other had hazed over. In his hand he held an arm…it might have been his own. Behind him, a small boy was making his way from the woods, crawling. His Transformer pajamas were ragged and dragging at his knees and the ends of his legs were gone, as though eaten by a wood chipper.

Tyler pushed another button, mashing it until his thumb hurt. The alarm finally shut off, but the damage was done. Six of the dead were coming through the woods…no, more than that, a dozen. Two dozen.

Tyler pointed the fob at the Toy, his breath wheezing out in frantic gasps. He no longer thought he was ultra-sharp, in fact, part of his mind assured him in a voice that sounded strangely like his old man that he had pissed his pants. Just a little, but still, piss was piss.

He grabbed the door handle and yanked. It didn't budge. He pointed the key fob again, mashed the button. The one armed dead man was closer. The Toy refused to unlock. Tyler glanced at the fob and saw that he was actually pushing the lock button…fuck!

The dead man was at his back, reaching for him. Fingers, cold and rubbery, brushed down the nape of his neck. Tyler screamed and finally remembered he could unlock the car manually. He shoved the key at the lock, missing, scratching the already worn paint. The fingers banged and bounced on his neck, on his back. What the fuck? He slid the key home, twisted and yanked the car door open. He spun to get in the car ass-first, feet already coming up so he could kick the guy away.

The man was reaching for him, but he was reaching with the severed arm. The fingers shook like a rubber movie prop, and the man moaned as if frustrated by his inability to grasp Tyler with the dead and shaking fingers.

Tyler kicked out, skinny legs strong with adrenaline, and sent the man flying back. He dragged the door closed. It thunked heavily into place. A split second later, the man thumped into the window, head tilted like a bird, milky eye on Tyler.

"Fuck you!" Tyler yelled. "FUCK YOU, FUCKER!" Spit flew from his lips and he was unaware of the tears stinging his eyes. His entire body shook with long, rolling tremors, chattering his teeth. The man bashed the severed arm into the window and it was the dull thump of a ham hitting the glass. Tyler laughed, hysteria turning it into a hyena yowl. "F-FUCK YOU!" he crowed again and raised both middle fingers. "EAT TH-THIS, F-F-FUCKER! EAT THIS!"

The man moaned and raised the severed arm again. He brought it down, hard, and the fingers bent backward with a crack and slid down the glass. The man stepped back and disappeared from sight.

Tyler stared in shock, made breathless with the man's sudden and total disappearance. He sat up, pushed himself toward the driver's side window. The man was lying on his back, staring with milky indifference up to the sky. The back of his head had a flattened look, as though it had melted into the blacktop. The crawling kid with the Transformer pajamas and no legs scuttled out from under the man. He had tripped. The one-armed man had tripped over the no leg kid and fallen, hitting his head hard enough to kill him. For real, this time.

Tyler laughed, incredulity and hysteria spreading his lips until the bottom one split. Blood trickled down his chin and he wiped it away without thought. That fucked up little kid had saved him! Holy shit! Now he could–

He reached for the door handle, confident of his ability to run past the crawler. Easy as shit. He laughed again and the sound rattled around the inside of the car, sounding multiplied, spooking him.

A thump on the passenger window made his jump and turn like a cat. Another man, this one a little fresher. Behind him, three more people. A thud on the hood. A girl clawed, trying to climb. Her eyes were bright and cold and she watched him intently as she gained a few inches, and then slipped back. Gained and slipped back.

The car was surrounded. He was trapped here.

No, get a grip. It's okay. He could just drive out. Yeah. Plenty of gas in the tank, just go. Run the fuckers over! Fuck 'em all up!

He grinned manically, fresh blood running down his chin. He bugled another mad laugh and reached for the keys in the ignition.

No keys.

What the fuck?

He shook his head, reached again. No keys. He leaned slightly to check. The ignition was empty. The car shook. He looked on the seat, scanned the floor. The car rocked as more of the dead piled on, so thick they began to block the light.

Keys…where are the FUCKING KEYS? WHERE–

No. Oh, fucking no.

He slammed his forehead into the window, craned his neck, and looked between the heaving bodies.

Yep, there they were.

Dangling from the door.

Ultra sharp.

CHAPTER 17

"We have to try!" Susan said. "We have to do something! We can't keep...we can't keep losing people!" She was worn and frazzled beyond anything she could ever recall feeling, worse even than the day she'd gotten the call about Billy. At least then, she'd had her ma and later that day, the baby. Sorrow had been the one spark of brightness that she'd been following doggedly as she climbed on top of the depression, but now this. Now it seemed as though she had nothing and what was left was dwindling. It made her angry because that small treacherous voice in the very deep, deep part of her mind kept asking, "What's the point, Susie? What's the point of anything, now? Can't we just let go?"

She slammed her hand into the thick glass of the cafeteria window. A few of the swarming dead–those closest to the building–glanced in her direction with mouth-hanging blankness. The sun was probably making the window into a mirror.

She turned to Floyd who stood next to her as stolid as Pit Pull. His face was filled with helpless sorrow as he watched the slow, rotted riot in progress in the parking lot. He didn't know what to do, either.

"He's gonna cook in there," Cal said from her left. "Hey, listen...are we even sure that it's Tyler in there? Christ, maybe they've cornered a cat or something. A raccoon."

Hope didn't even try to raise its rosy head in Susan's mind...it knew better. "They don't go after animals," she said. "Yesterday there was a dog in that crowd, and they didn't..." She sighed and scrubbed her hands over her face. The voice was getting louder, drowning her out, drowning her, asking, *"Oh, who cares? Who cares, Susie? None of it matters."*

"It's Tyler's car and he isn't in here with us," Floyd said. "The idiot probably tried to leave. Maybe he thought Cassie had the right idea."

At Cassie's name, a small light of injured anger flared with brief heat in Susan's mind, but petered out just as quickly. She was more hurt than angry, but too tired to maintain either emotion. Who cared? None of it mattered, did it?

The bodies shifted and for one split second, she could see Tyler. His face behind the glass looked so small, his eyes large with terror. His hands were on the window, palms flattened against the glass, beseeching. His helplessness pierced her heart and she gasped and put her hand on her sternum at the pain there. She bent over her knees.

"Fuck," she said, "Fuck…I think I'm…shit this feels like a fucking heart attack." Robert appeared in her mind, nattily dressed, standing in the office, telling his dry jokes. Robert with his tie pulled askew, gasping. Robert with his arm blown off, the dead empty of his eyes reflecting the plastic as it floated down over him.

She gasped again, tried to pull in air, but her lungs were tight with refusal. A hand on her back, heavy and warm–Floyd's hand. "F-f-fuck, fuck," she said. Her head began to swim, her vision blurring.

"Susan, listen to me," Floyd said, his voice low and very close to her ear. He massaged light circles on her back…patting her like a goddamned dog. "It's a panic attack. You're having a panic attack."

Who cares? Who the fuck cares? Let it be a heart attack! Let it come, let it happen. Let the wet, red muscle in her chest seize up for all time. Let it. Who fucking cared? There was nothing she could do for anyone. Everyone she loved was gone. There was nothing left.

A yell, faint but ululating wildly, came from the parking lot.

"Holy shit," Cal said. His words drifted down onto her and lit, like a spark. "That guy's straight-up crazy."

"Holy shit," Floyd echoed, his hand disappearing from her back. "What the hell is he doing?"

The yell came again, closer and stronger. It sounded like a lone Indian racing into battle against a militia–desperate and crazy, untamed but determined. The spark became full-blown curiosity and tugged her upright. She wanted to see.

A young man, possibly in his early twenties, shirtless, lean and handsome, ran past the building. He waved a hatchet over his head and sprinted easily, muscular and light as a gazelle, gathering the attention of the horde at the car. They turned one by one, peeling away, shuffling after the young man. His war cry rang out again as he doubled back along the line of the dead, teasing them with his life and vibrancy. They reached and stumbled, too slow to grab him. He laughed, head thrown back, and doubled again, drawing them further, drawing them across the parking lot.

A handful of the dead remained at the car. The ones that had the best view of Tyler. They banged the windows and moaned. An arm tumbled across the hood, trailing strings of rotting flesh. Black crumbles shimmered wetly in piles around the car.

Movement at the tree line caught Susan's eye. Five people–two women and three men–broke from the woods. They moved across the lot in a tight formation. Crouched low and silent, they approached the car without alerting the dead. Once at the car, they separated, each person raising a weapon.

"No guns," Floyd said. "See how they're not using guns? They know…"

One of the women buried an ax in the back of the neck of one of the dead, right at the base of its skull, dropping it. She tugged at the ax as one of the men in her group lopped the head off another of the dead. Another head thudded onto the car. Another of the dead dropped, its neck half severed by a machete. Once all the remaining dead were…well, *dead*…one of the men raised his arm, his hand in a tight fist. He nodded to a man who had leaned heavily on the driver's side door. The man turned and lifted the door handle, slowly, making no sound. The others formed a protective circle, faced out. The man opened the door, easing it with care, his face a frown of concentration. Tyler tumbled out like a load of laundry and the man caught him. Put a hand over Tyler's mouth, and shook his head. No sound.

Tyler nodded, his eyes dazed. His hair hung lank and sweaty over his forehead. It must have been over a hundred degrees in the car. He raised a hand, pointed to the building. The man looked, turned back to Tyler, shrugged. Shook his head.

"Shit," Susan said. "They can't see us!" She slammed the glass with a flat hand, shivering it. The man and the others all looked. One of the women drew a gun.

— — —

Tyler shook his head frantically. He pulled away from the man, stumbled, but then stood on his own. He pointed at the building again. Started to say something. The man made a cautionary gesture, then put his ear to Tyler's mouth. Listened. Nodded. The small group conferred and Tyler pointed to the front of the building. The man who seemed to be in charge, nodded. They started off.

"Let's go meet them," Susan said. She started for the door and Floyd put a hand on her arm, stopping her.

"Wait," he said. He looked from her to Cal. "There's five of them, six if the nut job makes it back. There's only four of us."

"So?" Susan said, impatient to get going. She was excited to meet new people. Four was not enough of a buffer; not a hopeful enough number. These people had survived, so then others had, too. It expanded the horizons she'd felt collapsing in.

"Susan, we don't know what their intentions are," Floyd said. "We've got a unique setup here. I think we should protect it."

"And do what?" Susan asked, thunderstruck by his words. "Turn them away? Forget it, Floyd. Just because we were here first, doesn't make it ours."

"Hell yes it does," Floyd said. He stared at her, his eyes half-lidded, beard thrust out. She stuck her own chin out. She wasn't afraid of him.

Cal stepped between them.

"Relax, you guys. We have to stay calm," he said. "Floyd, we need more numbers. That will only make us stronger. They're survivors, just like us. We're all after the same thing, here."

"You don't know that," Floyd said, but he stepped back and dropped his shoulders. "But you're right...we need to stay calm, and we have to stick together. Can I depend on you two?"

"Depend on us for what?" Susan asked. His manner was starting to get to her, making her nervous all over again. Those people weren't going to barge in guns blasting. In fact, Floyd was the only one with guns as far as she knew.

Floyd waved his hand in a vague way. "Anything. Just…we were here first. It's our school. Okay?"

Susan shrugged and nodded, but couldn't hide her irritation. Such a guy thing to be so worried about territory. She thought about telling him he should probably start pissing in the corners right now, but decided not to. She was frazzled and didn't make the best decisions in that frame of mind.

For now, she'd hold her peace.

CHAPTER 18

Susan waved at the people coming across the parking lot led by a worn and bedraggled Tyler. The boy's face was paler than ever and he stumbled twice. A man on one side of him and a woman on the other kept him from falling down.

Excitement, but something else, too, made Susan's stomach jump and clench. She wished Floyd hadn't voiced his nonsense; she'd be more able to greet the new people with ease if he hadn't planted that goddamned seed of fear. She shook it off and stepped outside to hold the door open. The faces that passed her were grim, their eyes catching hers and flicking away as they assessed her, Floyd, Cal, the school itself, the parking lot, and the woods beyond. Susan was still reeling from the enormity of their situation; how had these people gotten so savvy, so fast?

Once they were all in, Tyler leaned over his own knees, breathing hard, and not seeming one hundred percent aware of his surroundings. Cal and Floyd stood on one side of the hall, the new people on the other. As the silence spun out and both groups eyed each other, it began to seem like a standoff.

The woman who'd been at Tyler's side finally spoke. "He's very dehydrated," she said. "Can we get him some water?" She was tall and had long, coarse brown hair pulled into a low horsetail. Her clothes were simple: jeans, a plain, serviceable t-shirt, and heavy boots. A sweat-jacket was tied at her mid-section. She looked to be in her late thirties.

"Yeah, yes," Susan said. Something about this woman, maybe her height and hair, reminded Susan of her mom and it gave her a sense of comfort. This was a capable person and Susan liked capable people. "We can go to the cafeteria." She started down the hall but no one followed. "This way, come on."

The woman exchanged a look with the man standing closest to her side and turned her eyes to Susan again. She nodded. Then she smiled. "A cafeteria sounds good."

Susan almost reached for the woman's hand but then she stopped herself and put her hand on her own chest, instead. "I'm Susan. Susan Reed. This is Calvin Post and Floyd Abby...we're all teachers here. The boy is Tyler Bieler. He's a student."

"I'm Mary Sideski. This in my husband, Paul," the woman said, indicating the man at her side. He was tall, too, but there was something pale about him, shy and retreating and he glanced at his boots at her introduction. He wore tan Dockers and his fair hair was thinning. "This is Trish Marks, Al Tinsdale, and John Everson. The one running around in the woods is Charlie, but he never gave us a last name." She smiled at Susan. "I guess it sounds odd to say under the circumstances, but...it's nice to meet—"

"*Albert* Tinsdale?" Cal said. "The *scientist*?"

At Cal's tone, Susan realized that while she had recognized the name when Mary said it, she hadn't made the association. The man in question was older, his hair dusted gray at his temples, but obviously fit. He looked at Mary with unease and his shoulders lifted and dropped.

At Cal's words, all pretense of friendliness dropped from Mary's expression. Her eyes went half-lidded and she fisted a hand on her hip as she turned to Cal.

"Yes," she said, "that's right. Is that going to be an issue?"

"Why would it be?" Cal asked and his voice held nothing but honest confusion.

"Because he's the one that might be responsible for this whole disaster," Floyd said. It was the first time he'd spoken. Tension crackled the still air in the hallway as Mary eyed Floyd.

"You don't know what you're talking about," she said and her hand went to her waist. There was a large knife sheathed there. "Are you one of those religious nuts? Are we going to have a problem?"

Floyd's hand went to his back. "If we're going to have a problem, it's all on your end, lady. You came to *our* school...now get your hand away from that knife."

"Stop!" Susan said. She stood in between her group and the new one, her hands out, palms up at Mary and Floyd. "Everyone please just calm the fuck down. Floyd, for Christ's sake! Shut the fuck up, okay? You can't possibly–"

Albert Tinsdale cleared his throat. "He's probably right, actually; at least, in a way."

"What are you talking about?" Susan said, but it hit her all at once that that was why Mary was being so cautious, why the tension seemed so out of whack to the circumstances. Albert Tinsdale was a controversial figure, but Susan didn't know enough about the controversy to understand Tinsdale's words. "But you've been in jail, haven't you? How could you be responsible?"

"It's a long story," Albert said. He pulled glasses from the pocket of the jacket tied at his waist. He wiped them on his t-shirt and slipped them on. They magnified his brown eyes. "Maybe we should go to your cafeteria and converse. This boy really does need some water and we could use a rest."

"Tyler, shit!" Susan said. "I forgot all about you; I'm so sorry." She gripped him under his arm and he gave her a wan smile.

"I'm okay, just thirsty," he said and then he looked at Floyd. "These guys saved my life."

When Floyd didn't respond, Susan helped Tyler to stand. The two groups fell in together and began to move down the hall.

"Hey," Floyd said. He hadn't moved an inch. "What about your friend Charlie? Just gonna leave him out there?"

Mary gave Floyd a long look before she answered. "He'll go back to the hospital where we've been staying; it's right down the highway," she said. Her chin rose as she considered Floyd. "It's good of you to think about him. I don't feel like most people are thinking about their fellow humans in this kind of situation."

"*You* are," Floyd said, "you rescued Tyler. You didn't have to do that. I'd be willing to bet that most people–people like us here in the school–are just clawing for purchase. How are you guys so together?"

"Well, we might have been a little more prepared than most, but the four of you are doing remarkably well," Mary said, "given the circumstances." She half-smiled at Floyd and reached across the hallway to rest a hand on his massive shoulder. As she did, the tension left his body and he relaxed. "You're doing a good job, Floyd," Mary said and she and Floyd might have been the only two in the hallway; her tone was that confiding.

Floyd's head dropped and he kicked at the ground with one chain-jingling boot. Then he looked back up and Susan was knocked out to see a shy grin on his face, his cheeks red with heat. The big galoot was actually blushing!

"Thanks, thank you," Floyd said. All bark and bluster were gone. "It's hard, but I'm trying."

Mary squeezed his shoulder, her fingers barely denting the leather vest. "I see that, and I apologize for jumping on you like that." She squeezed again and then dropped her hand. Turned to address everyone. "We can all work together. The more people we have, the stronger we are, and we're going to need that strength...everyone is important," Mary said. She looked at Cal and Tyler. Looked at Susan. "Everyone."

Something seemed to settle in Susan, calming and quieting. The panic she'd been living with since this nightmare started was abating. The sadness was still there, the horror, too, but the dread seemed less insurmountable. Mary was right; they would all work together and get this figured out.

There was light, yet, at the end of this terrifying tunnel.

– – –

"At a certain point, we knew that something like this might happen, at least, in theory," Albert said. He toyed with the protein bar on the table in front of him. Mary sat next to Albert, Paul on her other side. Susan and Floyd sat across from them. Trish and John sat at the next table over with Cal and Tyler, but they'd turned their chairs to face Albert as he spoke. "It's why we were trying to bury the research, but we didn't act quickly enough. We had no idea how influential the Clergy Party had become in the company." When he looked up, his eyes were filled with tired disillusion. "This used to be America. How could we go to jail for doing *research*?"

Mary put a hand on his forearm. "It doesn't matter anymore, Al," she said.

"No, you're right," he said. He took a deep breath, his head down as he gathered his thoughts. "I'm not going to get into all the complications, but suffice to say that we were working on a gene therapy meant to reverse dementia. It was an adjunct project to work being done by the Devlan Group in Haiti. There was interest in a neurotoxin called tetrodotoxin, which, as I'm sure you're all aware, comes from the Tetraodontidaes, commonly called pufferfish; specifically, in this case, the Arothron hispidus, a White-spotted puffer. You see, if we look at the basic expression of..."

Susan ran a hand over her hair and realized that she was exhausted. Too exhausted to follow what was coming from Al's mouth–it sounded like a foreign language. Hadn't he just said he was going to skip the complicated stuff? She let her eyes drift to Tyler and watched him as he drank. He was shaken, but had already started to recover his bland indifference.

"Zombies?" Cal's incredulous voice snapped Susan's trailing thoughts back to the conversation at hand. "Is that what you're saying?"

"Well, yes, provisionally," Al said, and his hand went flat, palm down, "because of the so-called 'Immortality Gene,' but you have to understand–"

"No; no way," Cal said. "You're telling us that everyone has been turned into a Haitian zombie? And that it happened over*night*?"

Al's lips tightened and his face became ashen as the blood dropped from it.

"It's just a lot for them to adjust to, Al," Mary said. Cal started to protest and Mary amended, "For *anyone* to adjust to. Believe me, I know. It sounded like science fiction the first time I heard it."

"You picked it up very quickly, though," Al said. His tone said he was grateful for her words. "Luckily for me."

"Not that it helped. We still lost."

"That certainly wasn't your fault, Mary," Al said. He caught Floyd's confused expression. "Mary was part of my legal defense team. I had a *very* good team; the best that pharma can buy."

"Pharma?" Floyd asked.

"Pharmaceutical," Susan said before Al or Mary had a chance to answer. "The big pharmaceutical companies are–were, I guess, now–the richest companies in this country." She nodded for Al to go on.

"Yes, that's right," Al said. He gave Susan a long, speculative look and she tightened up at his gaze, but quelled it. No reason to be defensive.

He went on and Susan tuned in and out, as he spoke. She let the science slide in one ear and out the other. Who cared what had caused it? What were they going to do about that now…arrest someone? The time for reprisals was gone.

Al explained the research and the unintended consequences. He detailed the panic in the lab once they knew that the Clergy Party had control over the incoming director. Al knew the man and knew him to be an anomaly in the scientific community: a religious zealot, and dangerous because of it.

"It was a case of pure, unreasoned miscalculation and fuckupery," Al said. "By then, I was in prison along with my team, but I still received information from some of the people in the lab. They were afraid to protest the new head, the new regime, as it were, but they were more afraid of what they saw going on. What we had discovered was too powerful for someone with the new director's narrow scope of mind, and his political connections were more numerous than his brain cells. We all began to talk in terms of damage control, instead of prevention."

"Why couldn't you *do* something?" Susan asked. The anger had been growing in her as he spoke and now it thrummed through her like tuneless, pounding music. She would have done whatever it would have taken to stop what had happened. "Christ, you could have bombed the building! Had the guy killed! Something!" She slapped her hands on the table, palms cracking flatly. "This country is…it's gone! Fucking almost everyone is dead or one of those…one of those fucking zombies out there!" She flung her arm wildly, indicating the windows and the decimated world beyond. "You should have done *something*."

Al kept his eyes down, his hands clasped before him.

"Susan," Cal said, "listen, maybe–"

"No, of course, she is right," Al said. He looked up at Susan but it was merely a blind tilt of his face, like a plant to sunlight; he did not see her or anyone. His gaze was inner-directed; eyes blank and unfocused. "I can't justify it to you or explain it. We had checks in place, or so we thought, and we were hoping for the best. We knew *something* like this might happen, but believe me, we had no idea of the true potential of the disease, or of the scope."

"Al, it wasn't your fault," Mary said and by her tone, it was something she'd said many times before. She gripped his hand fiercely and turned his face to hers. "We've been over it. You did everything you could...you were in *jail* for Christ's sake! No one blames you."

His eyes focused on hers and he blinked. "I blame myself, Mary. I did the research, and I knew the implications, at least, the potential. I *am* responsible."

"We can't keep going over and over it," Mary said. "It does you no good; it doesn't do anyone any good. We have to work to hold it together."

His eyes drifted past hers. He nodded but even Susan could see the hesitation and dismissal of Mary's words.

Susan sat abruptly, deflated and regretful. "I'm sorry," she said. "Al? I'm sorry. I had no right. I'm just...we're all just, you know, fucked up right now. We're all fucked up about this whole thing. We need solutions more than we need answers." Her eyes found Floyd's. "I think we should try to go after Cassie and Dave. Bring them back, if they'll come." She addressed Mary and Al. "Cassie is a nurse and Dave was from the CDC. They–"

"Someone from the CDC was here?" Al asked, interest kindling in his eyes. "That quickly?"

"Yes, there were reports of an epidemic from the hospital up the road," Susan said. "I think that's what he had said. He flew in from California. I'm pretty sure it was California." It was hard for her to remember exactly what Dave had said. Too much had happened.

"Was he in contact with anyone on the west coast?" Mary asked and then without waiting for an answer, she shifted gears and stood. "We have to get him back here. My God, he might know how to get in touch with the military. They must still be operational. Maybe Fort Dix. That's close to here." At the excitement in her tone, they all began to stand.

"Yeah, okay," Floyd said. "I'll go after them on my bike. The *Zap* is no match for a hog."

Mary turned to him, her eyes filling with distress. "Was it a bright blue one? A dark-haired woman and a tall man who looked a little like Clark Kent?"

Floyd nodded and grew still. Susan's stomach rolled uneasily and she wondered just how much more bad news they could take. How much more before they all decided it would be better just to off themselves?

Mary sat back down. She dropped her forehead into her hand and massaged. "I'm sorry to have to tell you this," she said, "they're dead."

CHAPTER 19

"We couldn't help them," Paul said. He draped an arm over his wife's back and ran his free hand over his pale, tired face. Grey light from the windows lit on his scalp where the hair was the thinnest. "It happened right in the hospital parking lot and we still couldn't help them. Mary, let's go talk to Al. He seems done in. I want to make sure he's all right."

"Why were they at the hospital?" Cal asked as Paul and Mary walked away.

"They might have just wanted to check and see if there was anyone there; the hospital was Dave's original destination, after all," Susan said. "Or maybe they were going to get more provision, because they didn't take much with them." She didn't really care why Cassie and Dave had stopped. Like so many other things, what did it matter now? They were dead. The loss was greater than the loss of a nice lady (despite her suburban prejudices, which Susan already forgave Cassie for) and a displaced man. The loss was a loss of regular humans and by the evidence, there weren't very many regular humans left. They were dwindling and what was the rule about extinction? If a species gets below a certain line, then…goodbye forever. Hadn't Susan read something about that somewhere?

Al stood at one of the windows, far enough back not to draw attention to himself from anything outside and Floyd stood moodily a few windows down, his back turned to everyone, arms crossed over his chest. Al's hands were clasped at his stomach and he rocked gently heel to toe. Trish stood next to him and her mouth moved as she spoke, but it was inaudible to the others at the table. As Paul and Mary approached, she turned to them with relief, as if the burden of Al's depression was too much.

"They must have gotten out of their car before really giving the area a once-over," John, the other man from Mary's party, said. "By the time we saw what was happening it was too late to help them; they'd already been overpowered." John's blue eyes held Susan's and there was real sorrow in them. She wondered briefly what his story might be. Who had he lost? He went on, "I don't know if you all were very close, but if it's any consolation, they didn't turn."

"Turn," Cal said, bemused and Tyler blinked in his direction as though unable to understand Cal's preoccupation with the word.

"Yes, I mean, they didn't turn into zombies," John said.

"How do you know?" Susan asked.

John shifted, uncomfortable, and looked at his hands clasped between his knees. He glanced at Cal and Tyler and then looked steadily at Susan. "You want me to tell you? You're sure?"

She pondered and was about to shake her head no, after all, what did it matter?–but then Cal answered in the affirmative. John shot her another inquisitive glance and she nodded for him to go on.

"The lady...Cassie, you said? She had climbed onto a box truck. She had levered herself up, using one of the big front tires and scrambled onto the hood. From there, she gained the back of the truck, the box part. At first, it looked like she'd be okay up there. The zombies threw themselves at the sides of the truck, clawing at it, but didn't get anywhere. They don't seem very strong and they definitely aren't very bright. We were trying to think of a way to help her; Charlie had come up with the idea of leading them away. He had decided he'd take the dogs with him, extra distracting, right? But–"

"Dogs?" Susan said.

"Yeah, Rottweilers," John said. "They're Mary and Paul's dogs. Big, but nice."

"The zombies don't care about dogs," Susan said. "I mean, they don't go after dogs like they go after humans. Do you guys know that?"

"Yes, we've seen that, too," John said. "I guess that's good, I mean, at least the dogs are safe from them."

"I don't know if it's good or bad," Susan said. "There's going to be a lot of dead dogs before long with no one feeding them."

"We saw dogs eating the zombies, even the ambulatory ones," John said. His expression held a strange combination of nausea and humor. "They've got plenty to live on."

"That's so fucking gross," Susan said but a bubble of black laughter burned into her throat. She pictured it, almost like a cartoon: a terrier gnawing and growling, tearing at some unfortunate's Achilles tendon as it shuffled down the street, unaware. "Ugh."

"What happened with Cassie?" Cal asked in an impatient, get on with it tone. Susan looked at him with sympathy. Cal had a dog, too; a gentle, sweet-faced lab named Killer. He must be imagining the poor dog, trapped in the townhouse, dying slowly. When Susan's eyes met John's again, the humor, however grim, was gone from her mind.

"Yes, go on," she said. She grasped Cal's hand and he let her for a minute. Then he tucked both his hands into his armpits as he listened to the rest of John's story.

"One of the zombies fell over near the wheel and got trampled. Another fell on top of it and then another and they struggled with each other, kind of tangled together...they started to make a pile, you see? Finally, another one climbed onto the hood, using the tangled ones as a kind of ramp. Others followed the first one. It was easy for the zombies to follow the lady...Cassie...up onto the box. She kept backing up and up. She didn't have a single weapon. Then she got to the edge and she fell off. I saw her land. She landed square on her head. They tumbled off right behind her, like nightmare lemmings, making a kind of zombie mound. Some of them just broke apart. Guts and...that weird coffee ground stuff went everywhere. Eventually, most of them got up and shuffled away. One of them–a heavy man, older–his neck had been broken. You could see it; you could see the bones at the top of his spine, but he kept walking. He just..." John swallowed.

Susan imagined Cassie's fear, the panic when she realized the zombies had made it onto the truck. Maybe she had landed headfirst on purpose. Turning into a zombie was unimaginable.

"And Dave?" Cal asked. "Did you see what happened to him, too?"

John nodded, his lips tightening. He grinned and it was tight, horrified. His eyes sparkled with something that looked like incipient madness. "I gotta hand it to that guy," John said and his voice held dark, confused admiration. "He must have known, *really* known what was going to happen if those things got a hold of him. He put a knife up to his eye and–" John burped into his fist and shook his head in a warding off gesture. Then he took a deep breath and continued. "When the zombies were closing in on him, he held a knife up to his eye, turned, and slammed his head down onto the roof of a car, he–" John burped again and this time a gag followed it. He leaned over his spread knees and gagged again.

Susan pushed back, not wanting to be hit with throw-up, but John recovered. He took a few deep breaths, sat up, and ran a hand over his forehead. The hand came away wet. He tilted his head back and closed his eyes. "You get the idea, right?" he asked, his voice faint. "I didn't know him, but I admire him, I really do. That took guts."

"We didn't really know him, either," Cal said. "We didn't even know Cassie, actually. Although we worked with her husband at the school."

"You guys are both teachers?" John asked. His face was refilling with color and he seemed glad to change the subject. Cal and Susan nodded. John said, "I was a nurse. *Am* a nurse. That's why I was at the hospital. I was lucky to get out."

"Is that why you guys are here? You escaped the hospital?"

"No, actually, we came to check out the Vo-Tech. We thought we'd have better luck finding food. There's not much where we are."

"There's no food at the *hospital*?" Susan said.

"We're not actually in the hospital," John said, "that would be suicide. The hospital is overrun. We're just outside at the day surgery center. It wasn't open yet. Trish and I–she's an admin–patient liaison or something–we forced the door. Eric was there with a mute girl. Mary and Paul showed up with Albert and their son, Ethan, and their dogs, of course. Charlie showed up later.

There were three others–Anthony, I think his name was, Amy, and Rashida–but they were turned."

"How? What happened?" Susan asked and then realized that, once again, she didn't care about the answer. What did it matter how three people whom she did not know at all had died? Strangely enough, John either sensed her feelings or already felt the same way himself.

"They went out; they shouldn't have," he said without elaboration.

"It seems like an odd place to hole up," Cal said. "With an infested hospital one parking lot over?"

"Mary thought it might be best, especially if any kind of help came," John said. "It would make sense that they'd check hospitals, but I don't think anyone is going to come."

"How old is their son? I can't believe they left him behind to come here," Susan said. "That seems like a *really* bad decision."

"I don't know...he's little, though, like this?" John said and leveled his hand at about three feet from the ground. Then he shrugged and raised his hand a foot higher. "I'm not sure what age that would make him, but the center is *very* safe; much safer than bringing the kid through unknown territory," John said. "It's small, no windows, and there's only one way in and out. And it was deserted, so, no surprises. There just aren't enough resources. We were eating out of one vending machine...it wasn't going to last."

"Yeah, but still," Cal said, "you'd think one of them would have stayed behind, and they left him with strangers? Doesn't seem smart at all."

"You might not think that if you met Mabel and Turk," John said. He ran a hand distractedly through his hair and grinned. "I'd trust them with my life." He glanced toward the windows and something snagged his attention. Susan turned to follow his gaze.

Mary and Floyd were in conference out of earshot, Mary nodding gravely at Floyd's words. He finished speaking and shrugged, his hands going up in a 'what do you think' gesture. Mary's head tilted as she thought. Then she gave him a small smile.

Mary turned to the room to address everyone. "We have a change of plans."

— — —

"Tomorrow, we'll go to the hospital and collect the rest of the people there," Floyd said.

"We'll stay here tonight and get some of our go back. It's going to be dark soon, anyway," Mary said.

Everyone sat at two cafeteria tables, listening. The room was gloomy with shadow as the sun began to set.

"Mary, are you sure?" Paul asked. "What about the National Guard or the army? The CDC? You said they'd most likely come to the hospitals." His tone was not one of dissent but caution. He was her sounding board, her voice of reason.

"I don't think the Guard is going to come," she said and picked up his hand. It was a gesture as unselfconscious as a child's. She wanted comfort. "I think this situation is much worse than anyone could ever have imagined. For now at least, we're on our own."

"There's more food here, more water," Floyd said. "The solar system on this building is better than the hospital's, too. We have more raw materials here, and more ability to fortify. We have the knowledge and the skills to really make this place a fortress. And a refuge."

"Wait," Cal said, "just hold on a second." He had become more and more agitated as Mary and Floyd spoke. Mary thought she knew what was wrong–he was at the beginning stages of internalizing the reality they were all faced with. It was a tough pill to swallow.

"What is it, Cal?" Susan asked. She put a hand on Cal's arm and Mary wondered about their relationship. Were they just co-workers? She'd like to sit with each person individually and get his or her measure, but she'd have to do it on the fly, instead. She was good at it, too, a good judge of character.

"Well, I just think–" Cal said, "I think we're being too hasty. Just yesterday, we were talking about getting out of here. I still have my mom to think about. Susan? Don't you want to try and get Sorrow? And your mom? Tyler? Your dad?" He looked from one person to another, the distress in his eyes half anger, half disillusion. The pill was going down *very* hard.

"Cal," Mary said. He looked at her with unease so she kept her tone even and modulated. "Let's do this one step at a time, okay? We'll look for everyone, I promise you that, but we have to make sure we're as strong as we can be, first. We can make a stand in this building and make it safe. Then we can start bringing the others in. Once we're *truly* a safe haven. Does that make sense?"

"It doesn't make sense for us all to go tromping to the hospital to save *your* people," Cal said.

Mary kept her patience; she was good at that, too.

"We're not all going," she said. With an apologetic glance at Paul, she went on. "Just Floyd and I will go."

"Now, hold on there, Mary–" Paul said. He was a mild man but anger simmered in his eyes…it was because she had sprung this on him without discussion. She understood his anger. She'd have been pissed off if he tried something like that with her.

"It just makes sense, Paul," Mary said. "The fewer we have, the better off we are."

"You're going to have more coming back," Paul said, but his tone had dropped from angry to cautionary. He was already bending to her will.

"We'll have Charlie and the dogs, too, though," she said, "and they're good distracters. Don't worry, okay?"

"Okay, yeah; sure," he said, but the mild sarcasm didn't bother her. He wouldn't stay mad for very long, especially once she got Ethan here safe and sound. Having their son with them again would make everything better.

CHAPTER 20

"– dead…Mary? He's dead. It looks like…like he killed himself."

Paul's voice wound into her consciousness and the dream she'd been having began to fade. In the dream, she, Paul, and Ethan, were at a friend's horse farm and Paul was on a horse with Ethan tucked in front of him. Paul kept falling sideways and she had to keep pushing him upright. He was slumped over, boneless. Ethan cried on and on.

Then Mary woke fully and the crying was real. The room was very dark, but she sensed that it was almost morning.

Trish stood behind Paul, sobbing into her hands, face hidden and shoulders shaking.

"What?" Mary asked, sitting up. "What happened? Who's dead?" Panic whipped into her, but she controlled it with a will. Assess first, always assess before acting, she reminded herself. That mantra had saved her an immense amount of heartache through the years.

"Al is dead," Paul said. "Trish found him. It looks like he, well, like he might have killed himself."

"*Might* have?" Trish said, her voice raspy. "Are you kidding me? He *hanged* himself, Paul. He didn't t-trip and fall into the goddamned n-noose!"

Everyone was up by now, their faces bewildered in the light of a lantern Susan had lit automatically on waking.

"Where?" Mary said and scrambled up. He might still be alive. It was tough to kill yourself that way. She looked for John and saw that he was already up and ready to go. Floyd leaned over one of the worktables and grabbed a large pair of shears. Good, he was a quick thinker. She grabbed Trish's shoulder. "Trish! Where?"

"The b-b-bathroom," she said and collapsed over herself. Susan put her arms around Trish and hugged her as the others ran out.

The hallway was brighter with the emergency nightlights that came on automatically. The bathroom was halfway down the hallway. He had probably tied something–maybe his belt–around one of the stall supports and leaned into it. Maybe had even let his knees sag. It had compressed his airway enough to make him pass out, that was all. He was going to be embarrassed when they saved him, but that was okay. Embarrassed was better than dead.

Mary pushed into the bathroom, the door banging back against the wall. Her eyes went right to the line of stalls and her first feeling was one of relief–there was no one there. Either Trish was mistaken, or Al had already released himself and was maybe lying on the floor in one of the stalls, recovering.

She wanted so much to believe it.

"Al? It's me, Mary…are you–"

A creak to her left made her look up.

She controlled her anguish, quelling it. Now was not the time.

He had done it right, she had to give him that, but of course, he had, he was a smart man. A methodical scientist.

The rope–thick enough to hold his weight but not so thick that it would pad the choke–was wrapped three times around what looked like the sewer stack, and tied off neatly on the frame of the stalls. The noose looked like a slipknot. Exceedingly efficient.

He had also buried a silver pen in his right eye.

He had showed Mary that pen as they sat together at the defense table. It had been a twenty-year anniversary gift from his employer.

"Looks like it's just a pen again, now," Mary said.

Floyd gave her an odd, quizzical look and she shook her head.

"Nothing, never mind," she said. Her heart had sunk very low in her chest and she wanted more than anything to be sitting down with Ethan and Paul at the picnic table behind their house in Yardley. She wanted a sun setting, a mosquito whining, and the first flash of a lightning bug to pull Ethan from his seat into the yard in a daze of wonder.

She wanted it so much she felt almost weak enough to kneel, but she wouldn't. Maybe later. Not now. "Let's get him down from there," she said and reached up for her friend.

— — —

"Are you sure about this?" Paul asked. "About leaving him right there? It seems so..." Paul shook his head and looked to where Al's body had been tightly bundled and deposited near the front doors. Floyd stood past it at the middle door, scanning the dim, early-morning parking lot, seeming unaware of the conversation between Mary and Paul. Long shadows lay across the pavement and the sun glimmered behind the pines.

They had to get going. Now, while the lot looked empty.

Mary swallowed her impatience and tried for humor. "He's not going anywhere." But her words fell flat and Paul looked down. She was immediately sorry and put a hand on his arm. "I'm getting Ethan and bringing him back here. That's the only thing to think about right now. We'll figure out what to do about Al later, okay? In the meantime, get those other zombies killed–that Alfonse and the other ones behind the gate. Get the school cleaned out; make it safe for Ethan. This is going to be our home. Together."

He looked at her and she could see from the disappointment in his eyes that she had put him off with the badly timed joke. They'd been married a long time; she knew how he thought. He thought she was using the idea of Ethan as a tool to calm him down.

Maybe he was right, but she couldn't help being able to compartmentalize. She couldn't help being rational. Those traits were the ones that made her good at whatever she chose to do. It made her succeed.

"We'll be back by dusk," she said. "I love you."

He shook his head, but smiled ruefully, almost reluctantly.

"I love you, too, but–"

"Wait! Wait for me! I want to–" Susan called, jogging toward them. Paul's astonished glance stopped her short. "Sorry, I didn't see you talking." She tightened the hoody she had tied at her waist and ran her hands over her hair. She looked from Floyd to Mary. "I'm going with you guys."

Floyd turned from his contemplation of the parking lot and his eyes went from Susan to Mary, handing over the decision, but his eyebrows went up and the grim line of his mouth curved slightly–he thought it was a good idea for Susan to go with them.

Mary, who had been about to protest, relaxed. Floyd was fast becoming her number two and he was a very good number two. She trusted him.

"You need a weapon," Mary said. Impatience swelled in her again. Even the ten or so minutes it would take to outfit Susan, seemed like too much of a loss.

Susan reached backward over her shoulder and that was when Mary noticed the leather strap running bandolier-style over Susan's chest. It shifted as Susan tugged something from it, bringing it back over her shoulder–a homemade machete, easily three feet long with a blade that glowed with an almost mystical light in the darkened hallway.

"I've got this," Susan said and her smile widened at Floyd's long, low whistle.

"You made that?" Floyd asked with obvious admiration. He drifted closer to Susan, his eyes locked onto the business-like but somehow still beautiful blade. He put his hands on his hips as though to stop himself reaching for it.

"Yeah," Susan said and blushed and turned the blade to catch a little more of the first morning's light. "Kind of an extra-curricular project of mine."

"What do you do, again?" Mary asked. She, too, couldn't tear her eyes off the machete as a deep itch of want crept along her nerve endings. It was the perfect zombie killing weapon. If it could be reproduced, or, even better, *mass* produced, then everyone could be outfitted with a machete. Mary would make sure she was first in line to receive one.

"I'm a welder," Susan said. She caught Mary's eye. "A really good one."

"Obviously," Mary said. "Okay, then. Let's get this show on the road."

— — —

Paul watched them make their way past the handful of cars, and then his eyes moved past them as he scanned the woods at the edge of the parking lot. They would go that way, more or less backtracking over the route that had gotten him and his group here yesterday. His troubled gaze went back to Mary, to her solid back, the calm but alert swivel of her head. He had absolute trust in her judgment and ability to assess dangerous situations quickly enough to mitigate damage, at the very least.

But the world had become an extremely dangerous place and even though they'd had some advanced notice, it didn't change the fact. Even in their wildest and most speculative discussions of what would happen if the virus were to be loosed on the world, they hadn't come up with this almost instant decimation of the population. Even Al hadn't been able to predict the apocalyptic nature of his research. Or he hadn't wanted to.

Paul's eyes drifted to Al's corpse, tied in a white bundle and stashed in the hallway like something from a horror movie.

Maybe if Al's wife or children had survived, he'd have had some will to keep going. As it was, he'd had too much guilt and too much sorrow. How many might give up once they realized they had nothing left? Paul hoped not many. The world was going to need all the normal humans it could get.

He was glad to have Mary; glad that, together, they'd been able to keep Ethan protected. In their former life together, their life before this plague, she had been a protective mother, a doggedly loyal wife and friend, and a warrior in the courtroom, but this new world wasn't a courtroom.

The rules were gone.

His eyes strayed to Al's body again and he shivered.

Then he pulled forth the folding chair he'd stowed against the wall, unfolded it, sat, and settled in to wait.

CHAPTER 21

"Keep your weapons out and ready," Mary said, whispering, as she, Floyd, and Susan descended the wide concrete stairs. "Keep your eyes open. Look in every direction. Keep your ears open and listen carefully, because they don't always moan and groan. Sometimes they're dead silent. So to speak." She snorted a small laugh then sobered as Susan turned to scan Mary's face with mild surprise. "If you have to perform a task, stow your weapon first. You don't want to get startled into either dropping it or hurting yourself. We all watch each other's backs. This isn't going to be like one of those movies where everyone wanders away one by one and gets picked off. Okay?"

Susan said, "Got it," and Floyd nodded. Mary was glad Floyd and Susan were locals. When Mary had explained the route she wanted to take to the surgery center, they'd both known it and–even more confidence building–had both approved. They had both been on board with the no vehicle decision. Electric cars were quiet, but the potential for attracting attention was huge in a moving car against such a still landscape.

And the landscape had become *very* still since yesterday. Paul had even floated the idea that the zombies might have all lain down and finally died–but Mary didn't hold out much hope for that. *Put that in the 'too good to be true' category*, she'd told Paul with a wink and a smile he hadn't returned.

She looked over her shoulder. Paul was a dark shadow behind the door. She almost waved but then didn't, returning her focus to the task at hand. Susan had her machete out and held comfortably at her side. Floyd had a thin, matte-black baton that at first glance didn't look like much more than an antenna, but it was a cop's riot control baton, made of graphite, light and deadly. A solid rap to the head would do immense damage.

Mary hefted her ax and tapped the one tucked carefully at her waist. They were too small, really, too short handled and clunky, but she kept them. She'd already grown somewhat superstitious about it, which by turns caused her amusement and annoyance.

She had a gun for backup and Floyd had one, too. They'd have to gather more eventually, but for now, for this kind of foray, the silent weapons were better. The zombies were dumb animals, not much brighter it seemed, than a trundling line of insects. As with insects, the damage came about the same way–through the sheer force of their numbers. It was easy to squash one termite, but a nest could bring down an entire house.

Soon job one would be getting rid of nests. For now, though, it was getting people back together again.

The parking lot was still and silent, the new sun winking off the chrome of the few cars in the lot. Floyd's Harley sat near the base of the stairs, looking like a surrealist's idea of an alien with its tall handlebars and long, complicated, low-slung body.

As they'd passed by it, Floyd had reached out to caress the black seat, his face filled with longing and pain. The gas guys, they really loved their machines. Most people had gone willingly enough to electric, and as the cities filled up with the self-driving grids, society as a whole had rejoiced over the reduction in traffic jams and the decrease of carbon monoxide poisoning the atmosphere. The gas guys...no one could convince them to give up their hogs, or whatever they called them.

Mary had to admire their dedication.

A light shuffling sound snapped her attention to the right. A crow was flapping weakly on the ground near a *LaDoll Food Service* truck. A body, what was left of it, was puddled in a festering hump behind the crow. A chef's hat lay crumpled and bloodied next to it. There were a few scraps of torn looking meat on the ground near what looked like a hunk of thigh. Crow pickins'. The crow squawked and flapped again, its feathers rustling like dry leaves. Its black beak was streaked with brownish gore.

It was dying.

From eating an infected person?

It flapped again and half-rolled onto its back, one foot tightening in a spasm. Mary watched it, hypnotized. If the crow were dying from eating an infected person, would the crow come back as...as a crow zombie?

The thought brought a fear that wanted to make her run, screaming, back to the safety of the building. An image of zombie birds, mice, squirrels, snakes, raccoons...anything that might feed on the dead. Even dogs? Cats, certainly. The remaining humans might as well give up now and just stop fighting. How could they possibly defend themselves against a horde of zombie animals?

"Take hold of yourself," Mary said and closed her eyes. Counted out three seconds. Took a breath. Her fear walloped and struggled inside her, and it was like trying to hold onto a large, muscular snake, but she did it. She clamped down, hard.

Floyd and Susan had stopped and were turned back to her, questioning. Mary held up her index finger...*give me a minute*. The crow flapped again, managed to stand. Fell over. Let out one more tired squawk. Died.

Mary motioned Floyd and Susan back to her. She pointed out the crow, explained her thoughts.

"It's a disturbing idea," Floyd said, "but we can't just keep standing here waiting to see if it comes back."

"No, I know," Mary said. "That's why I want to bring it with us."

"Gross," Susan said. "I'm not carrying it."

"I'll do it," Mary said. She scanned the parking lot and her eyes alighted on the LaDoll truck again. One back door was open. Gingerly, being careful to step neither on the lumpy puddle of flesh nor on the crow, Mary nudged the door wider, using her ax to do it. The door screed on its hinges.

Mary turned, her face tight with alarm. Floyd and Susan were alert, scanning the lot, the woods, the building. Floyd looked back at Mary and motioned for her to go on.

She tucked the ax into the sheath at her waist, took a large step over a chunk of what looked like part of a calf, and peered into the back of the truck. Boxes with the LaDoll logo were stacked roughly against the walls. Mary reached for one the size of a shoebox sitting upended near the door. A roll of bologna lay near it.

She pulled the box out and dropped it on the ground next to the crow. The large bird would just make it. Using the toe of her boot, she nudged it into the box. One of its wings accordioned out, catching on one of the flaps. Mary's lips tightened with disgust and she pulled a sleeve down over her hand. She bent and reached for the wing. The bird convulsed. Mary jumped back, tripped over a hunk of meat. Her breath came in a gasp of alarm. She pin wheeled her arms, trying for balance. Fuck! She was going to land right on that pile of human squash!

Floyd's hand gripped her arm, steadied her. She got her boots solidly on the ground again, let out a breath.

"Okay?" Floyd asked.

"Yeah, just..." she straightened and gave Floyd a grateful smile, "thanks. I wouldn't have wanted to land in that."

Floyd looked at the remains and grinned. "No," he said. "That wouldn't be a good time."

Before she could psyche herself out completely, Mary crouched, tucked the crow the rest of the way into the box and folded the flaps over it. She stood, tucked the box under her left arm, and grabbed her ax. Hefted it.

"Okay, that's enough fun for now," she said and Susan shot her a grin before resuming her intent scan of their surroundings. "Let's move the hell out."

— — —

For Susan, it was the strangest walk she'd ever taken. The surroundings were both intimately familiar and completely alien. The parking lot was silent. No traffic noise, no student voices, no sounds of machinery running in the shops, no airplanes overhead. It felt as though someone had constructed a very realistic movie set of the Vo-Tech and surrounding areas, but hadn't yet populated it with cameramen and grips, extras and stars. No one had yelled "Action!"

It was eerie as hell. Even in the bright sunshine of morning.

She cocked an ear toward the box under Mary's arm. If that thing came back and started flapping, then they were all in trouble. Not even worth thinking about right now, though. She put it in the same place she was keeping her mom and Sorrow–in a 'think about it later' recess of her mind.

They crossed the parking lot and moved into the woods surrounding the Vo-Tech. Susan shivered at the temperature change. The soft floor of pine needles was like the stuff of nightmares where you run and run and never get anywhere. Every tree seemed capable of hiding a zombie. She wished now that she'd voted for a different route.

But from these woods, they would be able to see and follow the highway and still stay well screened. It wasn't a dense forest, just a fifty-foot or so buffer of scrub pines and spindly oaks. Wild blueberry bushes and Mountain Laurel were dotted throughout, providing extra cover. The woods would take them almost all the way to the hospital.

Almost all the way.

The hospital itself was surrounded by a crisscross of streets filled with fast food, gas stations, a chain pharmacy, specialist's offices, an imaging center, and the day surgery center where Mary's people were staying.

Contrarily, Susan began to feel that leaving the woods would be a bad idea.

Get your shit together, girl, she told herself. *Nowhere out here is safe. That's all there is to it.* A picture came to her mind of a wall–a tall, concrete block barrier with barbed wire on top. That's what they needed, a walled fortress. Like a prison.

That would be the way to keep the remaining people safe, but who the hell was going to build it? Not like you could just call up a few masons, get some estimates. Home Depot wasn't going to send out a crew.

But if they had enough people in one spot, they could pull together and build it themselves.

The idea appealed to her blue-collar nature.

They walked on and on. The highway stayed empty and the woods stayed quiet. Several times Susan thought she caught movement out of the corner of her eye, but by the time she looked, there was nothing to see. Could have been squirrels or birds. That made her remember the crow in the box under Mary's arm. It didn't seem as though it was going to come back.

They came to the edge of the woods. Susan's stomach dropped.

"Jesus Christ," Mary said, barely breathing the words. She motioned for them to stop and crouch down.

They were on a rise and the trees gave way to a sloping, cleared section of town dotted with businesses primarily related to the hospital. Directly before them sat a small brick building on a corner lot with an MD sign in the front. A pharmacy sat across the highway from doctor's office. An imaging center, long and low, sat next to the pharmacy. Buildings were lined up neatly along the highway and cross streets with barely a shrub between parking lots. The hospital sat in the center of the other buildings like a larger planet surrounded by its moons. Just beyond the hospital, sharing a section of its parking lot, was the day surgery center.

The lot between the hospital and surgery center was jammed with hundreds of the undead. They weaved and wandered senselessly, occasionally bumping into each other, changing course only when acted upon.

The wind shifted, ruffling through Susan's hair, and brought with it the moans.

"There's so many of them," Susan said unsure if she'd actually voiced the words or just thought them.

"Maybe that's why the rest of the town is empty," Floyd said, "they all came here."

"Why?" Susan said. Disorientation washed through her. Would her mom be down there? Would she have Sorrow with her? Terror and anger began to stir in her heart. "Why would they come here? It doesn't make any sense."

"Maybe they have some kind of communication abilities," Floyd said. "Maybe, I don't know, maybe this is something other than an organic fucking disease." He wiped his mouth roughly and swallowed. He shifted, a branch cracking beneath him. He seemed on the verge of standing. "Maybe we're under a fucking alien attack; did anybody think of that? Huh? Maybe–"

"No," Mary said and her voice was calm. She put a hand on Floyd's forearm, stilling his anxious movements. "Look at them, Floyd. It's mostly patients and healthcare workers. Look at the hospital Johnnies, the uniforms. It just looks like more people than it actually is. That's all."

Floyd swallowed again and his gaze stuttered across the zombies. Susan tried to push the disorientation away, think logically. Mary's calm and reasoned tone helped.

"Watch them closely," Mary said. "They're not organized in any way, they're not communicating. See the front doors of the hospital? The big double sliders? They're wide open. Look, there's a body holding them open. That's how they all wandered out into the parking lot. I'm sure there are still more in the building. Lots more. I'll bet that if–"

Susan glanced at Mary but Mary's eyes were locked on something in the distance. Her face was frozen in shock. "Oh…no," Mary breathed.

"What? What's wrong?" Floyd asked, still scanning the lot.

"Look, up there. The roof of the hospital."

Susan looked.

Three people were huddled against the knee wall that surrounded the top of the building. One of them was a woman in a nurse's uniform, one a man in street clothes, and the last a small boy in pajamas. Across the roof, on the far side of a neatly-lined helipad, stood what looked like some kind of large shed–the entrance to the inside stairs. The double doors were steel, windowless, and closed. Anything could have been on the other side of those doors.

The man gripped the child to his side and gestured with his free hand. The nurse shook her head. The man gestured again and the child began to struggle under his arm. The nurse reached a hand to the child but the man brushed her away. He gesticulated. They were too far away to be heard, but their actions were as clear as a pantomime. They were arguing over their next course of action. Of course, Susan thought, they might have been trapped up there for the last two days. If so, then they were getting desperate for food and water.

"We have to help them," Susan said her voice laced with horror. It was the child, of course, that made her stomach begin to churn. They had to help that little boy. He was wearing pajamas, fucking *footie* pajamas, for Christ's sake! Kids can't die in footie pajamas!

She started to rise.

Mary grabbed her arm. "Susan, no," Mary said, "there's nothing we can do."

"What? Are you fucking *serious* right now?" Susan looked an angry, distracted glance from Mary to Floyd. "Floyd? We have to help them, right? Right, Floyd?" Mary's grip on her arm tightened and Susan panicked. She flung her arm, dislodging Mary's grip, stumbled back and connected with a tree. Her teeth snapped together, barely missing her tongue, but the pain was jarring.

Floyd and Mary both watched her, Mary with sympathy, Floyd with something else, something veiled and cautious that made Susan very uneasy. She let herself slide down the trunk, the rough bark rucking up her shirt. The teeth clacking had started up a headache behind her eyes. She looked past Mary and Floyd and felt more than saw as their heads turned to follow her gaze.

Across the roof, a small group of the undead shuffled from where they'd been hidden from sight behind the shed. They were aimless and slow, occasionally stopping altogether to stand, swaying, as if to internal music. One hit the knee wall and stepped up onto it. It took one more shuffling, uncoordinated step and tumbled over, out of sight.

The man and woman on the roof seemed to have come to a consensus. The man hefted the boy onto his hip and the nurse got in front of them. She had a knife in her hand, a big industrial kitchen knife at least eighteen inches long, but knives weren't much help against zombies, not unless you buried the knife in an eye socket. Susan wished with the failing, falling sensation of a nightmare where you find you are mute that she could tell the woman to pick up something else. Anything *blunt*. To go for the skull. If they hadn't figured it out, then they were lost…Susan was powerless to help them.

The hospital's solar grid was small and only took about half the roof behind the helipad so there was no cover there. They would have to make a more-or-less straight-line approach to the door.

They jogged across the roof, trying to stay behind pipes and air conditioning units. Trying to be fast but quiet. The boy, slightly too big to be carried, clung onto the man. Even from this distance, Susan could see that the child's grip was the panicked clench of a drowning victim, but the man pushed on.

They were all the way to the helipad when one of the zombies happened to turn in their direction. The people froze. The zombie–slow and aimless to this point–shivered as if shot through with an electric current. It took one big, shambling step, like a slow and rusty to start toy. Then it began to run.

The run was clumsy and uncoordinated. Its arms flew without reason and it pogoed up and down, as its leg stomped too hard one step and its foot turned sideways on the next. It must have been moaning, too, because the others began to turn in its direction. They all started lurching toward the three on the helipad.

The zombies were between the people and the doors to the stairway. The nurse stood her ground, facing the zombies, knife held at chest level. She motioned behind her and she must have said something to the man because her head jerked in his direction, her mouth moving. The man shook his head, said something, and the boy in his arms began to struggle. The woman snapped a look back at them and Susan understood, all at once and with a horrible sinking sensation, that the boy was the nurse's son.

"Oh fuck, oh shit…no…no, no, no," Susan said,

Mary glanced at her and then back to the hospital roof.

The zombies were almost to the little group and the nurse flung her arm at the man–*get him out of here!*–and turned back to the zombies. The man turned with the struggling boy in his arms and began to run back the way they'd come. The first zombie fell toward the nurse and she thrust the knife forward, sinking it to the handle. A second later, her yell reached them on the rise; it was fierce and lost, forlorn. Susan began to cry as the nurse was overrun, disappearing into the confusion of roiling, rotten limbs.

The man crouched against the far wall. He held the boy's head to his chest, hiding the boy's eyes from the sight of his mother's death. He watched the nurse and then, turned his head and lowered it onto the boy's.

"No...*no*! Don't give up!" Susan said. Mary gripped her wrist, reminding her of her surroundings, quieting her. Susan snapped a wild and despairing glance from Floyd to Mary–*they had to do something! something!*–then she returned her gaze to the rooftop. Two of the zombies had left the nurse and they were almost to the man and boy. The man kept his head resolutely down, and a flash of childhood memory came to Susan of drawing the covers over her head to ward off the monsters. But these monsters would not be put off by shaking denial.

"Please," she whispered, "*please* get up. Please, for the boy...*please*." Tears rolled hot down her cheeks but she didn't notice. All her concentration was on the man and boy. The two zombies fell upon the man and a wail rose in Susan's throat, but she gritted her teeth against it.

The boy popped free and rolled back, unhurt. Susan gasped and Mary's hand tightened on her wrist again but this time with desperate hope. The boy ran twenty feet back toward his mother and then he stopped, undecided.

He was maybe six, maybe seven. Too little. Way too little.

Another zombie left the remains of the nurse and started toward the boy. This time, the boy ran back toward the wall and then along it, away from the man being devoured. He reached the corner of the building. Another zombie left the nurse and came toward the boy. Now the boy was trapped in the corner. Trapped.

He looked at the approaching zombies, looked over the edge of the building.

"No," Susan said and this time her tone was bereft of any feeling. Numb with shock, her mind slowed. She thought of Sorrow, of her mom. Had they had to go through something like this? Or, if changed themselves, were they putting others through something like this? She thought of her poor, doomed husband and with a jolt, realized he was the lucky one. He'd gotten out before any of this had happened. He was lucky to have died such an ordinary death.

The boy pulled himself onto the ledge, facing the zombies. They were less than ten feet from him. The boy turned and took a step on the narrow ledge, his little arms out for balance. Took another. Another. Missed his footing.

Susan looked away. Mary gasped and Floyd started to rise, his hands coming up, as if he could reach across the distance and catch the boy as he fell.

The boy's scream came to them, ghostly across the distance and all too brief.

Susan turned to the tree, leaned against the rough bark, and cried quietly into her folded arms.

CHAPTER 22

"Come on," Floyd said and reached a hand to Susan, "we have to keep going."

She looked up at him with shock-filled eyes and he had to quell a small rush of irritation. *Calm your tits, Abby, don't be a dick*, he told himself, using the buck-up, last name tone of guys who play sports. *She just watched a kid die. Course she is thinking about her own kid. Cool it.*

"I'll...hey, listen..." he started and then stopped and shuffled the toe of one boot through the pine needles. "You want me to hold your hand or something? I'll do it." It could have sounded jeering but Susan didn't take it that way. She tried to smile, but it looked bad on her pale, pixie face. He reached for her hand again. Pulled her up.

"Are we going back to the school?" Susan asked. She ran her hands through her hair, pulling it. "We have to just go back, right? Mary? There's too many of them down there. Right?"

Mary was still at the edge of the woods, facing the clearing. She didn't answer.

"Mary?" Susan said again, her voice unsure. "We have to go back."

Still Mary didn't answer. Floyd waited patiently while Susan tugged and fumed next to him, growing more agitated.

"Mary?" Susan said, "I think we have to go back to–"

Mary stood then, and turned. Her face was set in grim lines but her expression was not unkind. Not angry.

"I have to go down there. You can go back, both of you. I understand, but I have to go," she said. A small smile tightened her lips and then disappeared. "My son is at the surgery center."

Floyd hazarded a glance at Susan. Would she get mad? Would she ask then why they weren't going to find Sorrow? This was too close to the Cassie situation; Susan was a hothead and bound to get pissed. If she started yelling, it would draw the zombies. He'd have to–he'd have to do something.

She surprised him as she reached out a hand to Mary.

"I'm going with you," Susan said. She scanned the clearing, "But I don't know how the fuck we're supposed to get there."

"Very carefully," Mary said. "Here's what I was thinking–"

She set the box with the dead crow carefully aside, brushed away pine needles, and drew a rough grid. She mapped out the route that would give them the most cover, and also keep them furthest from the hospital parking lot. It would bring them up behind the surgery center where there didn't seem to be any of the undead.

"Once we're down there, we won't have this bird's eye view," Mary said, looking up from the drawing. "There's nothing *keeping* them in that parking lot, so they could easily make their way around by the time we get there. Plus..." she looked from Floyd to Susan as if to make sure they were really listening, "I don't know if there's a back or side door at the center. I assume there is, but, you know...*ass*ume, right? And even if there is, I don't know if they'll have anyone manning it. There's a chance we'll have to go right through the front doors."

Floyd nodded but he was having to work harder and harder to quell his impatience. It was already mid-morning or close to it, and he didn't want to have to spend the night next to those things. They had to get going *right now* if they were going to get there and back before nightfall.

Mary whacked his pant leg with the stick she'd been using to draw.

"Hey!" he said. It hadn't hurt, but it had startled him. Startled was not a good feeling right now.

"Pay attention, Floyd," Mary said. Her tone was not a scold but a command. Her eyes held him with their steady surety. "Two minutes of planning will only help, not hinder. Believe me. You on board?"

"Hell yes," he said. Beside him, Susan snorted a small laugh but he ignored her. It was good that she'd laughed. It meant she wasn't as frozen up.

"Okay, let's go," Mary said.

They went downhill, careful to stay behind the cover of the brick doctor's office. Floyd didn't like being out in the open even in this town he knew so well; everything seemed foreign and extremely dangerous.

If they had been able to take a direct route, it would have been only four blocks to the hospital but going around would double the trek. As they traversed the empty streets, Floyd had to keep quelling a mounting sense of disorientation. Occasional birds chirped and a dog barked in the distance, but there were no voices. The stoplights at each intersection blinked green to yellow to red, over and over, but no cars moved according to their direction. The smells of burning grew stronger the deeper they moved into the town and offhand, Floyd could identify at least three sources: gas, rubber, electrical. Smoke wafted distantly. The auto body station, most likely. But what else was burning? Did it matter? No fire trucks raced by with hysterical sirens and tremulous lights. No ambulances. No police.

Military. The military would be here soon. There had to be some government left, some group in charge. It would all get sorted.

But it won't.

Floyd trudged on, alert, eyes on everything. He met Susan's gaze and gave her a wink. She looked away but not before he caught her slow blink of gratitude.

If this had happened, whatever *this* was, as quickly and thoroughly everywhere else as it had here, then…no; no one was coming. No one was going to sort this mess out.

No one was in charge.

We're on our own, Floyd thought and the idea gave him a thrill that seemed more elation than fear. It seemed wrong to feel as though his time had come round to prove himself. To pit himself against the zombies, the elements, the situation. *The other normal people, too, Abby?* he asked himself with a stern inner voice. *Are you pitting yourself against them?*

He grinned behind his beard and then killed the grin, feeling shady as hell. Okay, he had a wide streak of self-preservation. That wasn't necessarily a bad thing. It didn't make him a bad guy.

Did it?

"See the bones?" Susan asked and he nearly jumped even though her voice was barely a whisper. They were at the pharmacy, tucked in the shadow of the big building as Mary looked around the corner, scouting their route.

Floyd shook his head and scowled at Susan. Raised his shoulders. *What are you talking about?*

"In the piles of clothes," she said. "Look at the road. At the parking lots. Anywhere open."

Mary had turned to listen to Susan, too.

Floyd looked, focusing his eyes close instead of in and around the buildings. Susan was right, the street was full of clothes. They were puddled and piled in random spots. Floyd had overlooked them in his intent scrutiny of their surroundings. There *were* bones. Under and around the clothes.

"Why the fuck would there be–" he started and then his mouth snapped shut.

"The zombies...they're eating people," Susan said. "Right down to the bone." Her tone was almost nonchalant, as if this newest atrocity had put her over the edge of concern. She kneeled suddenly, arms going limp, and her machete hung loose in her hand. "Those should all be bodies, but they're just bones...just bones, now." She sighed and the lost sound sent a chill up Floyd's spine.

Anger pulled Floyd's guts into a tight knot. He was incensed by the indignity of those carelessly tossed bones, of the implication, but also, by Susan's wide, shocky, detached gaze. "So the fuck what?" he said. He was practically growling in Susan's face as he hung over her.

"Floyd, listen," Mary said with a hand on his arm, but he shrugged her off and kept his attention focused on Susan.

"What the fuck do you think is going on here?" he asked her, his voice a furry hiss through his beard. "You think it's going to get better? It's *not*. It's *never* going to get better. You always acted so goddamn tough in the Vo-Tech...big welder, right? A woman in a man's field? Well, you better pull up your fucking panties, Susan. Or lay the fuck down and die." He flung an arm toward the road, indicating the piles of clothes and bone. "Like those fuckers out there."

Her mouth hung unhinged as she stared up at him. Then her hand curled around her machete as her lips thinned and tightened, going white. The lost, shocked quality left her eyes, replaced by irritation. "You shut the fuck up, Floyd." She struggled up, using the pharmacy's brick wall for support. She brushed at the knees of her jeans, avoiding eye contact. "Just…shut the fuck up."

"Four more blocks," Mary said. She shot Susan a glance and went on as if nothing amiss had transpired between Floyd and Susan. "That's all we have, so let's get them behind us. Okay?"

Susan nodded and grimaced at the ground. Floyd laid an arm over her back and the thin, slightness of her filled him with regret. He'd been too wrapped up in his own shit to recognize the genuineness of her distress. He vowed to do better.

"Almost there," Floyd said and she nodded and gave him a quick punch. It hadn't been an apology, but she didn't need one. Floyd's equilibrium settled back to level.

As much as it could in these circumstances.

— — —

The last thing between them and the back of the surgery center was a row of skinny, hip-to-hip Victorian townhouses with shallow back yards. It was harder to walk past homes, reflected in the blind windows; it felt weird and spooky. Were there people in there? Dead people slowly rotting away? Undead people wandering in the confined spaces with not enough brainpower left to unlock a door and get out? Pets resorting to…

The thought of pets made Mary think of the crow she carried. She knelt at the front porch steps of the last townhouse in the row. Floyd and Susan crouched, watchful.

"I'm leaving the bird," Mary said and set the box on the first riser of the porch. She lifted the lid for a quick glance, just to be sure. The bird was a pool of dusty dark in the less-dark shadows of the box. She re-closed it. "If it was gonna come back, I think it would have by now, but it bothers me."

"What does?" Susan asked. She was as sharp-eyed now as when Mary had first met her. Floyd's odd combination of tough and soft love must have bolstered her.

"Did it die from eating zombie?" Mary said. Her thoughts were on Mabel and Turk, her Rottweilers. They'd have to be trained *not to eat* corpses, especially ambulatory ones.

Susan and Floyd didn't answer. How could they? No one knew much of anything. All the more reason, in Mary's reckoning, to get as many people together as possible. Collective knowledge.

It was noon and warm. Their shadows pooled at their feet and Mary felt suddenly vulnerable. If they came around these houses and the undead had finally wandered to the back of the surgery center, she and her small team would be seen, but it was better to be able to see this enemy. They didn't seem very athletic, but they could be silent as death itself. Sure, they moaned sometimes, but when they didn't, their breathing didn't give them away...they didn't breathe.

She slid across the outside wall of the last townhouse in the row, staying as tight to it as possible. Then she reached the back corner. The townhouse had a small, tidy yard bound by a four-foot fence. Beyond the fence lay the parking lot at the back of the surgery center. The lot was empty and quiet. A row of parking spaces followed by a grassy area with two picnic benches led to a solid door set in the middle of the long building. The hospital stood beyond the center, looming in the near distance like a small mountain.

There was no outside handle on the door and no windows in the face of the building, but there was a small box with a yellowed plastic cover over a red button. A sign above the button said, FOR DELIVERIES, PLEASE RING BELL

She motioned Floyd and Susan to stay put.

"I'm going to try the bell," Mary said. "Wait here for my signal."

Mary trotted across the asphalt feeling vulnerable and way too visible. She skirted a picnic table and made her way up a short concrete apron to the door. She pushed the bell. Looked left and right.

She pushed the bell again. If it was buzzing inside the building, it was doing so somewhere she couldn't hear it. Why hadn't she noticed this door when she'd been inside the building? She and the others had been through every part of the facility, or so she had thought.

"Come on, come on," she whispered. She looked left and right again, scanning the long, blank back of the building. She looked back at the townhouse. Floyd watched her with sharp focus while Susan watched back along the side of the townhouse.

Mary pushed the button again, mashing it down. It had been too long. No one was coming. They would have to try the front of the building, but the front parking lot was jammed with zombies. They wouldn't–

Movement in her peripheral vision. She looked left, her heart sinking as two zombies came past the back corner of the building. They hadn't seen her. She mashed the button again then turned and pushed her back against the door, making herself as flat as possible. Run for Floyd and Susan? If she did that, the zombies would surely see her. Try to make it to the front of the building?

Another zombie came past the corner. Then another. Then a group of three. They wandered aimlessly and Mary was briefly reminded of the small robot that vacuumed her floors at home.

They would see her soon.

Which direction should she go?

Decide! You have to decide before–

The door opened inward with a rattling crash and she nearly screamed. She had forgotten the door! A face appeared at the crack and below the face, struggling and whining, the brown and black, pink tongued, bowling ball head of Turk, Mary's Rottweiler.

"Mary!" A man's voice, startled and glad. He opened the door wider, the dog struggling as the young man held him back with one leg. "Turk, geez! Cut it–"

A moan floated across the parking lot. The zombies had heard them.

"Charlie, grab Turk's collar. Get back," Mary said. She pushed her way in, and stood with her back propping the door open. She looked out, a quick glance across the back of the building. There were at least twenty zombies at the end of the parking lot, maybe more. A few were in street clothes. Most wore hospital uniforms or the blue Johnnies of patients.

One of them–an old, old woman–dragged a colostomy bag. An IV pole still attached to her wasted arm clacked across the blacktop behind her and a respirator tube jiggled in her mouth. She was nude save some unraveling compression apparatus on her legs. Her stomach was sliced open from hip to hip. Folds of skin hung loose and wrinkled over her caved-in mid-section. It looked as though most of her organs had exited her body.

Mary looked to where Floyd and Susan were waiting. If they ran now, they'd make it into the building. She waved them across.

They jumped from the cover of the townhouse and ran. When they appeared in the parking lot, the chorus of zombie moans became a dry roar.

"Close it! Close the door!" Charlie yelled. Turk whined and barked, trying to leap out of Charlie's grip. He held the dog's collar with two hands, shoulders jerking at each lunge.

The dead were nearly upon them. A steady stream poured around the corner of the building; their number seemed endless. Their moans changed again, became more urgent.

Susan and Floyd pounded past Mary and she pushed the door closed. She leaned her weight against it as the undead thumped and banged on the outside. Floyd joined her, adding his weight to the door. It shivered at each bump, but not much. The door was strong.

Charlie turned Turk loose and collapsed onto a nearby chair. He grinned as the dog jumped and spun in front of Mary, whining like a puppy reunited with his mother.

"That door locks on 'er own," Charlie said, "and it's strong. You should be good. 'Sides, those things'll forget pretty quick what they was up to."

The thumping had already decreased, seeming more accidental drag than a conscious assault.

"Not much brain power at work out there," Charlie said. His grin included Mary and Floyd and then his eyes strayed to the dog. "Turk! C'mere, you big baby! C'mere!" He grabbed the sides of

Turk's head and dragged the big dog to him, cooing and baby-talking as Turk panted, jowls stretched wide and tongue dangling.

"That's a big dog," Susan said.

Without letting go of Turk, Charlie turned his head to look at her where she stood pressed into the corner of the small office. She smiled tentatively at him and her shoulders dropped as her body seemed to catch up with the idea that she was safe.

"He big, but he mostly a big baby," Charlie said.

His accent had a southern kind of twang to it, but it might have been more south Jersey than South Carolina. Mary caught the rest of her breath as she watched Charlie manhandle the dog.

A set of metal shelves lay toppled over beside her, scattering paper, paperclips, staplers, tape…a small tide of office supplies. That must have been what crashed when Charlie opened the door. That's why they hadn't seen the door from inside the building; the shelves covered it.

"Charlie, this is Floyd and Susan. They're from the Vo-Tech," Mary said and then, as if it was a natural transition, "where's Ethan?"

Charlie's grin became one-sided, slanting across his young, amiable face. "He's with Mabel in the lobby, a'course. Why'dja think Mabel wasn't here with this big dummy?"

"What about Eric and the girl?"

"Aw, well, yeah. They're with him too," Charlie said. He tilted his head, considering his words. "Or, more like, they're *also* with Mabel. If you get me."

"Do you guys want to meet my son?" Mary asked and she couldn't contain the anxiety and excitement in her voice. Now that she was back, she allowed the thought of him to fill her mind. She had wrestled with the decision to leave him and like any good parent had second-guessed herself at every calm moment. That there hadn't been a lot of calm moments had been both good and bad.

The look she sent Susan was hesitant, almost apologetic, but Susan merely ran a hand over her worse for wear spikes.

"Of course," Susan said, "I can't wait to meet him."

— — —

Mary knelt and swept the small boy into her arms. The two big dogs sat to either side and watched with solemn regard as the mother and son hugged.

Susan had to turn away.

She put her fingers to her temple and pushed fiercely, as though a sudden migraine demanded the relief of pressure. She controlled the tears tightening her throat and tried to blink Sorrow out of her mind. *How often would she have to do that?* She wondered and fresh anger burned in her stomach. *From now until the goddamned end of time?* It was all so unfair. Every stinking bit of it.

But none of it was Mary's fault. Her good fortune to have her son with her was not something to be jealous of. It was unfair to be jealous.

Everything was unfair, same as it ever was.

She squeezed her forehead once more and closed her eyes.

She let the thought of him float up. Her baby, Sorrow, the best thing that had happened to her since her husband had died. The only thing that had kept her going through those numb, lightless days. She couldn't meet Mary's son. She just couldn't do it. It was too hard. It was too–

"Susan?"

The boy in Mary's arms looked to be four or five, with a tousle of dark hair. His cheeks were round and licked with pink. His fingers and hands were as lavishly lined as those of a plump infant, and he had one arm slung around Mary's neck. His brown eyes were swimming with tears.

He was already a rare thing in this new world.

A wave of fierce protectiveness crashed over Susan and as quickly as it came, it washed away, leaving her calm, washed out and sure. She didn't think she loved the boy, not on sight, but she would have laid down her life for his. If there was a point to any of this, then it was here, before her, hugging Mary and trying to smile.

"This is Susan," Mary said. "Ethan? Can you say hello to Susan?"

His smile widened, showing little teeth. He turned his shoulder shyly into his mother, even as his hand rose and his fingers opened and closed, opened and closed.

"He's a cute little guy," Floyd said. "Can you say hi to me, little guy? Can Floyd hold you?" He put out his burly arms and to everyone's surprise, Ethan tilted himself toward the big man. Mary let him go.

Ethan's attention went to Floyd as he patted the big man's beard and Susan caught Mary's eye.

"He's beautiful," Susan said and it was all she could manage. Mary seemed to understand.

"I want to introduce you to Eric," Mary said. "Floyd? You too."

A man and woman were to the side of the long reception area. The woman was young, mid to late teens, just a girl, really. She was dressed in nurse's scrubs but she wasn't a nurse, Susan would have put money on that. Too young. She was petite and pale and there was a lost, dreaming quality to her light eyes.

The man was older, heavy and gray haired. His yellow pallor and sagging skin bespoke of someone acquainted with a long history of ill health. He was in a wheelchair.

Susan wondered briefly if the wheelchair were a permanent thing–there would be no way to get him back to the Vo-Tech, if it were.

"Hi there," the man said, "don't worry about the chair, young lady. It was just sitting here so I parked myself in it. It's more comfortable than the waiting room rocks they have set up in here." He rose, not fluidly but with more ease than Susan would have predicted, and held out his hand. "I'm Eric, obviously. This young dear heart hasn't spoken yet, but I'm sure she will and soon."

Susan shook his hand and let her eyes skate over the girl, who had dropped her gaze to her lap. "I'm Susan," she said and returned her eyes to Eric's. He watched her keenly and she wasn't at all surprised he'd picked up on her reservations regarding the wheelchair. He might look sickly but he was sharp. Susan said, "Nice to meet you, or...well, you know."

"Yes, indeed I do," he said. His face broke into soft wrinkles as he smiled. Then he turned to Floyd. "Hello, Floyd."

Floyd handed Ethan back to Mary and shook Eric's hand. Then he stepped back and crossed his arms over his chest. The mute girl kept her eyes down and Charlie had drifted to the busted-glass front of a vending machine. He fished a candy bar from one of the ringed shelves. Mary picked Ethan back up and hugged him.

"Okay," Mary said. There was something that seemed both softer and fiercer about her now that she had Ethan in her arms. "Let's get back to the Vo-Tech."

CHAPTER 23

"I'm not sure how we're going to get out of here, Mary," Floyd said. He, Mary, and Eric sat behind the reception desk. Susan stood on the opposite side, leaning her elbows on the countertop, listening.

Floyd said, "This building is surrounded." He kept his voice low. He didn't want to scare the kid and he also wasn't sure about that mute girl, she seemed more than a little off the rails.

She was sitting in the same place, still staring at her lap. She didn't seem aware of the people around her. Charlie sat not far from her in the row of waiting room chairs, Ethan on his lap. They were sharing a candy bar. The dogs looked on in worshipful silence. Two lines of thick slobber hung from Turk's jaws.

"Last time I looked out, the crowd seemed a bit thinner," Eric said.

The two glass entryway doors had been covered with layers of heavy blankets blocking the view in or out, but Floyd glanced that way anyway. "They're around back, that's why," he said.

"Yes, but maybe they'll start to drift away," Eric said. "I don't know why they haven't, yet."

"The parts of town we saw getting here were empty," Susan said. "Maybe they're, like, herding or something."

"They could possibly be more comfortable in a group," Eric said. His hand rubbed unconsciously across his midsection. "Maybe there is some base instinct left after they die. That first death, I mean. Al might have had some better ideas because he was a natural theorist."

When Mary had informed Eric and Charlie of Al's death, Charlie had accepted the news without fuss, but Eric had grown agitated, just shy of angry, as he grasped the implications. *He was, potentially, the only one who knew anything about this disease and he took himself out of the game?* Mary hadn't tried to explain or defend.

"Doesn't matter why," Floyd said in regards to Eric's grouping hypothesis, but tucked away the term Eric had used–'first death'– with an inner grin of recognition. It was a good description of the zombie phenomenon and would make great shorthand. "The only thing that matters is that we're surrounded. Getting out the way we came in is going to be near impossible. Especially if we were thinking about bringing her with us." He raised his chin toward the mute girl.

"We're bringing her," Eric said, and his jovial expression hardened like quick drying cement.

"She doesn't exactly look capable of a hike," Floyd said and without intention, he assessed Eric as an adversary. The man was big, but he was also old, and that yellow pallor and the way he rubbed his hanging gut meant he'd been at the surgery center for a reason. Maybe he was using the girl as a crutch to hide his own infirmity. "I'm not putting everyone in jeopardy. If you–I mean *she*–can't make it..."

Eric stood, facing off with Floyd. Susan straightened. "Guys," she said, but it was as if she hadn't spoken.

"She goes with us," Eric said, "no matter what."

"Of course she does," Mary said. She laid a hand on Eric's shoulder but turned to Floyd. "It'll be okay because we're not walking." Her mouth was a line, but her eyes danced with anticipation. "Floyd's going to drive us all out of here."

– – –

"See?" Mary said.

"Yeah, I see," Floyd said, "but I don't think it's gonna be quite as easy as you made out."

The ambulance sat directly across from the entry doors, separated from the building by a mere ten feet of concrete apron. A zombie staggered between the building and the ambulance, and Floyd let the blanket drop back into place.

"The parking lot is still jammed with those walking corpses," he said. "It's going to be near im-fucking-possible to get that truck out of here." A tickle like excitement wormed its way up through his gut. *Cool your jets, Abby,* he told himself, but the tickle wouldn't go away. He *wanted* to make a try for the ambulance. Hell, he just wanted to run out and kill as many zombies as he could. His dreams, since that first day, had been filled with satisfyingly blood-drenched rampages, where he left a swath miles wide of decapitated zombies in his wake. *There's something wrong with you, Abby,* that inner voice cautioned. *You're not normal.*

Maybe not, but it was preferable to sensitively losing your marbles like the mute girl, or that guy Al opting out. Or, look at Susan, even! She was tough, had been, anyway, but she'd lost her shit several times since this mess all went down. Her toughness was all surface-tough, all pre-apocalypse tough.

"I'll draw them off," Charlie said from Floyd's side. "No prob."

"Charlie," Mary said, "I appreciate your desire to help, but there's no chance of drawing that many zombies away. You'd be killed. I think Floyd is right, we'll have to come up with something else."

"Nah," Charlie said, dismissing Mary's words with a comfortable wave of his hand. "I'll outrun 'em. Them's slow as shit, Mary. I'll run all the way back to the votechnical. Meet you folks over there. No probs, no probs." He bounced lightly on the balls of his feet as if to demonstrate how ready he was. Turk jumped up, barking and grinning, obviously as enamored with Charlie as he was with Ethan and Mary. Mabel looked on with something like doggy disapproval and shifted her weight tighter to Ethan.

"I'll take the Turkey with me!" Charlie said and grabbed the dog's front paws. "He listens good, don't you, Turkey?" Man and dog danced across the lobby floor, Turk's muscular haunches swaying like a stripper's. Floyd had a sudden realization that he was watching a fellow crazy. He caught the reckless twirl in Mary's eyes as she hid a smile in a cupped hand and he knew that the crazies were at least three strong.

Was that good or bad?

He decided he didn't give a shit and laughed at Charlie's antics. Good or bad, it was the crazies who would get the normals to safety. He felt that in his bones with a deep surety that he knew he'd never be able to explain. It just *was*.

"Yeah, we'll give it a try," he said. "What's the worst that can happen?"

Eric and Susan looked at him with identical frowns, but next to him, Mary burst into laughter. She controlled it quickly, but the gleam stayed on in her eyes. Only when she picked up Ethan did her gaze sober completely.

Charlie dropped Turk's paws and sank into a lobby chair. "I need something to make a muzzle for him, Mary. I don't want him chomping no zombie, not after what you all told me about that crow."

Mary and Ethan followed Charlie back toward the nurse's area in search of suitable muzzle material and Floyd lifted the blanket again, checking the parking lot. The zombies were thick between the surgery center and the hospital. Most wandered until something bounced them off their trajectory, but some merely stood, heads down and swaying. Why? Did it have something to do with how fresh they were or weren't? Was it something to do with the manner of death? Did it matter?

Susan ducked under his arm, squatted, and looked out. He thought about dropping the blanket, but he didn't want Susan to get cold feet. She merely watched, her face impassive.

"You think this is a good idea?" he asked, more to gauge her state of mind than out of any indecision on his part. "That's an awful lot of those things out there. More than we've come across yet."

"There was that big group that went past the Vo-Tech, remember? Right at the beginning?" Susan said. She still hadn't taken her eyes off the parking lot.

"Yeah, but we didn't drive out into them."

She turned and looked up at him. "Cassie and Dave did," she said. She stared at him a minute longer, then straightened and wandered to the vending machine. "We should fill a bag with what's left in here."

Mary came back with a set of keys in her hand, towing Ethan. Charlie was right behind them, holding Turk's collar. Turk had been turned into a half-mummy, gauze twisted and twined around his nose and mouth and tied up behind his ears.

"Is that going to hold?" Eric asked. He motioned Turk to him and examined the make-shift muzzle.

"Only for so long," Mary said. "If something should happen..."

"He's gotta be able to get it off if something happens to me," Charlie finished. He didn't seem distressed by the thought. "Anyone pack up that vending machine yet? I'd appreciate a coupl'a them candy bars."

Eric held up the cloth sack that in another life would have held a patient's belongings and Charlie went to him, face lit up like a kid trick-or-treating.

"Okay, here's the plan and it's pretty simple," Mary said. "Charlie and Turk will leave by the back door, since there's less zombies that way. They'll circle around to the highway side of the building, show themselves to the ones right out front, and draw them off. Floyd will exit the front door, get to the ambulance, get it started, and then back it up to the doors. In we go and off we go. Okay?"

"Sounds easy enough," Susan said, and Floyd gave her a sharp look. Was she being sarcastic? She stared back at him, her expression bland. He'd really trusted her, back at the Vo-Tech, and he'd thought she'd been someone like himself: a survivor. Now, he didn't know. Was she really this calm or was she teetering on the edge of another breakdown?

"Well," Mary said, "I don't know about 'easy'...I'm just hoping for doable right now."

"Maybe we should–" Eric said, but Charlie cut him off.

"Okay, Charlie out. Charlie and Turk out, I mean," he said and laughed. He nearly thrummed with pent up energy as he bounced. "I'll make sure that door locks behind me, don't worry. I'll holler when I get to the side, you'll hear me. Then me and Turk'll see you all at the votechnical." He grinned in Mary's direction but didn't quite meet her eyes.

The kid was a little strange all right, but his heart sure was in the right place. Floyd punched him lightly on the shoulder. "See you there, kid," he said and Charlie's eyes skated over his and away, his grin widening.

"Later, gaters," Charlie said. He slapped his thigh, and he and Turk bounced from the room.

He seemed to take some vital momentum with him. The others looked at each other blankly. Mabel whined from her place next to Eric, her eyes anxious as she watched Turk disappear. Eric dropped a hand onto her head. Then she stood and barked, just once, as if to tell everyone to get a move on, the sooner they got going, the sooner she'd have her Turk back.

Mary crouched to unlock the front doors, her hands just under the blanket, working nearly blind. The snick of the deadbolt sliding back was nearly silent. She handed Floyd the keys. She whispered, "Soon as you're ready."

Floyd lifted the blanket sideways. It was bright outside and dark in the lobby, so they should be nearly invisible inside the building. Still, he was cautious only to shift it as much as he needed. The less zombies that saw them, the better.

He glanced over his shoulder. Eric stood with Mabel's collar in one hand, the mute girl's arm in the other. The girl was still catatonic looking, but she had stood on her own, going willingly when Eric directed her to the doors. Hopefully, she would go as easily into the ambulance.

Susan held Ethan on her hip, her machete up and ready. Her eyes were still calm, eerily so. Floyd wished there was some fire of life and fight in them. It made him uneasy that she held the boy, but she would hand him over to Mary as soon as he was out the door, so it should be okay.

Should be.

He turned back to the door. The zombies were just as thick. He watched as one's arm fell off, hitting the blacktop with a sickening slap. What the fuck kept these things going? Disgust made him shake his head. They were like–

An ululating call came from somewhere to his left. Charlie. Turk barked and Charlie whooped again, half war cry, half cackling laugh. The zombies began to turn.

Floyd tensed, his hand on the horizontal metal bar that said 'PUSH'. Wait. Wait one more second.

The zombies struggled and shuffled toward the sounds of Charlie and Turk. Their moans became louder and louder as more and more were alerted. The realization flowed through them like ripples on water, spreading...spreading...

The ones closest to the building wandered out of Floyd's sightline.

He pushed the door open. He was to the ambulance in three long strides, the key out and ready in his hand. He didn't bother with the automatic lock, didn't want that little *weep, weep* to give him away. He fitted the key smoothly, turned it, opened the door and slid into the passenger's seat. He pulled the door behind him, easing it shut. In the sudden silence, the release of his pent-up breath was the loudest noise–he hadn't realized he'd been holding it.

He looked back at the building. The blanket was back down, and the door shut as though no one had come out. It gave him a bad feeling. Deserted, although, technically, he was the one who had done the leaving.

Then Mary appeared and she gave him a quick thumb's up, her face a question. He raised a finger...*hold on*...and shifted into the driver's seat. The ambulance had a gas engine, many public service industry vehicles still did. There was no need for an ambulance to be governed by the automatic speed restrictions that controlled most electric cars. Plus, fossil fuels had become a nice little budgetary plum for those trying to justify expenditures.

Floyd slid the key in the ignition and turned it a quarter turn. The dashboard lit up and the gas indicator went to three-quarters of a tank. So, no problem there. He took another breath. Another. He looked out across the building, trying to see Charlie, but the tide of corpses obscured his view. Now or never.

He keyed the engine to life.

The zombies nearest the ambulance turned in his direction with sludgy interest.

He slammed the ambulance into gear and swung it out into the parking lot. He slammed the brake, slid the lever to 'R'. More and more zombies had turned toward him. Charlie yelled from somewhere closer by and they turned again, swaying with seeming indecision.

Floyd looked in the rearview mirror. He hit the gas. The wheels screeched as he backed up. Mary's face disappeared for an instant and then the blanket fell away from the door. She stood with Ethan in her arms, the others in a dim line behind her.

She raised her eyes and her face fell, her mouth dropped open in shock. Her hand came up, palm out to him.

Floyd had a split second to wonder–*what the fuck?*–then the ambulance slammed to a halt. He registered a crunch somewhere above and behind him as he was thrown back and then violently forward. His face bounced off the steering wheel. White pain shot into his head, as heat cascaded over his mouth and chin.

Above the doors, there was an overhang that protected entering and exiting patients from the elements. He had backed right into it.

— — —

Mary put her hand up, palm toward the door, her head tilted back. Susan followed the direction of Mary's gaze and she saw the problem. The ambulance would never make it under the overhang. Floyd was going to crash.

She pushed past Mary and hit the door straight-armed. The ambulance crashed into the overhang, shaking the building. The moaning of the zombies became the shushed roar of ocean waves as they swarmed toward the ambulance. Even Charlie's yells were drowned out.

She gave the back doors of the ambulance a quick yank, pulling them open.

"Floyd!" she yelled into the echoing cavern. She could just make out his shoulder where he was slumped over the wheel. The impact had been hard, but not hard enough to kill him. He was still alive. She knew he was. "Floyd, wake the fuck up!" Beyond him, the first zombie crashed into the front of the ambulance. It struggled there as if pinned, reaching for Floyd across the hood. Another piled into the first. Another.

In less than three seconds, they'd be overrun.

"Floyd! Come ON! Wake UP!"

His shoulder twitched. He shifted. Okay, he was coming around. With relief, Susan turned and motioned for Mary and the others.

A zombie staggered around the open ambulance door. Susan screamed and her heart dropped. They were done for. They never should have tried this. They should have stayed put and waited for help to come.

Behind her, Ethan cried out in fear.

Rage blew into her mind like a black and coldly sulpherous cloud. He was the point, the baby, the baby was the point.

She had to save the baby.

She raised her machete and its clean and shining edge gleamed in the sun. She brought it down in a wide arc and sliced through the zombie's neck. Her arm wanted to falter as the blade hit spine, but the rage gave her strength. The body fell in a heap. The head rolled. Susan had a brief flash of pride–proud of her blade, proud of her aim and her arm–and then another walking corpse stumbled over the first one's head.

Susan yelled and brought the machete back the other way. She chopped the zombie's head off. She lunged forward and stabbed the machete into the eye of another close on the heels of the first. She was only dimly aware of the noises behind her as the others piled into the ambulance.

The zombies no longer looked like humans to her, or even like corpses. She saw each one as its own target, her eye picking out vulnerabilities as though they were bathed in divine spotlights. Her blade never faltered. She could do no wrong. She chopped, swung, and sliced...and she laughed. Without fully knowing it...she laughed.

Finally, Mary's voice cut into her whirring, blood-soaked mind.

"Susan! Let's go!"

Susan glanced back. Mary hung out one door, having pulled the other closed. Eric and the girl sat on a gurney inside. Ethan stood just behind his mother, his hand on Mabel's back, his eyes huge in his small white face as he looked anxiously out at Susan.

"Close it!" Susan yelled. She pushed a zombie that had gotten too close, her hand nearly disappearing into the spongy mass of its chest. It toppled over and she swung the blade down, into its eye. "Close the doors!" she yelled over her shoulder. She straightened and brought the blade up. Sank it into the soft area under a zombie's chin, pushed up with both hands on the handle, skewering the brain.

The ambulance doors closed with a solid thunk. Red and blue lights strobed the building. The siren whooped and echoed across the parking lot. It pulled forward, braked, and backed up. Floyd leaned across the seat, pushing the passenger door open.

"Get in here, you maniac!" he called to her. She pushed another zombie back. Kicked another. Sliced a throat.

She jumped into the ambulance.

Floyd gunned it and the door slammed shut just as a zombie reached in. The wheels screamed as he pulled the heavy vehicle into a tight turn, rounding it on itself like a dog chasing its tail.

"Cut those fucking lights!" Susan said, her hand white-knuckle tight on the sissy bar above the window. She reached across and slammed down the switch for the siren. "Are you nuts? The fuck are you trying to do? Draw every fucking zombie in the county?" Anger burned the edges of her vision but laughter continued to bubble up like uncontrollable gas.

"Me? What the fuck are *you* trying to do?"

His laughter met hers and they glanced into each other's frantic eyes. Susan swallowed and grew solemn. Floyd said, "Man, that was–"

Susan screamed and yanked her feet off the floor. Floyd hit the brake in reaction and then hit the gas again. "What?" he yelled. "What's wrong?"

She bent into the well under the dashboard. When she came back up, she held a hand in hers–it must have gotten chopped off when the door slammed shut. She powered down her window and threw the hand out with a tight moue of disgust on her face.

"Fucking *gross!*" Susan said, and with that, they were both laughing again.

The ambulance careened through the parking lot, as Floyd dragged the wheel left and right avoiding the zombies. Hitting one of them head on would be like hitting a deer–it might do tremendous damage to the ambulance. They couldn't risk it.

Mary leaned into the space between the seats and pointed him toward the exit. "Please stop laughing," she said. "You're scaring Ethan."

That sobered them.

He couldn't completely avoid the walking corpses and few got at least a glancing blow from the ambulance's bumper. Susan turned her head to track a leg that flew across the lot, twirling like a baton. Ribbons of muscles and skin flapped from the severed-thigh end.

"That sucker was *ripe*," she said.

Floyd said "Huh?" and glanced toward her. He looked back to the road and a zombie stepped directly into their path. Floyd dragged the wheel to the right. The ambulance hit a half-crumbled chunk of cement threaded with re-bar. It bounced hard and Susan yelped. Eric cursed from the back. Sparks flew out from under the ambulance as the rebar, trapped underneath, ground across the tarmac.

The ambulance began to slow. Zombies piled into it from both sides, thumping meatily. "We're caught on it!" Floyd yelled. "We're hung up!"

Fresh anger, so wild and hot it made her earlier anger seem tame by comparison, burned across Susan's mind. The world became a black and red swirl. "Gun it!" she screeched. "Gun the fucker!"

Floyd tromped the gas pedal and the ambulance bucked, while the engine screamed and sang. For a second, it seemed as though it wasn't going to help. Then the ambulance bucked again and broke free, the back end lifting and thumping back down with a bone-jarring thud.

Then they were out on the highway. The zombies thinned. Disappeared behind them. Floyd turned to Susan, a wide smile splitting his beard. "We did it!"

She looked at him and tried to smile. Couldn't. With a shaking finger, she pointed at the gas indicator. The three quarters of a tank was already at a half, and dropping.

CHAPTER 24

"They should be back by now," Paul said. He stared out the front doors although it was too dark to see much of anything. The streetlights were still coming on, but the ones in the Vo-Tech parking lot hadn't.

"It's Mary we're talking about, Paul," John said, standing next to him, "she'll pull everyone through. You can count on that."

Calvin sat further down the hall in a folding chair. He'd felt outnumbered since Floyd and Susan had left, although he knew–intellectually–that the feeling didn't make any sense.

He wanted to say, "Floyd and Susan have a say in it, too, you know," but he quelled the impulse. John was just trying to get Paul to calm down. The man had been a wreck since nightfall. Calvin felt more sanguine. Maybe they had decided to stay overnight at the surgery center and come back tomorrow morning. There was just no way to find out. They should have tried to find some cell phones, or at least, kept either Cathy or Dave's. But who knew if they'd even work at this point, anyway? No one was out fixing anything anymore.

"Are you worried, too?" Trish asked, making him jump a little. He hadn't heard her come down the hall.

"Not yet," he said. She was a good-looking woman, probably about his age. Average height, really nice hair and eyes. Nice body. She unfolded a chair and planted it next to his. "Paul's pretty worried."

"He would be, though, right?" she said after a brief glance in Paul's direction. "It's his wife out there. His child."

He glanced at her left hand–no ring. "Did you, I mean, do you have any? Kids?"

"No, but a lot of nieces and nephews. I hope they're okay."

Calvin didn't say anything to that. Trish probably wasn't a stupid person–what had John said she did at the hospital? Some kind of admin?–so she must already know that the chances of her nieces and nephews being okay were not great.

"You don't," she said.

"Don't what?"

"Have kids."

"No," he said. He sat back and crossed his ankle over his knee, settling firmly into shadow. "How did you know?"

"You don't seem very, you know…vested. In this situation, I mean."

He was glad he'd tilted himself out of the light so she couldn't see the hurt she'd caused. He turned his face sharply away from her as if studying John and Paul.

"I'm sorry," she said. She reached across and hovered her hand over his knee as if uncertain whether she should touch him or not. "I just meant…you're more like me–a little detached. In this situation, I mean. You were single, too, right?"

He shrugged without looking at her. Like all pretty women, she assumed too much and spoke without a thought to consequences. "You were pretty upset when Al killed himself," he said, and didn't care that there was a mean undercurrent to his words. "That's not so detached."

"Yes, I was upset," she said and her tone held no defensiveness. "I didn't feel particularly close to him, it was really more of the shock. Plus, at dinner that night, when we were all in your cafeteria…remember?"

Calvin acknowledged her with a glance.

"He had been telling me," she went on, "that he felt…you know…pretty despondent."

Calvin's foot came off his knee and he sat forward to study her. "You knew he was going to kill himself?"

"No…no, no, nothing like that," she said. "I'd have told Mary if I thought that. No, I mean, it just added to the upset, you know? That I wasn't much help to him, but I'm not…I'm not a very…warm, I guess…person. In general, I mean."

He studied her downturned profile. She looked up and gave him a brief smile before turning her gaze back to Paul and John. "I don't know which is better," she said.

"Which...*what* is better?" He had an urge to grab her hand but didn't. She was an odd one.

"Is it better to be, you know, unencumbered? Like me? Or is it better to have a loved one to hold onto?"

He was intrigued by the hesitations in her speech as she offered him her hypothesis. She didn't seem to have much confidence in what she was saying.

"I don't know," he said, "but I don't know if it matters, either."

"No, of course, you're right," she said, "but...it might, though. I mean, in any decision making process."

"How do you–"

"There's Charlie!" Paul said. He pushed through the door and Calvin jumped up, panicked.

"Wait!" Calvin said. "Be careful!"

"I've got him," John said but Paul had stopped right outside the doors. He waved to someone out in the parking lot.

"Charlie!" he waved and whisper yelled. "Here! Over here! This door!"

A shadow twined and twisted through the cars, got closer, split into two shadows. The young man, Charlie, bounded up the steps and a large black and tan dog loped at his heels. Paul grabbed Charlie in a bear hug and the dog barked. The bark had a muffled quality. His snout was wrapped in white gauze. Had the dog been bit, or what?

"Get them in here," Calvin said. John pushed the door open and grabbed Paul's shirt, tugged.

Paul turned, grinning, and led Charlie into the building. He knelt and rubbed the dog's head between his hands, grinning, then kissed him on his furry head. "Man, am I ever glad to see you guys," Paul said to Charlie. The dog struggled to lick him from between the white folds looped over his mouth and nose. "Yes, yes, you, too, Turk. I'm happy to see you, too."

"Mabel's gonna be beside herself," Charlie said. He had sunk into one of the chairs, obviously exhausted. "Is this the longest she's been separated from this old boy of hers?"

Paul looked up from Turk. In the scant light from the doors, his face was pale and ghostly. "What do you mean?" he asked and his voice barely registered. He cleared his throat. "Charlie...where's Mary?"

Charlie sat bolt upright as though he'd been stung. "She ain't here?"

"Charlie," Paul said as he stood. John put a restraining hand on Paul's arm but he brushed it off. He stood in front of Charlie. "Where...is...*Mary*?" He grabbed Charlie's shoulders and shook him, shouting. "What *happened*? Where *is* she? What did you *do*?"

"She was headed back here!" Charlie said, his voice a bark of protest. His head snapped back and forth but he seemed unable to bring himself to defend himself. He grabbed Paul's wrists. "Everyone was with her! Ethan was with her!"

Paul stepped back. He looked at his hands as though he wasn't sure whose they were. He swallowed and looked at everyone standing in the hallway and then ran a hand down his front, smoothing his shirt, calming himself. He looked at Charlie.

"Tell me everything."

— — —

"I'm going out there," Paul said. His voice was calm and sure on the surface, but Calvin figured if *he* could hear the uneasiness running just beneath, then everyone could.

"You can't," John said. "Listen to me, Paul, you know that's not a good idea. You'd have no idea which route they were taking back."

"That's what I mean, see?" Trish said quietly to Calvin so only he would hear. He dragged his eyes from the arguing men to look at her.

"Huh? What are you talking about?"

"Paul...he's not making a clear-headed decision, because, you know, it's people he loves out there."

Calvin stared at her for a long minute, studying her as she watched Paul and John. He knew that what she was saying was a little clinical, a little detached, but she could have pulled the words directly from his own thoughts. She glanced at him with an unhappy twist of a grin on her lips.

"See now? What I meant?" she asked him.

"Yes," he said.

"I'll go," Charlie said. "I'll just double on back and–"

"Anyone can see that you're exhausted," John said. "You can't run right back out there. You'll make dumb mistakes. Even the dog is exhausted."

Turk lay near the doors, the makeshift muzzle lying in a forgotten puddle beside him. He had his head on his paws, sound asleep despite the arguing.

"I have to go, John," Paul said. His voice had taken on an almost monotonous quality. "It's my responsibility. It's my–"

"*Guys*!" Tyler's voice echoed down the hallway to them. He'd been in the cafeteria, on watch. "There's a shit ton of zombies coming up the road!" He jogged down the hall on quiet, sneakered feet. "They're coming right toward us. Hey, what's up?" He nodded to Charlie.

"Yo," Charlie said, returning Tyler's nod. The two probably weren't that far apart in age.

"Charlie," John said, "were there a lot of zombies out there? Did they follow you?"

"Not so's I noticed," Charlie said. "Not followed me, anyway, tho there was a lot of 'em at the hospital. Like I told you about."

"If these zombies were at the hospital," Paul said, "and they're here now and Mary *isn't* here, then she must have…she must have…"

"She must have holed up somewhere," John said, "that's all, Paul. You know Mary would get everyone under cover. You know that she–"

The sighs and moans had reached them, loud enough to penetrate the glass doors. Under the streetlights out on the highway, shadows began to appear, herking and jerking along. The woods on the far side of the parking lot rustled with movement. More zombies. A whole herd of them.

Turk sat up, hackles rising. He began to growl deep in his chest.

"Charlie, get Turk back, take him further down the hall," John said, his voice low. "We can't have him barking."

Tyler had drifted to the doors and he stared out with something like fascination. "Lots of doc and nurse clothes," he said. "Lots of people in those what do you call its? Those hospital dresses."

"Johnnies," Paul said, "they're called Johnnies."

Calvin put a hand on Tyler's back, drawing him away from the doors. "Everyone move back," he said, whispering. The balm of detachment ran through him. *Maybe it* was *better*, he thought, looking at Paul's haggard, tortured face. The man was falling apart. *At least I won't be devastated if anyone is killed.* He thought of funny, spunky, tough-talking Susan. Yes, even losing her was survivable, he decided. He glanced across to Trish where she stood just out of the light, watching the slow flood of the undead. Her face was impassive.

Part of the herd staggered into the parking lot. They bumped into cars, tripped over detritus. In the dark, their condition was less immediately identifiable, and it would be easy to imagine that they were not what they were. The mind, seeking escape, could change the listing stagger of one into that of a drunk, the moans and gibberings of another into that of a mental deficient, but Calvin's mind remained clear.

"We'll wait until morning," he whispered, making sure that Paul was close enough to hear him. "Then, if those things are gone–we'll go look for the others."

"Sounds good, but I bet they'll be here by then, anyway," John said. "Paul? You hear that? Sounds good, right?"

Paul didn't answer. His eyes were trained out the doors. Calvin could only imagine what Paul must be seeing, the terrible thoughts that he conjured in regard to his wife and child.

They'd have to keep an eye on him for the remainder of the night.

CHAPTER 25

The chunk of concrete and rebar must have punctured either the gas tank or gas line. They were lucky they hadn't been blown sky high when they were throwing sparks, but now the ambulance was almost on E. They were fucked.

Floyd checked the rear view mirror again, compulsively. They were back there, coming on. They were distant, but still on the move. He glanced at Susan, glanced past her. "Where would be the best place?"

"I don't know," she said, a swell of impatience in her voice. He'd asked her the same thing about eight times already, but he felt helpless not to.

"All this shit is goddamned *retail*," she went on. "Look at the giant goddamned *windows*! There'd be no way to secure a building with windows like that!"

Her hands twisted together in her lap. She leaned over and grabbed the machete from next to the seat. It seemed to calm her.

"We need somewhere enclosed," Susan said, "somewhere that they can't–"

The ambulance hitched. Hitched again. Bucked.

"Fuuuuuu–" Floyd breathed out. He tried to goose it, knowing it would do no good. The ambulance coughed. Jumped. Coughed again and then sputtered and died. It rolled to a stop. The sudden silence was shocking.

"We're fucked," Floyd said. His hands gripped the steering wheel. His nose was killing him, throbbing with pain. He looked in the rearview again, but this time looked at himself.

He looked like a monster. The lower half of his face was drenched in blood, just beginning to crust a little in his red-soaked beard. There was a nasty bulge across the bridge of his nose and his eyes were already blackening. He grinned to see the blackish blood in his teeth.

"Gross, you look, gross, okay?" Susan said, her patience breaking. "Stop checking yourself out, you sick weirdo." Floyd sneered at her, showing her his bloodied grin, and she covered the smirk that tried to form on her lips. She hissed at him instead and he would have laughed if his fucking face didn't hurt so much.

"Guys, listen to me," Mary said, her voice snapping from the back of the ambulance. Under her words, Eric groaned. Whatever he'd been at the surgery center for had caught up with him almost as soon as they'd discovered their leaking gas tank. Mary appeared in the front between them. "Find a place. A close one. Find it now."

"We'll have to hoof it, Mary," Floyd said. "Can he–?"

"We can roll him," Mary said. "If we can get the gurney figured out." Her tone became quieter, distracted as she faded back. "We need a damn doctor."

"The doc's office!" Susan said. She slapped the dashboard. "We passed it on the way in. Right at the edge of the woods!"

"I remember it," Floyd said looking around, trying to get his bearings, "but, I think that's pretty far, Suze."

"We just have to cut around a different way," Susan said. She turned in her seat. "Mary? Get him strapped in. You and I will push Eric," she said to Floyd. "Mary can take Ethan and the girl."

"Yep, yep," Floyd said. That tickle of excitement was back. Ridiculous, yes, but there it was anyway. He glanced back the way they had come. The zombies were on the horizon, a shuffling horde of the undead. "We gotta get a move on."

They exited the ambulance and Floyd had a second's worth of grief over leaving the vehicle behind. He'd only been an ambulance driver for about fifteen minutes, but he'd enjoyed the hell out of it. Mostly.

They yanked and pulled, searching until they found the catches on the gurney. Floyd rolled it forward and lowered the front wheels, then Mary levered it out and Susan dropped the back ones. Eric groaned and held his stomach. His face was dead white, his eyes clamped shut and sweat pouring off him in rivers.

"Okay, let's roll," Floyd said. Susan and he each took a side.

Mary had Ethan on her hip and held the mute girl's wrist in her free hand. She told Mabel to heel and the dog stuck herself to Mary's knee.

"Up there, through that alley," Susan said, indicating the way with a nod.

"Up a hill? What the fuck, Suze," Floyd said, but he started to push. The ride was not a smooth one for Eric and he groaned again. As if in answer, the first moans of the zombies came to them on a light breeze.

"I didn't make the town," Susan said. The gurney kept trying to turn in her direction as she tried to keep up with Floyd's greater strength. They weren't making good progress. The zombies moaned again. Floyd didn't know if it was his imagination, but they sounded closer.

"Suze, push harder," Floyd said. "Come on!"

"I am, I *will*," Susan said gamely. Then the gurney swerved into her again, running over her foot. "Fuck!"

"Watch your language," Mary said. She was sweating and trying to smile as she hitched Ethan higher on her hip and tugged the mute girl along. "Or I'll have to–no, wait! Stay with me!"

The girl had wrenched free and she stood, staring at them.

"Ah, shit," Floyd said, "she's gonna bolt!"

If she did, they wouldn't be able to stop her or save her. She'd be on her own. The gurney slammed into Susan again and she yelped.

The girl hesitated for a second longer, and then she joined Susan at the side of the gurney and began to push. Floyd stared, mouth sprung. Then he got his shit together because the gurney squeaked in his direction. Between the three of them, they got it righted and pushed it up the hill.

The doctor's office was two blocks over from there on a more or less flat road. They made better time, the gurney rattling and chinging at each dip and pebble. Floyd hoped it would hold together.

"See there?" Susan said. "Brick. Solid. No windows. Good, right?"

"Yeah," Floyd said, panting, "it's great. Now push!"

They were at the handicap ramp that led to the front door when the zombie came around the side of the building. She was relatively fresh looking, her clothes not even very disheveled. Another, smaller zombie staggered after her...a little boy of maybe seven. It looked like a mother and child, but that wasn't possible, was it?

Susan froze and the gurney nearly careened off the ramp.

Eric groaned, but even his groans had become weak.

"Susan!" Floyd yelled. The zombies were on Susan's side. He'd never get over there in time. "Your machete!"

Susan pulled the machete from its place on her back, but she did so slowly, as if she were dreaming. Ethan cried out and Mary shushed him. Floyd motioned Mary to go behind him, past the gurney, and to the door.

The zombie woman's moan was very nearly a scream as she fell on Susan. Susan brought her arm up in a short, sharp arc and the woman's head dropped back, mostly severed. Sludgy black blood streaked down her chest and blackened the edge of her knit top. Her mouth continued to move although no more sound came out. Her hands waved blindly and Susan stepped neatly back out of the zombie's reach. She brought the blade down, severing the zombie's spine. It dropped, and its head boinged on the wooden ramp.

Then the boy zombie was to Susan. He was a little more sluggish and his tentative movement gave him a sad, distracted air. Floyd knew, suddenly and for a hundred percent, that Susan would not be able to end the boy zombie. She would be bit instead, while she stood there, rooted in shock, unable to dispatch a child.

Floyd struggled the carbon fiber baton from his belt and lifted the side of the gurney, groaning with the strain. He would dump Eric off and leap right over the gurney; save Susan. Christ, Eric looked like he was dying, anyway. He'd probably–

With a short, sharp movement, almost like a snake's strike, Susan rammed her machete into the kid's temple. The kid staggered and fell. Grew still.

She turned back and took her side of the gurney. She gave Floyd a look of surprise as her eyes went from his upraised weapon to his hand holding the gurney inches off the ground. He dropped it and it rattled, shaking Eric from side to side.

Floyd grinned at Susan. "I was getting ready to help you," he said.

Susan raised her eyebrows at him.

"Door's open," Mary said. "Get him in here."

Susan, the girl, and Floyd pushed Eric the rest of the way up the ramp and into the building. Mary pushed the door closed behind them and snapped the deadbolt into place. It seemed sturdy enough and anyway, it would have to do.

— — —

"Stay here," Mary told them. "Watch Ethan."

She went from the small reception area to the even smaller office behind it. From there, she went into the hallway. There were four doors, two to a side. Each door had a brown plastic chart holder attached to it.

Mary opened the first door and scanned the small space…sink and cabinet, examining table, rolling stool, a poster depicting proper sneeze technique, another showing the circulatory system, and a rack of pamphlets on diabetes, asthma, and avoiding the flu. The other three rooms were similarly outfitted. Standard GP office.

She went back to the waiting room. The mute girl seemed to have lapsed back into her catatonia and sat passively in the row of chairs against the wall. Susan had rolled the receptionist chair around to the waiting room. Her machete lay on the floor next to her. She held Ethan in her lap and Mabel sat before them, panting hopefully. Ethan laughed around a mouthful of corn chips. Floyd was standing at the one, long slit window that gave a view of the front parking lot. The bottom of the window was at least five feet from the floor and the entire opening was only a foot or so high. It was strange looking construction, almost militaristic. Eric was still on the gurney, but he had quieted. His eyes were closed, but his face had dried.

Quick recovery, Mary thought, *for everyone*. They were already getting used to the horrors of this new world. Ethan would grow up in it (she reassured herself), and what kind of person would that make him?

"He's better?" Mary asked, catching Susan's eye and nodding toward Eric.

Susan opened her mouth to answer but Eric spoke before she could. "I'm better for now," he said. He sat up with a groan and Floyd turned from the window to steady him. Eric gave him a smile of thanks. "It's my gall bladder. It'll probably kill me if I don't get it fixed, but at least it will be a long, slow death." He wheezed out a laugh.

"Antibiotics would help reduce the inflammation, if it's infected."

The soft, feminine voice startled Mary and she looked first to Susan, but it was the mute girl who had spoken. It was the first time Mary had heard her.

"My name's Kim," the girl said and her speech was clear but her eyes still distant.

"Are you a nurse, Kim?" Mary asked. "Is that why you were at the surgery center?"

The girl shook her head. "My mom worked there. She was a surgeon." Her gaze flicked to Eric. "She was probably the one who was going to take your gall bladder out."

"She didn't make it?" Mary asked, her tone quiet.

Kim's mouth twisted to the side and her expression was one of someone horribly cheated. "I drove to get her that morning. I was scared. There was no one logged in for school and the house was so quiet. The news was screwy. Everything was messed up...I could just *feel* it."

"Yes," Susan said, "I know what you mean. I couldn't exactly put my finger on it, but I knew something had gone really, really wrong." She hugged Ethan and laid her cheek on the top of his head.

"You pick up on things you're not even *aware* that you're aware of," Eric said. He struggled from the gurney and sank heavily into a chair. He sighed and rubbed his gut again. "In this case, actually, it was the *absence* of things you probably keyed into. No planes flying, and no one, or hardly anyone, on the roads if you went out early enough that day–as I did to get to the center for my surgery. I was on the road before dawn–you didn't see it as well. Later on, it became clearer." He looked at Kim. "No one showed up for work besides your mom and one nurse. I'm sorry, I never put it together. I only knew her as Doctor Morrone. You're correct that she was my surgeon that day. What happened to her?"

Kim dropped her eyes into her lap. For a while, Mary didn't think the girl was going to speak and when she did, it was a mumble. "Same thing that happened to everyone else," she said.

Mary was wrenched with pity but had an instinct that it wouldn't do the girl any good to hand her platitudes and commiseration–she needed to keep busy. "Kim, can you find an antibiotic for Eric? And, I don't know…maybe some aspirin? For the inflammation."

"You don't want aspirin," Kim said, "that might aggravate his stomach. I'll dig up some Ibuprofen. This place is sure to have it." She stood. "The antibiotic might be tougher to find. Hopefully, they have some sample packs."

Floyd had returned to his post at the window. "They're running thick out there," he said. "A lot of them are just kind of peeling off and drifting away, though. Like they've already forgotten they were chasing us." He leaned onto his elbow, one leg cocked behind the other as he stared out. The window didn't even have any kind of softening trim or mullions and it didn't open…it was just a piece of thick glass and it looked retrofitted into the solid brick.

Once again, Mary was reminded of something military like those bunkers out in California, built right into the cliffs on the coast.

Susan must have caught the drift of her thoughts. "Kind of neat, huh?" she said.

Mary glanced back at her. Ethan had turned himself in Susan's lap and his feet dangled perilously close to the machete. "Clean that blade, okay? And stow it," Mary said. Susan looked down as if surprised to see her machete next to her.

"Oh, crap," she said and lifted Ethan clear. She hissed with pain and massaged her right arm with her left hand, grimacing.

"You need some ibuprofen, too," Mary said. She bent to retrieve the blade. "I'll wash this off for you. What's neat?"

Susan looked up, confused, and then her features cleared. "Oh. This building, I meant. It's neat, isn't it? It's part of a small missile base that was dismantled in the mid-seventies. The silos were still around until the nineties."

"Really?" Floyd had turned from the window as she spoke. "I didn't know that."

Susan shrugged and held out a hand to Mary. "I'll clean that," she said. "There's sinks back there, right?"

"That must be why this view is so sweet," Floyd said, turning back to the window. "It's all spread out below us...from this elevation, I can see everything."

"Everything but what's behind us," Mary said. She sat to dig through the bag of provisions. "Not much in here. Ethan, do you want these?" She held out a package of fig bars, but he shook his head and climbed onto a double chair. His eyes were heavy and he seemed half asleep before his head hit the cushion.

"How about you, Floyd," Mary said. "Hungry?"

He glanced over his shoulder. "Not for those nasty things."

"I'll take them," Eric said but Kim, just entering the room, intercepted the package before he could grab them. She scrutinized the label.

"These have too much fat," she said and handed them back to Mary, "you can't have them." She bounced pills in her other hand. "Let me find whatever has the least amount of fat so you can take these pills with something."

"Good luck," Floyd said, "that bag's full of candy."

"I'm not even looking in the bag," Kim said. Her tone implied the 'duh' that she didn't voice.

Mary smiled after the girl. Being helpful certainly agreed with her. Everyone needed a job to do...it gave the mind something to focus on other than the horror of their current situation.

"What do you think, Floyd?" Mary asked. She dug a candy bar from the bag and stood to hand it to him. "Can we leave soon?"

He scanned the room to see who was listening to them. Eric had closed his eyes again and Ethan looked to be solidly asleep. Kim was still hunting whatever she was hunting and Susan hadn't come back yet. He turned his gaze to Mary.

"There's a lot of them," he said. "More and more every minute. Listen, Mary…it's really bad."

Mary searched his eyes, her stomach beginning to turn at the dread she saw forming there. She stood on tiptoe to look out.

The zombies were everywhere.

A kind of herd of them were still on the highway and disappearing in the direction of the Vo-Tech, but there were so many more that must have just wandered away from the main group. They staggered through parking lots and bounced off the sides of buildings. They swayed in small groups and tripped over each other. A handful had wandered into a cart corral at the pharmacy and they just stood there, corralled.

The small front lot of the doctor's building had already acquired two zombies and dozens more shuffled along the streets nearby. Their moans had quieted as their quarry vanished from their minds.

"There must be hundreds of them," Mary said. She couldn't keep the dismay from her voice. For the first time, probably in her life, she felt utterly defeated. "There's no way out of here."

She hoped Floyd would contradict her.

He didn't.

— — —

Mary watched Ethan sleep as her mind turned and turned on itself, formulating and discarding plans. They'd never be able to fight their way out. As soon as they made any kind of noise, the zombies would be on them from all directions. They were trapped in here. There was just no other way to see it.

The room was dark, lit only by one small flashlight. Kim had fashioned a cone of paper around the end, diffusing the light, making the beam more like the softer light of a lantern. She had also found a handful of crackers still in their cellophane packs and given them to Eric along with the ibuprofen and antibiotics. She had removed the gurney cushion and put it on the floor for Eric to sleep on, and now she dozed next to him.

Floyd had stuffed magazines into the window to block the light. He sat next to Mary, shoulder to shoulder. Susan was sitting next to Mabel nearer the little home-fashioned lantern, running her hands over the dog's head, dreamily playing with Mabel's floppy ears.

"I could go on my own," Floyd said. "Go back to the Vo-Tech and get more help."

"Floyd, you wouldn't make it twenty feet," Mary said, "besides, Charlie's probably there already. He'll figure it out. They'll come for us."

"They don't know where we are," Floyd said, his voice low.

"Right, of course," she said and tipped her head into her hands with a sigh. "I knew that."

"Know what I was thinking about?" Susan said. She had stretched out on the floor next to Mabel and her eyes were focused somewhere in the middle distance. Mary was reminded of slumber parties and a feeling of warmth and contentment tempered with a dash of girlish exuberance wafted through her mind like a nostalgic dream.

"What?" Mary asked and without conscious thought, she leaned closer into Floyd's warm bulk. "What were you thinking about?"

"Way back, when Cassie and Dave were still at the Vo-Tech," Susan started and Mary, confused by Susan's words, could have asked for clarification. She opted instead to see if it would resolve itself in context. "There was the one night–remember it, Floyd? When a whole bunch of them wandered into the parking lot." She quieted, still staring, and Mary looked from Susan to Floyd. He shrugged.

"Yeah, I remember, Suze," he said. "We thought the shotgun might have drawn them."

Susan flapped a hand with light impatience. "Yeah, but...not that part, I mean the dog."

"Dog?" Floyd said.

"Yeah, a little terrier. He was following one of the zombies, a little girl one."

"Well, it had probably been her dog," Floyd said, "that's why it was–"

"No, I mean...the things, the zombies...they weren't bothering with the dog. He was jumping and barking, but they didn't react to him at all. It was like they didn't see him."

"Mabel," Mary said, catching on. "We could send Mabel out there...is that what you mean?"

"Yes, exactly," Susan said and sat up. Her eyes were lit with excitement. "We could put a note or something on her collar. Let them know where we are."

"It's a good idea," Mary said, tempering her words. She didn't want Susan to feel too let down. "But Mabel doesn't know to go to the Vo-Tech. She might just run back to the hospital, or more likely, she'll just hang around outside."

Susan smiled like she knew a secret and Mary looked a question at Floyd, but he just raised his hands...whatever Susan was getting at, he hadn't picked it up, either.

"She can follow Turk's trail," Susan said. At the mention of Turk, Mabel's head came off her paws. She tilted her head at Susan as if trying very, very hard to understand the words.

Mary sat back. She shook her head. "We don't know if they came this way. We don't even know whether they made it this far."

"No, but it's worth a try," Susan said. She knelt and began to draw on the thin carpet. "Look...where we are...it's the perfect kind of funnel spot if you were trying to make it to the Vo-Tech. Especially if you were trying to lose the zombies by going through the woods. Charlie would have known that he could only lead them so far before he'd have to break away." She looked up. "Which way had you come before? When you all found Tyler in the car?"

"Through the woods," Mary said, "the highway was just too open."

"Exactly!" Susan said. She put hand over her mouth when Eric snorted and mumbled in his sleep. She waited for him to quiet before she went on, "Exactly," she said, her voice lower. "You came up on the far side of the Vo-Tech. I remember."

"Yes, but I don't know if we went into the woods anywhere near here. I don't recognize it."

"We were kind of busy when we got here," Floyd said. "Is it possible that you came at least somewhere near here but just didn't notice?"

"I don't know. I guess so," Mary said. She didn't have much hope for the plan, though. Rottweilers were not bloodhounds.

"It's worth a try," Susan said. "We can't just sit here and hope for a flood to wash the zombies away."

"No, but that would be *really* nice," Mary said.

"You're damn right it would be," Floyd agreed with fervor.

"Okay, let's try it," Mary said and Susan pumped her fist in the air with a quiet but heartfelt '*yes!*'

"What do we put in the note?" Kim asked, rising. Mary was startled; she hadn't been aware the girl was listening. "Just the address? I saw specimen bottles in the back–plastic with tight lids–they would be perfect."

"Yes," Mary said, "that sounds good, Kim, thanks. As far as the note, I think the address, but our names, too. We'll tell them we're all okay but also let them know about our, um, limitations."

They each glanced over at Eric. He looked bigger lying flat on the gurney cushion, his stomach standing up like a rounded hill. Had it swollen even more just since they'd got here? It was hard to tell in the dicey light.

"Susan, find some paper and a pen. Kim, find some rolled gauze when you get the sample cup," Mary said. She knelt before Mabel and ran her hands over the dog's meaty jowls. Mabel panted and looked at her from warm brown eyes. Mary kissed the dog on her wrinkled brow, the dog's fur soft under her lips. She tilted her forehead against Mabel's. "We're counting on you, girl," she said. She kept her head against the dog's. She didn't want Floyd and Susan to see her cry.

CHAPTER 26

Turk rose from his spot beside the sleeping Charlie and shook himself. He lifted his nose and sniffed the air in the small janitor's closet. Nothing was unusual to him, but nothing was overly familiar, either, except the smell of Charlie. His pack-mate.

He nosed the door open and walked into the dark hallway. He sniffed the air again and looked up the hall, toward the delicious smells of cafeteria and gym clothes. Then he looked down the hall, toward the smells of asphalt, cars, woods, and the other humans–the rotting ones. It wasn't a good smell like rotting groundhog or rotting deer...this was a bad smell, full of disease and sadness. Turk blew out, almost sneezing, ridding his nostrils of it. As the air passed over his sensitive olfactory receptors, he detected something else, very faint but very, very dear.

He turned in the rotting human direction of smells and took a few steps. Charlie hadn't wanted him to come down here, had told Turk to STAY, in fact, but that smell. Something...something. He sniffed again, head up, eyes closed. He took a few more steps toward the doors, as though compelled. There it was again. So faint. So dear.

He glanced back and then moved even closer to the end of the hallway, toward the glass doors. He passed another man who was slumped over in a chair, sleeping.

Turk looked back again, to the half open closet door. If Charlie wasn't going to tell him to STAY, did he have to STAY? Maybe not. He drifted again, eyes closed, nose up, and it was as if the scent eddied him further along.

When he opened his eyes again, he was at the doors. The diseased humans were still out there, he could smell them even if he couldn't see them. He pressed his nose to the crack between the door and the frame and breathed in.

He smelled his pack mate. His best friend. She carried with her an even fainter scent of the boy, THE BOY, his very favorite human of all.

Turk whined and danced his front feet, toenails clicking and ticking on the tiles. A shiver of excitement ran through him. He whined again and pressed his nose to the crack. Breathed in. There she was, even stronger. Turk's tail whipped, shaking his backside. She was coming! She was almost here!

He voiced a strangled little *yark*, doing his best not to bark–Charlie had told him NO BARKING–but his pack mate was so close! So close! He whined and it cycled up and then the sound of his own whining made him even more anxious. He danced again. She was closer...closer!

"Turk!" the man in the chair said and Turk flinched. "Quiet down."

Did Turk have to listen to this man? Maybe, maybe not. He put his nose to the crack, sniffed. She was closer! Almost here!

He barked!

He barked again!

"Turk, dammit!" the man said and his chair clattered as he stood. Turk flinched again but this time, kept his nose to the crack. The man put a hand on Turk's collar, and Turk growled to let the man know that he wasn't leaving the crack, wasn't leaving the scent of his pack mate.

The smell of the man's sudden fear was a satisfaction.

"Charlie! Come get your dog!"

Then Charlie was there, but he didn't yell STAY, and he didn't yell STOP BARKING. He knelt down beside Turk and wrapped an arm around him.

"What is it, you turkey? What's got your wind up, big boy?"

Turk whined and licked Charlie's face. How come Charlie didn't know a pack mate was close? Why were humans so dumb?

Turk whined and stuck his nose to the crack again. *Come on, you nose blind human! Follow my lead! Get your nose up here and–*

Charlie looked out, across the parking lot.

"Hey! It's Mabel!" he said, standing. Happiness sang from Charlie's pores and Turk liked it, he liked it a lot!

Charlie pushed the door open, leaned out as Turk danced and whined at his feet. A low, carrying whistle came from Charlie, a sound so organic it could have been a bird.

Across the lot, where she'd finally lost the scent of Turk and Charlie as the woods transitioned to macadam, Mabel's bowling ball head came up. She'd found them!

She began to run.

CHAPTER 27

"It says they are *completely* surrounded," Trish said. "Paul, listen–"

They were in the cafeteria and a thin light behind the trees indicated that the sun was about to rise. Paul, Trish, Calvin and John sat at a table, while Tyler and Charlie were in the kitchen feeding Mabel and Turk.

Paul shook his head, his face set in stubborn lines. Trish glanced at Calvin, and Calvin understood her slightly raised eyebrows–*see? See what I mean about not making good decisions?*

"Eric is sick. He'll never make it out on foot," John said, pointing to the note on the table. "That's Mary's own words, Paul."

The original elation at discovering that Mary, Floyd, and the others were alive had faded, as they realized the limitations that had been placed upon recovery. Paul's refusal to see any kind of reason was not helping the situation in the least.

"Charlie," John called across the space, "how many would you say were in that hospital parking lot? How many zombies?"

"Oh, um," Charlie said and dropped another chunk of bologna into Mabel's makeshift dog dish, "I dunno. Hundreds? Maybe a thousand?"

"A *thousand*?" Calvin said. "Charlie, do you have any idea how many 'a thousand' people *is*?"

"It's not impossible, I'm afraid," Trish said. "We had close to eight hundred beds. Not that they were all full, of course, but tack on doctors, nurses, aids, janitorial, security, admin…plus the ER was jammed. They were calling in everyone they could."

"Jesus Christ," Calvin said. He rubbed his temples and wondered if there was any extra-strength anything in any of the nursing classrooms. "I know the building they're in. It's part of an old Nike missile base from the seventies. It's a solid building, all brick, so they should at least be safe."

"We can't hike to them. It's just not feasible if that many zombies followed them from the hospital," Trish said. She stood from the table and walked to the window. "We could try to drive, but we'd have to stay on the road. If we came upon a big group, we'd be sunk." Her voice took on a bitterly amused air. "Gee whiz...I guess all we really need is a tank."

A tank.

"Holy shit." Calvin stood, his chair clattering away behind him. "We might have one."

"What are you talking about?" John asked, but Calvin ignored him as he turned to find Tyler.

"Tyler! Do you remember what they did in Mr. Yeung's class?"

"Last year's senior project," Tyler said and grinned. He tossed the bag he'd been eating from onto the counter and wiped his hands on his jeans. "The Monster Masher."

"Yeah...the Monster Masher," Calvin said. Tyler and Calvin started laughing as the others looked on in confusion. Even the dogs sat back on their haunches with twin looks of perplexity.

After catching his breath, Calvin led everyone to the largest of the auto body shops.

The truck stood in the middle of the floor, garish in orange and black, jagged white teeth painted across the pugnacious grill. A 1999 Stewart & Stevenson M-1078; an army cargo truck, flat-faced, beefy, and very tall. Across each cab door, one of the more talented spray painters had written out 'Monster Masher' in lurid green balloon letters.

"It's from an old song," Calvin said. "One of the ones they used to play before the holidays were outlawed."

"They weren't *outlawed*, exactly, geez," John said. "They were only taken off the government calendars. I swear, the religious nuts acted like–"

"Not the time," Trish said and put her hand up in a stop gesture. "We have more important things going on. Let's stay focused here."

"Will it run?" Charlie asked. He gazed doubtfully at the array of machine parts scattered across the room.

"Yes," Calvin said, "I'm pretty sure." He scouted the bed of the truck. It had metal slatted sides but was otherwise open. He wished that Susan were here to weld some metal sheets or something onto it, but the floor of the bed was high, at least. High enough to keep zombies out.

John pulled himself onto the running board at the driver's window and peered in. He turned to the others, his mouth in a twist of discouragement. "Anyone know how to drive a stick?"

"What's a stick?" Trish asked, blank-faced. Charlie and Tyler looked equally as blank and Calvin's heart sank. He had at least *heard* of a stick shift, but he sure as hell didn't know how to drive one.

"I'll drive," Paul said. "I grew up on a farm. A little organic outfit over in Pennsylvania. All the equipment had manual transmissions."

"Okay, Paul's the driver," Calvin said. "Who else is going?"

Charlie raised his hand. "I'm up for that. I want to ride in the truck!"

"Yeah...me too," John said, sounding a little distracted as he fished through tools on a long workbench. He hefted a screwdriver that was at least two feet long. "There's lots here we can use for weapons. I'll pile them in the back."

"I'm going, too," Tyler said. His shoulders had sunk and his hands were shoved deep into his pockets, but he glanced at Charlie with an almost worshipful air. Charlie lifted his fist to Tyler and Tyler looked at it, confused.

"Bump it," Charlie said, grinning.

"Oh!" Tyler said and yanked his hand free of his pocket. He bumped his fist to Charlie's. "Cool!"

"It's an old school thing," Charlie said, "my gramps taught me."

Calvin watched Trish to see if she was going to volunteer, too. She had gone to where John sorted tools but she hadn't said anything as she began to pull useful looking ones loose and set them aside.

"I'll stay back with Trish," he said and tried to keep any defensiveness from his tone. "Two is better than one if something goes wrong here. We'll keep it safe for if...I mean, *when*...you come back."

John turned and gave him a long, strange look.

"There's some big knives in culinary," Calvin said, his voice a shade too bright. He backed out of the shop. "I'll go grab them up."

— — —

The truck growled and rocked from side to side as Paul piloted it slowly out the garage door. He was glad he had buckled in and hoped the guys in the bed had braced themselves. From the ground, Calvin gave him a wave and then turned and scanned the back lot, his hand on a button that would close the door. Trish stood on the other side of the truck, one of the big screwdrivers ready in her fist. She said something to the guys in the back, but Paul couldn't make it out over the sound of the engine. He waved to her, but she didn't see him.

Once he was clear, he looked in his side mirror in time to see Calvin and Trish disappear behind the door as it rolled into place. It made him feel lonely and scared, as if they were shutting that door against him.

He wished John or even Charlie was sitting in the cab, but they had decided as a group that it would be better if the guys had the freedom of the bed. In some ways–even though he was behind glass and metal–Paul was in the more vulnerable spot. The cab sat much lower and only had the two exits, and there was no hood to this vehicle, just a flat front. He felt kind of like he was sitting in a fishbowl.

He mashed the clutch and dropped the gear into second. The back of the building was quiet, no movement. The solar field between the parking lot and the woods caught the first morning light and glittered it back into Paul's eyes. It felt weird to be out in a truck so early in the morning...it had been literally years since he'd done it. Without thought, he reached to pull the brim of his cap down and then, with a shock, remembered he hadn't worn a cap like that since he'd been seventeen and running the thresher.

He rounded the building and saw the first zombie. A young man, clothing torn and very disheveled, stared up at the building, head tilted at a grotesque angle. Paul dropped the truck back into first, slowing it as it hitched and burped, almost stalling.

Sounds of dismay came from the back but Paul ignored them, concentrating. He didn't want to hit any of the zombies at any kind of speed, not unless he absolutely had to. The windshield before him was too vulnerable.

The zombie turned toward the sound of the truck. Its head was half off, sliced at the side of its neck, its cheek resting solidly on its shoulder. As Paul drove past it, it reached for the truck, but stumbled, and its head rolled forward and fell, rocking side to side against its chest.

Paul shook his head and pushed the shift back into second, picking up speed as they started down the driveway to the highway. The walking corpses were dotted here and there, some in the woods, some in the parking lot. As the truck rolled past them, they turned to track it with their blank eyes, like sheltered country folk seeing newfangled technology for the first time.

He dropped it into first and drifted onto the highway, big tires screeching lightly. He clipped a Prius, sending it into a Mazda. This time, the sounds from the bed seemed like shouts of triumph as the two small cars embraced in a metal-crunch kiss.

Paul started to smile as he put the truck into second.

If everything went well, he'd be to Mary in less than fifteen minutes.

CHAPTER 28

"I hear something," Floyd said. He was at the window and had been all night. Susan scrambled up. She was too short to see out, so she turned the back of a chair to the wall and climbed onto it.

"What do you hear?" Mary asked, her voice groggy. She pushed herself into a seated position, pulling Ethan up to her shoulder. "Wake up, Ethan. Wake up, sweetheart."

"Is it a truck? I think I hear it, too," Kim said. Her hand went to Eric's forehead and she laid her wrist across his brow. "He's cooler. The antibiotic is helping."

Susan eyed Eric's distended belly with reservation.

Ethan said, "Where's Mabel?" his little boy's voice croaky and out of sorts, on the verge of tears.

"Shhh, shh, baby," Mary said and rocked him. "Mabel went to find Turk. Remember I told you?" Mary looked up at Susan, anxiety drawing her brows together. "Do you see anything?"

Susan turned to look. She saw lots and lots of zombies. Everywhere her eyes lit, zombies. She felt Floyd watching her and turned, expecting to see her own fear reflected in his face, but he met her gaze with a wide, goofy grin.

"What the hell's funny?" she asked.

"They brought the Monster Masher," he said, "didn't you see it?"

At first, his words meant nothing to her. What the fuck was he talking about? Then it hit her and she looked again.

Three long blocks away, appearing and disappearing behind buildings, was the orange and black monstrosity that last year's senior shop class had built and then given to Mr. Yeung as a gift. The Monster Masher, an army truck conversion.

"Holy shit," she breathed, "I forgot all about that thing!"

"What is it?" Mary asked. "What do you see?"

Instead of answering, Susan jumped down from the chair. "They're coming for us," she said. "Get everything together. Eric, are you awake? Kim...can you see if he can get up? We have to–"

Mary stood, still cradling Ethan. "They're here? They've found us?"

"Yes!" Susan said and laughed. She ran both hands over her hair, mussing it into wild peaks. "They're here, they're here!"

"Oh...shit," Floyd said. There was no longer any excitement in his voice.

Susan scrambled onto the chair again. Looked out. "What? What do you–"

Then she saw it, too. She hadn't noticed the first time because the truck had been in and out behind buildings. Now it had turned onto their road and she could see it clearly. A parade of zombies followed the truck, hundreds of them. The truck was picking them up like seagulls around a fishing boat.

"We'll never make it out the door," Floyd said. "Even if they pull right up next to the building...there's too many zombies out there. We're fucked."

"We could go out the window," Mary said, "if they pulled right up to it."

"A couple of us could," Floyd said. "Ethan and Kim, maybe Susan. No way would you or I squeeze through there. Eric, definitely not."

"We have to do something," Mary said. "We have to–"

Floyd shook his head and raised his hands, palms up. "We have to what? What the hell can we do?"

"Something! *Some*thing!" Mary said. Ethan had begun to cry in her arms. She looked at him, her eyes filled with terror. She looked back to Floyd. "Floyd, please...we have to *do* something!"

Floyd growled like a trapped lion, and dragged his hands through his beard.

"Okay!" he said, his voice rough with anger and frustration. He closed his eyes. "Okay...I'm going out there." He took a breath, filling his chest. Took another. Calmed. "I'll try and lead some of them away. You make sure–"

"I don't think we have that option," Susan said, her voice flat. Outside, the truck was still coming. It had left the road and it bounced and bounded over medians and through parking lots. Tyler, Charlie, and John were in the bed, standing behind the cab, waving like madmen. Paul was at the wheel, his face set and grim. Zombies fell before them, some shunted violently aside, others pulled under and crushed by the massive tire treads. Now she could hear the three men, yelling as they waved. Paul blared the air horn.

Susan turned to look at Mary and Floyd. "I think they're gonna make their own window," she said and jumped from the chair. "A *really* big one."

— — —

Paul hoped they'd heard and understood. *Get them back, Mary, get them safe. Keep Ethan safe. I'm coming for you, my love. I'm coming for both of you.*

The guys pounded on the roof of the cab, shouting, egging him on. The truck hit a zombie and its head exploded against the bumper, spraying brain and gelatinous black sludge across the windshield. Paul hit the wipers, smearing the sludge into a crescent of gore.

He blared the horn.

"*I'm coming for you, Mary!*" he yelled and banged the steering wheel as if keeping time to hard driving country music. They hit another zombie. Another. There were too many to avoid and the truck bounced over each one that was dragged under. With each bounce, the cheers from the back grew louder, almost savage.

A wild exuberance burst into Paul's mind like bright, bright light and it pushed out the last dregs of fear. Farming had never been like this!

Almost there, Mary...I'm almost there!

— — —

"Help me!" Kim yelled, "Help me get him back!" Eric was only half-aware, groggily disoriented. Kim shoved at him, but she was too small to move the man.

Mary started toward Kim, Ethan bouncing and crying on her hip, but Susan grabbed Mary's shoulders and shook them. "Get in the hallway! I'll help Kim! Just go!"

The air horn blared again as if to underline Susan's words. Mary turned sharply and disappeared down the hallway.

Susan said to Kim, "Get back! Get yourself down the hall!" The truck engine was loud, louder. Now Susan could hear the meaty, muffled whump, whump of zombies being hit. The truck was seconds away.

Kim stared at Susan, open mouthed with shock and indecision. Susan pulled the girl up, shoved her. "Go! Follow Mary!"

Without waiting to see if Kim listened, Susan turned back to Eric. Floyd was already there, dragging the big man by the shoulders. The air horn blared, seemingly right in Susan' ear. She grabbed Eric's legs. He screamed as they heaved him up. Floyd stumbled and regained his footing. His eyes were wide and white with alarm. Susan pushed, screaming, "Go, Floyd, go, go, GO!"

Behind her, the corner of the building burst inward.

Susan screamed again, a raging, angry, primal wail of terror. She pushed as Floyd collapsed back, pulling Eric with him. Susan fell onto Eric, crashing into his gut, and he screamed in pain. She screamed right along with him.

Bricks flew and the window crunched, caving inward. The truck engine roared and morning light filled the space. The flat front of the truck tore half the wall away, its windshield cracking. One tire, almost as tall as Susan, ground waiting room chairs under its treads, turning them into kindling.

The engine chugged, coughed, and then stalled.

Everything went quiet.

– – –

Paul opened the driver's side door and stepped down into the rubble. A brick fell from the jagged edge of the wall. Charlie jumped into the waiting room from the bed of the truck. "I'm back!" he yelled, with a grin. The grin faded.

"Guys?"

"You in here?"

Paul's heart seemed to stop and he held his breath. The waiting room was a ruin, bricks and glass, paper and splinters of wood everywhere, but no bodies.

"Mary!" he yelled. There was one doorway leading off the room. It was too dark to see down it. He stumbled across the bricks, nearly turning an ankle. "Mary! Are you back there?"

"Paul!" Mary called out and Paul heaved in a relieved breath. She called to him again, "Paul, we're back here!"

Ethan said "Daddy!" and Paul's heart squeezed so hard he thought he might die. He got to the opening. Susan popped up, her face a smear of brick dust and sweat. He pulled her up, and then, for him, time slowed down.

"Get in the truck, go," he said. He passed her off to Charlie. He was surprised at how calm his voice was and how calm he felt. Everything hung as if in stasis, serene and tranquil.

It would not last.

"Eric..." Susan said, but Paul was already pulling him up, Floyd pushing from behind. Eric groaned and stood, gasping.

"Charlie, put Eric in the cab of the truck; he won't be able to climb in the back," Paul said and the mute girl from the surgery center appeared behind Floyd. "Floyd, help her get in the truck, too. Hurry."

Outside the building, the zombie roar and moan increased steadily, like someone slowly turning up the volume on a radio station. John yelled something unintelligible. Tyler called for them to *hurry, please fucking hurry, we're surrounded!*

"Mary..." Paul said as his wife and son emerged from the dark. They were disheveled but unharmed. He pulled them close, closed his eyes for a second and breathed them in. "Mary."

"Paul..."

"Come on!" Floyd yelled. "We're being overrun! Let's get out of here!" and for Paul, time sped back up.

Mary shoved Ethan into his arms. "Put him in the cab with you," she said. "I'll help the others." Before he could say anything she had spun away to clamber through the rubble. Floyd reached down from the bed of the truck and she grasped his hand, yanked herself up and over the metal slats.

Paul squeezed Ethan tighter, then turned and slid him into the cab, pushing him over next to Eric. Even though Eric's eyes were still closed and his face dripped with sweat, the big man put an arm out, drew Ethan close to his side. "Hang onto me, son. It's gonna get bumpy." Ethan gripped Eric's arm, his eyes round with terrible fear. He buried his face in Eric's side.

Paul jumped in, slammed the door behind him.

He turned the key.

The engine didn't start.

– – –

"Why aren't we moving?" Susan yelled. She punched her machete between the slats, skewering a zombie in the eye. Another climbed up behind it, reaching for her. She screamed as she tried to yank her machete free. John reached across and chopped off the reaching zombie's hand. Tyler rammed a long screwdriver into its temple and it fell. Kim handed Tyler another knife and then spun to jam a broom handle between the slats and pushed another zombie off.

Floyd kicked a zombie away from the back, kicked again as another took the first one's place. He jammed a piece or rebar straight down, burying it in the top of a zombie's head with a crunch of bone. "Mary!" he yelled, "More rebar!"

She tossed him a three-foot piece and he caught it neatly, turned it, and skewered another zombie in the temple. Beside him, Charlie kicked another away. He brought the blunt end of an ax down onto the head of another, crushing its skull. Brains flew out, shards of bone. Mary tossed Floyd another rebar, turned, and kicked a zombie off the side of the truck.

The zombies were frenzied, in their own semi-sluggish way, and as unrelenting as a swarm of army ants. The truck would soon be overrun.

Below them, the engine finally started and Floyd bellowed with something like relief as he hammered the forehead of a zombie. Its ocular cavity crunched like a coconut and the eye flew past Floyd's face, the iris still contracting. He bellowed again and beside him, Charlie whooped a war cry.

The truck jerked. The engine roared, screamed. The truck jerked again but gained no ground.

"We're stuck!" Susan said. "We're fucking stuck on something!"

"Just hold on!" Mary yelled. She grabbed a slat with one hand, pushed a zombie back with the other. "Hold on, it's gonna–"

The truck bucked hard and jumped...then it began to roll out of the building. Bricks rained down, dust flew up in a cloud. Susan grabbed the side, raised her machete and whooped in triumph. Zombies began to fall off as the truck picked up speed. John faced Susan, grinning. "We're gonna make it!" The truck jerked into second gear and he grabbed the side to steady himself. "We're okay!" he yelled to Susan, his face alight with savage joy.

A zombie grabbed John's wrist, yanked itself up. Bit John's forearm.

Susan stared with horror, frozen. John tried to pull his arm back but the zombie gripped harder, began to gnaw. Susan screamed. Mary shoved her aside, planted an ax in the zombie's head. It tumbled down the side of the truck and hit the ground like a sack of wet laundry. The back wheels rolled over it.

Then they were clear, the zombies too lethargic to keep up with even the slow moving Monster Masher. John stared at his arm, his mouth bent down in a bow of shock. He held it out to Mary. "I got bit," he said. It was barely a whisper but they all heard it. Floyd and Charlie turned to him. Tyler turned away with his hand over his mouth.

"Ah shit," Floyd said and it was a mournful sound, drawn out with unimaginable disappointment. "Jesus Christ." He sat abruptly, the hammer clattering from his hand. "I really thought–"

Mary stared helplessly at John.

Susan sat down next to Floyd. She huddled against him. "I thought so, too," she said. "I really thought we were home free." He laid an arm across her shoulders. She was glad of the weight pinning her to the truck, because, otherwise, she thought she might float away.

Mary moved some tools, guided John down. His eyes never left hers. "Mary?" he said.

"It's okay," she said. "Just take it easy."

Charlie kneeled at John's side but addressed Mary. "What can we do for him?" he asked in a low voice. She shook her head. Tried to smile.

Tyler leaned against the back of the cab and stared ahead. The wind blew the hair from his forehead. Kim leaned against the cab next to him, her eyes far away.

They swayed as the truck bounced over a curb and pulled onto the highway. The zombies–their ranks thinned–had fallen behind. There would be plenty of time to get into the Vo-Tech.

Susan really had thought they would be okay. Hadn't they come through the worst of it? Didn't they deserve a win? She pushed herself tighter to Floyd, but turned her head to watch the scenery pass by. She had known this town, had, in fact, lived here her whole life, but she didn't know it anymore.

She didn't know anything, it seemed.

Almost to the school, the truck slowed and then stopped. Susan lifted her head from Floyd's shoulder. "Why are we stopping?"

"I don't know," he said. He disentangled himself and stood.

The driver's side door opened and Paul jumped down. He slammed the door behind him and then looked up at Mary where she stood in the bed. He shook his head and continued around to the passenger side door. He opened it and reached in.

He pulled, tumbling Eric out. The big man hit the pavement with a thud.

"Paul?" Floyd said. "What the hell are you–"

"He's dead," Mary said. Her voice was flat. "Eric's dead."

Paul pushed the door closed. He looked up at them, his expression unreadable in the gray morning light. He started back around the cab.

"Wait!" Mary said. She clambered up the side and over, grabbing Charlie's hand to help steady her. She jumped to the ground and looked back up. Reached her hand to Floyd. "Hand me some rebar, Floyd," she said. He did as she asked.

She knelt next to Eric and ran a hand over his forehead, smoothing the lines. She smiled, kissed her fingertips, and placed them on his cheek. Then she put the rebar to his temple and pushed, punching it home.

From the truck bed, John peered through the slots with dread fascination.

CHAPTER 29

WELCOME! TO SAFE HAVEN!
Are you a SURVIVOR? Are you TIRED of going it alone?
!!!! JOIN US !!!!
Grab your weapons, know how, and remaining family and friends
and JOIN US at the BURLCO VO TECH ON ROUTE 73 IN
MARLTON, NEW JERSEY! There's safety in numbers, so band
together with us and we'll work as a team to get our country back
on its feet!
YOUR FUTURE DEPENDS ON IT!
We're easily accessible via FOUR major highways: 70, 73, 30,
295, and don't forget the New Jersey Turnpike. To access the
building, ring the bell as the back door marked 'VISITORS' and
PLEASE wait to be buzzed in.

— — —

"What the hell is this?" Mary asked and Trish's face clouded. She snatched the paper from Mary's hand.

"Calvin and I were working on it while you guys were out," she said. She looked at the paper with a quizzical tilt to her head as though she couldn't understand what Mary had failed to understand about it.

"*Out?*" Mary said and looked at Floyd with raised eyebrows. Her voice held a shade of incredulity. She reached past Trish to accept Ethan as Paul lifted him from the truck. Susan helped John down and walked him to a shop stool with Charlie right behind them. Tyler wandered to the back of the shop, desultorily looking over the tools hung on the shelves, hands jammed deep in his pockets. Floyd watched him and thought, *he's like a cat—he wants to be with us, but just not too with us.*

Kim jumped from the truck and then sat, Indian-style, and began to cry. Floyd was proud of her for waiting. She had a lot of potential, that one.

Trish looked up at the sound of Kim's sobs. She blinked in the girl's direction, and then looked at her paper again. "Is it the mention of the highways?" she asked, looking up at Mary. "Is that part too confusing, like, we've given just way too many options?"

Mary hitched Ethan higher on her shoulder, gave Trish a long, long look, then turned away.

"Are Mabel and Turk in the cafeteria?" she asked Calvin, who stood near the shop entrance. He nodded without speaking and dropped his eyes.

"I'm going to lay him down with the dogs and then I'll be back," Mary said and began to walk out.

"Hold up," Paul said, jogging to catch up with his wife. She waited for him, her cheek on the top of Ethan's head. Ethan sucked his thumb and watched the others with a glassy, wide-eyed stare as though in shock.

"Geez," Trish said. She shook her head at Calvin like, *what the heck's wrong with these people?*

"Here, let me see it," Floyd said. His curiosity had gotten the better of him, but before he dropped his eyes to the paper, he looked at the truck, which still dripped gore and had a spider web of cracks on the windshield. Then at John, who was obviously in an incredible amount of distress…not to mention the fact that Eric clearly hadn't made it back with them…what could Trish find so important that it seemed to override the fact that they had just returned from a short trip through hell?

He dropped his eyes to the paper, read it, and handed it back to her.

"It's good, right?" she asked him with a small, self-satisfied smile. "You understand it, don't you, Floyd? There will be other survivors. It's really important that we get as many people together as we can." She looked at the paper again, considering. "So, of course, when we do, it's going to be even more important that we have rules in place. Codes of conduct. Governances. That sort of thing."

Floyd tugged at his blond beard as if contemplating her words. Kim had gotten herself under control. John had grown very quiet. Susan still had a hand on his shoulder as she spoke into his ear, but her other hand was behind her back, tight to her monstrously beautiful homemade machete. Charlie knelt on the other side of John. A short piece of rebar jutted from his back pocket.

Tyler was still contemplating the tool wall.

"Trish," Floyd asked, "what did you do? Before?"

"Oh, I was hospital admin," she said. Her eyes had gone back to the paper and they traced back and forth, greedily eating up the words. "I was the head of HR."

"Huh," Floyd said, as if he found that interesting. He *did* find it interesting, and also, damned funny. "Well, I think it's okay," he said and she looked up with a smile. "The only thing I would suggest," he said and her smile dimmed, but he went on, "is we should call ourselves something catchy…something that will really speak to people."

"Okay, sure," she said and her tone said, *as if anything could be better!* "What do you think we should call ourselves?"

"How about we go with Zombie, Inc.," he said. He winked at her. "We'll be the first start up in the new world."

Her face suffused with an entrepreneurial light and from his spot at the doorway, Calvin gave Floyd a look of seething disgust. Trish might not know that Floyd was making fun of her, but Calvin sure knew it.

Floyd tipped him a wink, too.

Then he joined Susan and Charlie as John began to slump over.

CHAPTER 30

She cried out, throwing her head back. Then she clenched, clamped down, and pushed. She screamed again. Her eyes, savage and full of miserable determination, met his. "You have to save the baby!"

"No! I'm not leaving you, Annie!"

Dry air baked the man's throat, and he swallowed against a cough. Annie groaned and clenched. She cried out again. A red-slicked, slimy bundle slid from her into the man's hands and then came a new sound, a mewling cry. He looked at the baby as if unsure of how she had got there. She opened her mouth and mewed again, her little hands clenched and waving.

"Please," Annie said. Her voice was barely a breath, exhausted, her eyes closed. Yellow and orange light leaped and flicked as the fire grew around them. She reached for his hand. "Save the baby, please...save the baby."

"I'm going to save *you*, Annie," the man said. His voice caught over a sob. How had this happened? The world had changed overnight into a hell populated with the walking dead. He swallowed back another sob as Annie's face clenched in pain. "I'm going to save you."

He laid the hot, slippery bundle on his wife's stomach. He scanned the beam across her shoulder and arm that held her pinned to the floor.

Do something! Do something about her arm! His mind ranted nonsensically. A wave of unreality washed over him and he swept a hand in front of his face as if to bat the sensation away. Do? What can I do?

Amputation...cut it off! Get her OUT of here!

His eyes went to Annie's as if checking to make sure she hadn't overheard the thought. Her eyes were red-rimmed slits, filled with tears. Her free arm, the arm with the fresh bite, had gone to the baby. Her fingers danced shakily over her daughter's head, brushing the thin hair into a gore-soaked little clump.

Annie smiled and blood glowed darkly in her teeth. "It's a girl, Carl," she said. "We have a little girl. Sarah...Sarah, remember? We're going to call her..."

"Annie, save your strength," he said, his hands running over his wife's hot skin. He didn't, *couldn't*, look at the baby. "You have to save your strength for when...for when we get out of here...please, Annie. Please." He wiped viciously at the tears on his cheeks.

She was dying. He couldn't stop it, couldn't help her.

But he had to. He had to stop it from happening. He couldn't *do* this, *any* of this, without her.

She sighed and looked at him from calm, almost sleepy, eyes. Her fingers had found the baby's ear and she traced the delicate curve. She took in a short breath and sighed again, the breath going out and out. Her hand sagged away from the baby. More blood pooled beneath her, under her legs. A trill of it ran from the corner of her mouth.

It was red at first, and then it blackened, became thick. The firelight jittered in her open, glazing eyes as if trying to burn life back into them.

"Annie?" He ran a hand down her cheek. "Annie? Can you hear me? Can you hear me?"

As if in answer to his question, the baby mewled, a tiny, helpless sound. Horrified, he tore his gaze from Annie's dead but grotesquely animated eyes and gaped at the baby. She struggled on Annie's belly, the umbilical cord shining and slimed with clots of blood. It had blackened where it came from Annie's body. The black was headed up the cord, toward the struggling infant. Annie's baby. His baby.

Sarah.

He hated her.

Oh, how he hated this baby that had caused them to hole up in this house. Had caused them to be slowed down. Had caused Annie to die.

He reached for her and–

–stumbled out of the small, burning house that wasn't his in a town he didn't know. He was far too far from home. Her clenched his hands into fists; blood squeezed between his white fingers. A group of three people ran past without seeing him. He dropped to his knees and turned his eyes to the black bowl of the night sky. He unclenched his hands, and let them fall to his sides. There was a full moon. Smoke ran across it in rivulets, turned it gray. Everything turned gray.

Then it went black.

07.2037 (ten years later)
EPILOGUE

He hitched the machete higher on his shoulder and tapped the gun on his hip. Neither weapon had gone anywhere–why would they have? He was a careful man, almost superstitiously so.

"Is that it?" he asked the younger man next to him. They were on their bellies, shoulder to shoulder on the flat roof of a CVS, staring at a tall concrete block wall. The wall looked much, much newer that the buildings that sat inside it.

"I guess," the younger man said. He lifted a pair of binoculars to his eyes. "It's hard to tell for sure, but that wall looks…oh, hey! Look at that!" He laughed and lowered the binocs.

"What? What did you see?" The first man asked but the second kept laughing. "Chris, for Christ's sake, what the fuck do you see?"

Chris handed him the binoculars. "Chill out, Carl," he said, still laughing. "Look…look further down…" the laughter kept bubbling out of him, "…down past that burned up hotel…see it? You see the…the gate?"

Carl gave Chris a look of disgust, then located the burned husk of the hotel and raised the binoculars. Just past the hotel parking lot, where the wall snaked over a cross street, a large gate stood closed and forbidding. At the side of the gate stood a zombie, tethered to the wall by its neck via a very short length of chain. It walked and walked and walked. The ground beneath its feet had worn down–like the area around an outside dog's doghouse. Next to the zombie, a sign had been erected. It read:

ZOMBIE, INC.
ALL ARE WELCOME!
Please Ring The Bell And Face The Camera To Be Buzzed In*
(*DON'T RING THE BELL MORE THAN ONCE. PREPARE TO DISARM. HAVE ID READY IF AVAILABLE. ALL VISITORS WILL BE SEARCHED. YOU WILL BE GIVEN A VISITOR'S BADGE AND LANYARD. PLEASE WEAR THEM AT ALL TIMES WHILE ON ZI PREMISES. ALL VISITORS MUST REMAIN WITHIN THE GROUP. VISITORS FOUND WANDERING IN RESTRICTED AREAS WILL BE REMOVED.)

A worm of misgiving inched into Carl's mind, but he'd come all the way back here from Florida to find this place. He shouldn't let a funky sign put him off, right?

"You're goddamned right," he said, his voice low and vehement and Chris gave him a careful look.

"You okay, Carl?"

"Yeah, sure," Carl said. He lowered the binoculars and handed them to Chris. "Let's go ring that bell."

They made their way carefully off the roof and into the CVS and Carl, out of habit, scanned the decimated shelves. Ten years after the apocalypse, there was nothing left. It had made the trip back up from Florida much harder than the trip he'd made down there nine years ago. Outside, the streets were quiet, but Carl was careful to keep his eyes open, noting every landmark. He was a methodical man. Being so had kept him alive.

Once they got to the gate, it was difficult to stand next to the tethered zombie and not kill it. Everything in Carl urged him to chop the thing's head off with his machete. It reached for him and Chris but it didn't moan–its throat had been removed.

"Man, I really want to shoot it," Chris said. Carl didn't say anything. He didn't know Chris very well. They'd only teamed up in Delaware when they'd found they had this common goal. He pushed the small red button under the sign marked: BELL, RING ONCE, ONLY.

After a short time, a buzzer sounded and something on the gate clicked and it opened inward by a quarter of an inch. Carl pushed it the rest of the way in to find they were in a kind of concrete vestibule. A guy stood there, a biker-type with a beard and leathers. He held a machete in one hand and a gun in the other.

"Close it up, Abby," he said and Carl did so, but not without irritation.

"My name's Carl and this is–"

"Don't tell me, Abby," the biker said. He was young, just a kid, really, and the beard was more wishful thinking than anything else. "You'll tell yer super who y'are. I don't give a good, clean shit about it."

Another gate opened behind the biker and *another* biker stood there. This one was a little older with dark curly hair and no beard.

Was this just some kind of biker compound? That's not how Carl had heard it, but rumors were hard to trust. He put a hand on his gun.

The darker biker saw the movement and he laughed, raucously. "Come through, Abby," he said and motioned them forward. "Drop yer weapons before you, do; Floyd here should'a said." He kicked the younger biker on the calf, nearly collapsing his leg, and laughed again. "Doosh."

"Yer a doosh, Floyd," the younger biker said and the older one hawked a loogie and spit at his feet. Carl and Chris jumped back as the younger biker crouched and leapt into the older biker's mid-section. They wrestled and Carl drew his gun, but who the fuck was he supposed to shoot?

The bikers were laughing. Carl relaxed his arm and let the gun sag. They were laughing? What was going on in this crazy place? The rumors Carl heard said that this was some kind of high tech company compound where they made zombie defense systems, and gave employees a safe place to live. Carl just wanted a job...he didn't want to have to deal with crazies.

"What the fuck is wrong with these guys?" Chris said in his ear and Carl shook his head. He really didn't know.

As abruptly as it had started, the wrestling ended and the bikers stood, pounding each other on the shoulders.

"Yer a good one, Floyd," the younger biker said and Carl frowned in confusion. Hadn't the older one called the younger one 'Floyd'? Why was–

"Floyd!"

Carl turned in alarm at the whip crack voice. A woman stood at the inside gate with a clipboard. She was glaring at the bikers. "Enough! This is counter-productive!"

The bikers gazed to her with identical looks of chagrin, but even Carl could see that mischievousness danced in their eyes. They were unbowed.

"Sorry, Ahb–" the younger biker started but the older one smacked him across the back of the head. Hard.

He grinned at the clipboard woman and the grin was wide, showing all his top teeth. "Sorry, *Trisha*," he said and the woman's cheeks flared a dull red.

"It's Trish, as you well know, Floyd," she said. Her voice was tightly controlled. She turned to rake Carl and Chris with flinty eyes. "Have you disarmed them?"

"We're about it right this second," the older biker said, "if you'd let us take care of it, Trisha." His toothy grin widened.

The woman gave him a look that could have wilted a cactus. Then she turned and walked away.

"Drop your stuff here, Abby," the older biker said, "Floyd'll watch it fer ya."

"So, wait," Carl said, "which one of you is Floyd?"

The bikers laughed again and then, mystifyingly, the younger one teared up.

"Aww, Floyd," the older one said with surprising gentleness and put a rough hand on the younger's neck. "It'll be okay, honey; e's happier where e's at. Up there, the zombies is all gone and Floyd just rides and rides and rides that hog on safe roads and 'e never crashes."

The younger biker wiped the tears away and tried to smile.

Whatever was going on here was well beyond Carl's understanding and he had misgivings about the lady with the clipboard. But beyond her, he had glimpsed a tallish building with lots of people going into it. More people than he'd seen in one place in a long time. The grass was mowed, the parking lot neat. It looked almost like the world before the apocalypse. Before he'd lost Annie.

He gazed at the Floyd's and he could see that there was genuine care between these men. That, too, was hard to come by in this world. He knew because he had been on his own for a very long time.

Carl disarmed and walked through the gate.

−The End−

CHECK OUT OTHER GREAT ZOMBIE NOVELS

VACCINATION
by Phillip Tomasso

What if the H7N9 vaccination wasn't just a preventative measure against swine flu?

It seemed like the flu came out of nowhere and yet, in no time at all the government manufactured a vaccination. Were lab workers diligent, or could the virus itself have been man-made? Chase McKinney works as a dispatcher at 9-1-1. Taking emergency calls, it becomes immediately obvious that the entire city is infected with the walking dead. His first goal is to reach and save his two children.

Could the walls built by the U.S.A. to keep out illegal aliens, and the fact the Mexican government could not afford to vaccinate their citizens against the flu, make the southern border the only plausible destination for safety?

ZOMBIE, INC
by Chris Dougherty

"WELCOME! To Zombie, Inc. The United Five State Republic's leading manufacturer of zombie defense systems! In business since 2027, Zombie, Inc. puts YOU first. YOUR safety is our MAIN GOAL! Our many home defense options - from Ze Fence® to Ze Popper® to Ze Shed® - fit every need and every budget. Use Scan Code "TELL ME MORE!" for your FREE, in-home*, no obligation consultation! *Schedule your appointment with the confidence that you will NEVER HAVE TO LEAVE YOUR HOME! It isn't safe out there and we know it better than most! Our sales staff is FULLY TRAINED to handle any and all adversarial encounters with the living and the undead". Twenty-five years after the deadly plague, the United Five State Republic's most successful company, Zombie, Inc., is in trouble. Will a simple case of dwindling supply and lessening demand be the end of them or will Zombie, Inc. find a way, however unpalatable, to survive?

CHECK OUT OTHER GREAT ZOMBIE NOVELS

900 MILES
by S. Johnathan Davis

John is a killer, but that wasn't his day job before the Apocalypse.

In a harrowing 900 mile race against time to get to his wife just as the dead begin to rise, John, a business man trapped in New York, soon learns that the zombies are the least of his worries, as he sees first-hand the horror of what man is capable of with no rules, no consequences and death at every turn.

Teaming up with an ex-army pilot named Kyle, they escape New York only to stumble across a man who says that he has the key to a rumored underground stronghold called Avalon..... Will they find safety? Will they make it to Johns wife before it's too late?

Get ready to follow John and Kyle in this fast paced thriller that mixes zombie horror with gladiator style arena action!

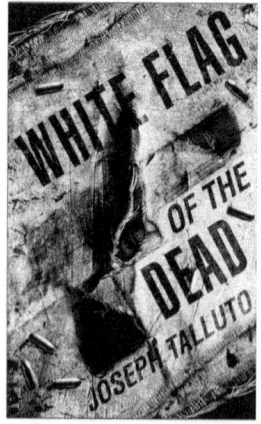

WHITE FLAG OF THE DEAD
by Joseph Talluto

Millions died when the Enillo Virus swept the earth. Millions more were lost when the victims of the plague refused to stay dead, instead rising to slaughter and feed on those left alive. For survivors like John Talon and his son Jake, they are faced with a choice: Do they submit to the dead, raising the white flag of surrender? Or do they find the will to fight, to try and hang on to the last shreds or humanity?

CHECK OUT OTHER GREAT ZOMBIE NOVELS

Z BURBIA
by Jake Bible

Whispering Pines is a classic, quiet, private American subdivision on the edge of Asheville, NC, set in the pristine Blue Ridge Mountains. Which is good since the zombie apocalypse has come to Western North Carolina and really put suburban living to the test!

Surrounded by a sea of the undead, the residents of Whispering Pines have adapted their bucolic life of block parties to scavenging parties, common area groundskeeping to immediate area warfare, neighborhood beautification to neighborhood fortification.

But, even in the best of times, suburban living has its ups and downs what with nosy neighbors, a strict Home Owners' Association, and a property management company that believes the words "strict interpretation" are holy words when applied to the HOA covenants. Now with the zombie apocalypse upon them even those innocuous, daily irritations quickly become dramatic struggles for personal identity, family security, and straight up survival.

ZOMBIE RULES
by David Achord

Zach Gunderson's life sucked and then the zombie apocalypse began.

Rick, an aging Vietnam veteran, alcoholic, and prepper, convinces Zach that the apocalypse is on the horizon. The two of them take refuge at a remote farm. As the zombie plague rages, they face a terrifying fight for survival.

They soon learn however that the walking dead are not the only monsters.

www.ingramcontent.com/pod-product-compliance
Lightning Source LLC
Chambersburg PA
CBHW070743180626
46818CB00007B/2970